THE ACCIDENTAL *Swipe*

Accidental Lovers
Book 1

Y. M. NELSON

Charlotte, NC

This book contains adult content and a few scenes and mentions that may trigger some people. For a list of triggers, scan the QR code below:

For all the online daters who came up empty, here's some wish fulfillment for you.
And perhaps some encouragement as well.

One

Fortune

FORTUNE HAD TO OWN up to it. She was grocery-store stalking this guy, plain and simple. She'd been here at least three times this week, and she hoped he wasn't catching on.

Well, *stalking* was a little harsh. More like ogling while buying unnecessary items. She picked up her third bag of fine-ground, expensive-as-diamonds coffee while she scanned the produce aisle in front of her just to get another glimpse of him.

Spotting him wearing that odd green apron and bright white name tag—"Graham R.," and under it, "Store Manager"—in the produce section thrilled her. With skin a golden tan, a shade darker than the beige onions he was stacking, and a face so clean-shaven and smooth, she wanted to reach out and touch him to confirm that he was real and his jaw wasn't, in fact, made of marble.

Fortune pushed the cart slowly down the juice aisle, and then the cereal aisle, and now she was rounding the corner to canned and dry goods, trying not to make any noise. Her list was completed, but her fill of seeing him stocking shelves wasn't. As manager of the store, he rarely rolled up his sleeves to put cans of soup on high and low shelves, but when he did ... Jiminy Christmas, what a sight. The bending, the reaching, the way the muscles in his arms and back and thighs worked? Delicious. Just one more peek around the corner of the aisle.

Sheesh. This was not healthy.

As she cautiously rounded the aisle, she saw him stacking boxes of rice. His feet stayed flat on the ground as he stretched to the back of the top shelf, pulling the boxes to the front. She always marveled at how some people were tall enough to reach the top store shelf, when at five foot four, she always had to ask for help. Maybe that's how she could get his attention this time. But what would she pretend to reach for?

"How are you today? Can I help you find something?" His cheery voice broke through her reverie.

Yikes. He'd spotted her midogle. In fact, there might have been drool.

Eek. She couldn't play this off with idle conversation, and she was too far away for her shelf idea to work. Fortune fidgeted, yanking the hem of her T-shirt down in the back, pulling it away from any visible bumps, then shook her head. Why was she even doing that? He had seen her enough times to know how fat she was. "Um ..." She looked around. *Just go, crazy woman*. "No. I'm fine, thanks! Have a nice day!"

He looked at her with a half smile and a confused eyebrow furrow, then went back to his task, squatting next to boxes of jasmine and long grain.

She had been discovered. Her face hot with embarrassment, she scooted away from the aisle.

The grocery store outing had been a pleasant—minus the embarrassing bit at the end—pit stop on her way to her best friend Louis's house, a small ranch on a square patch of yard in the middle of what Louis called "The Gayburbs" of Charlotte—a once-forgotten suburban neighborhood on the edge of town that had been taken over and revitalized by a few very prominent, openly gay couples in real estate.

Fortune stepped over the threshold, bags rustling even though she held them as still as possible. She always came in through the most awkward part of the house, the side door closest to his driveway. "I'm here!" she yelled, trying to mask the bag noise.

But he called her out on it. "Why did you go to the store? I told you I had everything."

Fortune whipped around from closing the door to staring Louis in the face. "Guess I didn't hear that part."

All shuffling ceased. They locked in a death glare for a full minute. Fortune caved first. She could never win at the death glare, especially when he held a glass of her favorite pink Moscato. "Okay, okay. I wanted some of those mini chocolate chip cookies. You know I love how their bakery does those. So soft. So chewy."

He looked in her bag, then back at her. "You don't have any cookies in this bag."

She blinked. Oh yeah, right. *I left the cookies because I didn't want Graham R. to see me with them.* Then she sighed and handed Louis the bag and took the wine. "Okay, okay, okay! I wanted to get a glimpse of this guy. Store manager. He's ... good-looking."

"Now, that I actually believe. Why can't you just search for pics of hot guys on the internet like everyone else?" He took her superfluous groceries into the kitchen.

A massive kitchen island separated the living room from the dining room, and with Louis's humongous wall-mounted flat screen, you could see what was playing from either room. Today's feature: a *Stranger Things* binge-watch session.

Fortune followed him through a doorway and sat on Louis's living room couch in front of the TV. She crossed her ankles on the bottom rung of his two-tiered coffee table and cradled her glass like it was a precious jewel. He brought in binge-watch survival provisions—popcorn, candy, and the opened wine bottle—and they hunkered down.

While the credits rolled on the fourth episode, Fortune mused about Graham R. "I think I'm going to ask him out. I got caught staring, and now he's going to think something is up." She'd kept her stalker sessions under wraps until today. Now that she'd been spotted, she might as well put everything out in the open. Plus, she couldn't keep anything from her BFF Louis. Especially after a few drinks during a binge-watch weekend.

"Are you saying you like this guy? What is he? A forty-year-old bag boy?" Louis plopped on the sofa beside her with a fresh bowl of popcorn, two bottled waters, and a bag of mini candy bars. Only four episodes in, and they'd run out of the snacks and drinks they'd sat down with.

"Will you stop with the hate, please? And he's the store manager, not that it matters."

"It does! You're an independent accomplished woman; he's got to represent or get out of the way. Listen, if you're that hard up, you should just find somebody on SwipeMatch. So, if it doesn't work out, he won't be staring death rays at you from aisle five every time you need a box of cereal."

"Swipe what?"

"SwipeMatch." He pulled out his phone and flipped through a couple of screens before finding the app, then handed her the phone. "It's like Tinder for plus-size beauties like yourself."

Her—a plus-size beauty? Hah. Plus-size yes, beauty no. She browsed through the screen. It looked a lot like Tinder, except the colors were pink and blue, and there were heart logos everywhere instead of the signature Tinder flame. She sighed. "I did the online dating thing five years ago. Remember my summer fiasco with that string of ODating4U.com guys? One guy had the nerve to—"

"Meet you at Capital Grille in a tank top and board shorts. Yes, I remember." He shuddered. "Hideous."

"Hey, why are you on SwipeMatch, anyway? BBWs aren't your thing."

"But I love a BBM every now and then." Louis waggled his eyebrows and smiled. "Sometimes, my usual skinny nerdy type just won't do it for me."

"An equal opportunity plus-size dating app. Sure. No problems there." She lowered her eyelids in a sarcastic look.

"Stop it now! You can modify your preferences, see?" He snatched the phone away and went to the profile settings screen. "Men Searching Men" was highlighted on his profile, but Fortune saw other selections: "Men Searching Women," "Women Searching Men," and almost ten others. With a couple of taps, he changed his preferences to "Men Searching Women" and went back to his potential matches.

Photo after photo of curvy women went across his screen as he swiped left for her to view. "Not much competition," he said. "You're more attractive than all of these women combined."

"You're supposed to say that. You're my bestie."

"Uh, no. As your bestie, I'm supposed to tell you the truth. Some of these women need a makeover. An *Extreme Makeover*."

Sometimes Fortune wished the show still aired, because she would totally apply. She would lose seventy pounds, tighten the flab on the undersides of her arms, get a breast lift, get a full-body "facial," and change her hair color. If she could go to work with hot pink highlights, she would, but for the office, she'd have to settle for a lighter red. She'd been rocking the short dark auburn curls for a few years now, while everyone else was doing streaks of white, purple, or green, even shaving one side of their heads while wearing hair extensions on the other side. She would save the wild colors for her nail polish instead.

Could she be—gasp—boring? No way. But how could anyone stand out on a dating app looking like she did? Ugh, online dating. She should have kept her mouth shut about her Graham crush. Now, Louis was going all in on finding her someone, and he wasn't going to stop.

"Don't make your straightness an excuse for a life of singledom, sweetie. You are painfully single, and you need to get over that with a quickness." He wagged his finger in front of her like a mother warning her child of bad consequences to her actions. Louis was such a drama queen.

"I'm not painfully single. Just the regular variety." What was *painfully single* anyway? She was too busy to date: work, book clubs, activity groups, volunteer projects. And then there were the weekends of endless binge-watch marathons. How could she keep up with discussions about *Stranger Things* if she didn't use her whole weekend to catch up? Being single was not painful. It was exhausting, really.

"Do you want to stay that way all your life? Forget your life, my ball is only three months away. And that's a date thing, sweetie. You can't go stag like you did last year."

And there it was. It was always about Louis, even her single life. Why did he care if she took someone to one of his drag-queen shows? "You know straight men don't go to drag balls. Especially straight Black men."

"First off, it's not that kind of ball. It's the annual ALZ fundraiser gala for UICC." Louis had been development director at United in Care Charities for over four years. UICC promoted several causes, and Louis worked a little on some of them, but his focus was on Alzheimer's awareness and cure research. He threw himself into preparations for the Alzheimer's gala so completely every year, the annual fundraiser was now unofficially nicknamed Louis's Gala.

"Wow, that came around fast. I thought I'd volunteer this time around."

"Sorry, sweetie. We've got all the volunteers we need this year. Special guest this year is that hunk of manliness Javier Firestone from that reality show—" Louis pointed to the TV, which was not playing the show he was talking about, and then to her.

She pointed back at him with recognition, as if she'd picked up the rest of his thought and agreed. They had been friends so long they could draw and decipher thought from each other's brains like Dumbledore and the Pensieve. She sighed. "Yep! Oh well."

"And secondly, there are all kinds of men on SwipeMatch. Who's to say you'll end up with a Black guy?"

"I'm a Black woman in the South. Odds are—"

"Is this Graham guy Black?"

"No." She envisioned Graham at the onion bin again. He could have been Mediterranean, but he was not a Black man. And that had been one of the things she'd noticed the least about him until Louis had brought it up.

"I know you, Ms. Rainbow Bright. Your eyes don't see skin color after they've spotted 'hot' and 'hunky.' Come on, let's help get you a profile."

Louis and his stupid ball. She would rather go alone than be stuck with some sex-crazed Neanderthal from the internet. But if he said she needed a date, it was out of love and understanding. He knew she was uncomfortable in places where there were crowds where you had to make small talk. While she could function at an activity-based event where everyone knew everyone else (like last week's college reunion cookout), or where everyone was a stranger and not expected to interact (yesterday's seminar on caring for aging parents she'd attended for work), she was horrible at mingle-and-network shindigs without a buffer. Fortune had almost cried last year when she'd left the charity ball early. She'd wondered if he'd noticed; now she realized he had.

"I drank too much of that Moscato. I'm going to have to sleep over tonight," Fortune declared.

"You know where the linen closet and the spare bedroom are."

"I love you, Louis."

"I love you, too, but you're not getting out of creating this profile. Please tell me you have a better photo than this DMV-looking thing here."

She leaned across his shoulder to see what he was seeing and laughed. It was a frantically taken headshot she'd done for work. She hated photos, especially ones where she was wearing boring work clothes. But Louis had kept at her to send him a photo so he could attach it to her contact info in his phone. His threats of taking one of her while she was midchew at his house finally had gotten to her, and she'd sent him the work photo. "I'll find something. Let's finish the binge-fest first, shall we?"

Her and Louis's TV binge-fests were never long enough. They always watched a few shows, talked about their lives, and got sidetracked until after midnight when one of them would get up and say, *We have got to do this more often*, and leave.

But this time, she was staying over, and Louis was needling her with questions to add information to her profile.

"Is this the best you can do for a photo?" He was looking at the snapshots she'd just added to her online album and shared with him.

"What do you want from me? I hate taking pictures." What was Louis even thinking? She'd say *no* to the SwipeMatch profile and go to the ball alone. She was a big girl. "I can go to a charity fundraiser by myself. I promise I won't be like last year."

"You're just anxious about meeting someone new. Now"—he settled into an armchair across from his sofa and began typing furiously on his phone with his thumbs—"what do you do again?"

"I'm a burlesque dancer." She blew a raspberry and crossed her eyes.

Louis played along with her sarcasm. "No need to get them salivating now. They can find out about the burlesque part after they meet you."

"I'm a seminar creator; you know that. It's boring to anyone who doesn't do it. Do we have to write anything for that?"

"No, we don't. There's no spot just for a job. It's just a big box that says, 'Write something here.'"

Fortune hopped off the couch and started pacing in front of him. "Let's be more creative than that." She went to the kitchen and came back with another bottle of Moscato. "This is going to require a little thinking juice." She poured each of them another glass and continued pacing.

"Okay, Peggy Olsen," she quipped, nicknaming him for the *Mad Men* character. "Take this dictation. 'I'm the cute girl. That's my iceberg description. My friends know that I'm also a TV nerd, a baseball fan, a volunteer, a spontaneous baker, and a good-hearted person. What else would my boyfriend know about me? That's for you to potentially find out.'" She took a bow and then a big gulp of her drink.

Louis finished the dictation, dropped the phone in his lap, and started clapping. "All right, Mr. Draper! Reel them in with that creative bravado!"

"You're a mess! Why am I following you up?" She grinned.

"Because you need a new adventure, and this is going to be a good one."

He was right about her needing a new adventure. But was this going to be something good? Or was it going to crash and burn like the ODating4U massacre?

Two

Jason

JASON WATCHED FROM HIS car as Tina unlocked the door to her place. That was as gentlemanly as he wanted to be with this woman he could describe only as a succubus. From the way she'd acted tonight, him escorting her to her door could be misconstrued as walking down the aisle. Every nice gesture and every instinctively chivalrous act he'd made had caused her to cling to him like his neighbor Mrs. Kosinski's dog's hair clung to everything—too much and unwanted.

When they'd gotten in his car—after a dodgy and frustrating dinner in which he'd found out more about her boob job than her brain—she'd climbed halfway over the console, wound herself around his side, and suggested, "How about we go back to your place?" in what could be described only as a longtime-smoker's version of a deep, sexy voice.

He'd almost offered to take her to the drugstore instead for some throat lozenges or a packet of Nicorette. Instead, he untangled himself as gently and politely as he could. "Um ... I'm, um ... kind of between places right now." He lied. "I'm staying on a friend's couch."

"Graham didn't say anything—"

"It's another friend," he added hastily.

She snaked a hand under his arm and across his abs. "I can be quiet."

"They don't allow guests. Sorry."

"Another time, then." She smiled.

That smile made him sick to his stomach. It was like staring at a viper. "I don't think so. Let's just call it a night."

Crap. Another failed date. His mood was going downhill fast. Jason would never let Graham set him up again. In addition to being clingy, Tina was vapid and self-absorbed, which was probably why Graham thought she and Jason would get along. Graham had the biggest ego of anyone Jason had ever known, and they were best friends.

After Tina gave him a flirty wave and disappeared inside, Jason sped to The Graveyard, ready for a few beers and to tell Graham exactly what he thought about his "sure thing."

The Graveyard was the guys' favorite hangout bar and nothing at all like a graveyard. It was part sports bar, part man cave, with wood tones and leather upholstery everywhere. The walls and high exposed-beam ceiling did nothing to contain the white noise of conversations and TV commentary, giving the bar a stadium atmosphere.

He spotted two of his friends, Graham and Seth, and wondered where his friend Ranjan was. Oh right, he'd had a date tonight, too. At least someone was having a decent date night.

As happy as he was for Ranjan, Jason would miss his presence tonight. Ranjan was the voice of reason in the group, the one who kept the rest of them from falling off the deep end. Seth with his conspiracy theories and insults, Graham with his self-important opinions, and Jason with his sensitivity and emotions.

In fact, he was already feeling restless and frustrated. It was harder to meet a pleasant woman than it was to craft a response to an RFQ to renovate bathrooms in a government building. Why was everything going well in his life but this one thing? This—not so little—screw-up of a love life.

He'd seen his sister meet and marry her husband and start a family, his mom and dad grow old together, even Graham and his girlfriend, Dani, repeatedly get back together after their millions of breakups. Even though he had a smidgen of free time to date between his construction business and substitute teaching, he still felt the void of being single around a bunch of couples. In reality, he was a little jealous and a lot lonely.

Jason ordered a beer and joined his friends, venting—extra loud and with dramatic arm flails, sloshing his bottle of craft IPA—about how there were no good women left. "I have been out with every single woman under forty in Charlotte in the past six months." He took a swig of his beer. "And they all suck."

"If they all sucked, why are you complaining?" Seth snickered. "If they didn't suck, now that's the real problem."

Jason narrowed his stare at Seth. "Is that all you think a woman is good for? Giving you head?"

"No. She also needs to make me breakfast. Eggs, bacon, and hash browns are my favorite morning-after breakfast."

"Hash browns? Who asks someone to make them hash browns after sex?" Jason pointed the bottle at Seth, and the drink spilled on the table. "You're a jackass."

Graham snatched the beer out of Jason's hand. "You're getting beer everywhere. What is it this time?" He grabbed a roll of paper towels from the table behind him and dabbed at part of the spill nearest him.

God forbid Graham should get beer on his overpriced, dry-clean-only, Egyptian cotton shirt, Jason thought irritably. He pointed to Graham. "This is your fault. Setting me up with Tina."

Seth piped up. "What's your deal? Tina's hot."

"She's clingy and full of herself! She talked about her workout and her diet all night, then tried to jump me before we even left the restaurant parking lot!"

"I don't see the problem." Graham shook his head and shrugged like he really didn't get it.

Jason wondered if, even after all these years, his friends really knew him. Maybe they assumed he'd only wanted something casual because that was all he ever talked about. He hadn't had a steady girlfriend since Lily, and that had been years ago. "The problem is I don't want a hookup. I want something serious."

Because he had gotten it so wrong with Lily, it was almost as if he wanted to redeem himself. Lily was his best friend from high school, and when he'd come back from Arizona State, it was like she'd been there waiting for him. They'd shared a ratty two-bedroom with astronomical rent on Charlotte's southwest side. Correction, they'd shared a roommate. A roommate who was now Lily's soon-to-be wife.

Yep, he needed to redeem himself all right—in more ways than one.

"Stop enabling him, Graham, and make him find his own date. Online." Seth sneered at Jason. "That'll teach you to appreciate a good setup."

Jason snatched his beer back. "Like I haven't been online. Everyone's already on Tinder anyway."

"No, not Tinder. This one." Seth fiddled with his phone, then held it up to show a download screen for SwipeMatch.

Jason saw the screenshots of voluptuous women, mostly face shots, but some scantily clad, full-body images. Words like *inclusion*, *plus-size*, and *curvy* jumped off of the screen at him. What was this—a dare? Seth must have forgotten Jason never turned down a dare. "Are you daring me to make a profile here?"

"You've got to make a profile, match with someone, and go out with them. No more yelling at us about women we set you up with."

Graham looked over Jason's shoulder at the app and barked out a laugh. "Seth, that's not a dare."

"No! I'm tired of this emo mooding up our hang time." Seth pointed his bottle of Budweiser at Jason. "We need a healthy Dare or Dare session."

"Truth or Dare," Graham corrected.

"I said it right the first time."

Obviously, Seth had either had too much to drink, or he'd never paid any attention to the women Jason liked. While none of them would call themselves plus-size, he loved women with curves—breasts that were more than "bee stings," soft curves, and thighs that touched each other, for goodness' sake. Jason didn't want a small girl, because he wasn't a small guy.

At six foot two, he was still a few inches taller than any of his friends and a good head taller than most of the women he'd gone out with. But for a forty-one-year-old who never said no to sweets, he didn't have a dad bod. He wasn't exactly a gym rat—the only six-pack he owned was the locally brewed IPAs in his fridge—but swinging a sledge and carting around building materials all day kept the muscles in his arms, legs, and back toned and his chest and torso solid.

Plus, Lily had once described his eyes as bottomless ocean blue, and he still had his hair—even though today it was especially unruly with brunette spikes and waves all over the top of his head. He'd have no problem matching with someone on this app.

He laughed to himself. *Seth thinks he can one-up me with this?* "Fine. I'm dared. I'll do it. You SOBs make me sick." He drained his beer and went to the bar for another while the app downloaded.

On top of being the jackass of the group, Seth always sucked at Truth or Dare. Jason drank his beer, hung out with his friends, and forgot about his merry-go-round of a dating life for the rest of the night.

A few days later on a rare day in his office, Jason got a text from Seth.

Seth: Found someone yet?

Jason had forgotten all about the dare; he'd been so consumed with getting the scope of this proposal perfect. If his company won this commercial contract, he'd have steady work for his crew for at least two years.

It was yet another reason why he was single. When he told women he was a business owner, they saw dollar signs—never mind that he'd had to scrounge for every dollar he'd earned and allocate all of them after he'd earned them. Owning Reed Reno & Construction meant he had to be conservative during the good times to weather the bad times.

But something about Seth's dismissive attitude and ridiculous attempt to insult him with this half-cocked dare got to him.

Hunched over his desk covered in blueprints, a sub sandwich in one hand and his phone in the other, he scanned the few desks in front of him for approaching employees. The one-room office he'd had when he started the business had expanded to include a conference room and a small break area just big enough for the essentials—coffee machine, fridge, and microwave. Still, with the expansion and the glass fronts for all the enclosed areas, he could see anyone coming and going. His assistant, Gabi, had gone to meet Austin, his longtime general contractor, and a few others from the crew for lunch.

Satisfied he was alone, he pulled up the SwipeMatch app. *Couldn't wait until you got home, could you, Reed?* He put down his sandwich and swiped left through numerous women's profiles. Every picture portrayed a variation on women he'd already dated—straight blond hair and blue eyes, straight brown hair and brown eyes, straight ...

Wait a minute.

Jason's finger hovered over the directional buttons as he took in the face on his screen. Diva3000 was mesmerizing. Short, auburn curls framed an open, cheerful face and bright chestnut brown eyes. Her lips were full and pouty, even without that God-awful duck face women made. He took a bite of his sandwich as he imagined kissing those lips, running his tongue along the bottom one. And even though the shot was cut off, ample cleavage hinted at breasts he'd love to get his hands on. Yep, he was hard up. But she was gorgeous.

He swiped right before he even looked at her profile, which had been created only days before his. *No-brainer. Diva3000 is my next date.* Jason always beat Seth on a dare.

Oh yeah, I forgot. I've got to match with her first.

Three

Fortune

THE SMELL OF EAST Asian spices hit Fortune when she opened the door to the office kitchen. She glanced in the trash can by the door: Someone had thrown away a bowl of ramen without putting the lid on it, releasing the scent. The remaining ramen bowls on the kitchen table were sealed, serving spoons resting on their respective lids. The salvaged ramen bowls were the only neatly recovered items from the afternoon meetings. Cartons of leftovers crowded every horizontal surface: the counters, the dining table, and the bar counter across the back wall. Some were covered, but most were not and had serving spoons sticking out of them, as if someone just moved them from the meeting straight to the kitchen to die. The longer she stood in the kitchen, the more the food smells combined, giving Fortune a mild headache. The employees at Davies Marketing, especially the seminar creators, were notoriously messy and ate in the office a lot.

Though she was also a seminar creator, Fortune was not messy, nor did she eat in the office. Her desk was so clean, she could eat off it. And she never had any lunch meeting leftovers, no matter how much someone raved to her about how good they were. Well, not in front of anyone, anyway. If they'd seen a plus-size Black woman shoveling food into her face at her desk, mockery and ridicule would be sure to follow, along with a healthy dose of speculation about her work ethic.

No matter that she was a senior marketing creator, and she was probably eating at her desk because she was working through lunch on a stellar idea or an award-winning campaign. It didn't matter that she'd never caught anyone ridiculing or speculating. Shoveling in leftovers in the breakroom between meetings in front of this group? She might as well wrap her short, curly hair and call herself Aunt Jemima. Even though all the years of breakfast pastries or pasta lunches at meetings and heavy hors d'ocuvres gently forced on her at networking events with an excited "you've got to try this!" did little to keep her from what her doctor called "morbidly obese." One would think if they put "morbid" in front of something, they would at least have a healthcare treatment plan that was more than "eat less and move more" and actually worked.

But who cared when yoga pants came in all kinds of sizes? She'd never been skinny, but neither had anyone in her family—men or women on both sides of her family. The men were huge and burly with barrel chests and strong backs. The women were similarly built, but with curves and fleshy parts where the men had straight lines and angles. Fortune was no exception, with a torso defined only by her ample breasts, swimmer's legs and thighs, and smooth medium brown skin to cover it all.

While she did wish to lose some weight, she never thought less of herself because she hadn't. No one looked like her in the fashion magazines, but that was their fault for not seeing that beauty came in more than one package. She knew she could turn heads. Her last boyfriend, Thomas, had nicknamed her Luscious Lucky. She preferred to remain Fortune. The name didn't stick, and neither did he. But it wasn't because of her waistline. Their breakup was all him.

A woman walked through the kitchen door and immediately turned back around.

"Hey, Elaheh," Fortune called.

"I'm on it," Elaheh called back over her shoulder. She returned with a young skinny guy. "Josh, can we get this cleaned up before the next meeting is over?"

"Yes, ma'am." Josh was this summer's intern from the local college. He went to work, matching lids to containers and then throwing away most of the leftovers.

Elaheh went to the fridge and got her afternoon iced coffee. Every afternoon around three-thirty, she would sneak out of whatever meeting she was in for a bathroom break and a bottle of cold caffeine. Fortune always met her coworker and friend in the kitchen, most of the time to gossip about work, sometimes to plan their weekends.

Since Josh was cleaning, Fortune steered clear of the gossip. "Have you caught up on *Stranger Things* yet, Elaheh?"

"I'm still on season two. I can't get enough daylight to finish watching it."

"It's not that scary!" Fortune laughed. "If I can watch it, then anyone can."

"I jump when my house settles in broad daylight." Elaheh took a gulp of her iced coffee. "What are we doing this weekend? My mind's already on Friday."

"It's only Tuesday."

"Still." Elaheh stared at her blankly.

Going out with Elaheh was a tricky business. She was that friend who knew everyone, whether she did or not. And with her size eight Coke-bottle body and penchant for long blond hair, flashy jewelry, and skintight clothes, she looked like a Middle Eastern version of the EDM singer Erika Jayne. Next to her, Fortune felt like a giant troll. And not one of the cute pink ones either.

Elaheh in clubwear looked almost nothing like she looked right now. "Turndown Tuesday," as she referred to it, meant sporting her natural black, shoulder-length hair, modest earrings and necklace, and a pantsuit with a short, fashionably cut jacket. The only hint of her wild side was the sparkly silver top underneath the jacket, which she probably wore only because tonight was date night for her and her husband, Geronimo.

Geronimo was one of the basemen on the local minor league team, so Elaheh kept herself out of the spotlight. And even though she'd been photographed at only a few of his games, and she sported a huge diamond wedding ring, men still flocked to her wherever they were. Most guys were just attracted to the shine—she literally sparkled every time she went out—but some guys ignored the diamond and tried to hit on her. A few knew who she was and took advantage of the rare moments when paparazzi would catch her to ask about her husband and talk stats.

Fortune always stood by like the wing woman who wasn't needed. Elaheh getting all the attention with Fortune getting none was a fact of life, a rule of their friendship. But Elaheh was an attentive friend, and since she was happily married, she never left Fortune at a club with no way home for some guy.

"I want to dance," Fortune said. "When was the last time we went out clubbing?"

"Probably a millennia ago, give or take a few years." Elaheh looked over her shoulder and saw Josh still cleaning, so she turned back to Fortune with a secretive look and a lowered voice. "There's this new spot I've been wanting to try. I'll text you the address and time, okay?"

"Sure," Fortune answered. "Are you going back to your meeting?"

"Not until they stop wasting my time and say something meaningful. I've got real work to do." Elaheh walked out of the kitchen.

A high ping sounded above Josh's rustling. Fortune pulled out her phone and read a text from Louis.

Louis: Have you checked out the SwipeMatch profile?

She hadn't even opened the app yet. What was his hurry?
Oh right, the gala. This was becoming a chore, and Louis
was transforming into her mother. The next thing he'd text:
I only want you to be happy!

Looking forward to a night out in a few days and overly
optimistic about her chances of meeting someone then, she
texted Louis back.

Fortune: Nothing yet. But I doubt I'll need it much
longer. Going out with Elaheh Friday!

Louis: The Persian princess? Ask her to tone it down
so you can shine. She's already got a husband.

Fortune rolled her eyes at Louis's text.

Fortune: Doubtful that will happen. But I'll ask.

No way would Elaheh do that, and no way would Fortune
ask. Elaheh was one of the few girlfriends she had and the
only one she worked with.

Fortune's ten-minute meeting reminder flashed over her
screen, so she pocketed her phone and rushed out of the

smelly kitchen to a conference room to finish setting up her presentation for their newest potential client.

When she arrived, most of her coworkers were there, but the new client they were meeting with hadn't been brought up from reception. The room was chilly and so were the people. Six of her team occupied a row of black metal armchairs along the back wall, and most of them looked uncomfortable or tired. Why would they meet with a new client at four in the afternoon instead of first thing in the morning? But that was Tracey. Fortune's manager's schedule was haphazard and busy when it came to accommodating clients, and they just adapted to it.

The room, like the rest of the office, was done in grays and blacks—cold, sleek, modern, and nothing like the warm, caring, friendly attitude they endeavored to project to clients. The chairs were black, executive-style, and un-comfortable if the meetings went longer than an hour. For-tune wondered if that was by design. At least snacks and coffee provided some warmth. Ugh, sugary snacks. Fortune whirled away from trays of even more food toward the A/V equipment.

She'd barely had enough time to get set up before the client walked in. Or rather, the procession of severe-looking executives with perpetual frowns who all looked like they had swallowed hot peppers and vinegar before arriving. The woman heading the procession was smaller and shorter than Fortune and had long, black hair pulled severely into an elaborate bun. She looked like she was in her mid-fifties, but her body looked like it belonged to a twenty-something personal trainer. Intimidation must have been this woman's middle name.

The woman extended her hand to Fortune. "Thank you for accommodating us. I'm Aileen Davenport. I believe we spoke on the phone?"

Fortune shook Aileen's hand. "Yes, and it was no problem, Aileen."

"I prefer Mrs. Davenport for now."

Fortune stiffened while the department director swooped into the room beside her to greet the client. "Great to meet you, Mrs. Davenport. I'm Tracey DeJager."

Tracey leaned down to Fortune and whispered, "She's our client, and this is a big account. Don't mess it up." Then Tracey took her place at the table.

Great. Just what Fortune wanted to hear before her presentation. Tracey was usually more poised than that, but she was probably nervous, too. This account could net the company six figures—a significant amount for a nonprofit to spend on marketing.

Fortune stood and addressed the room. "Thank you, everyone, for working with our client's schedule." She focused on the client. "Mrs. Davenport, at Davies Marketing we pride ourselves on our high standards of customer service in addition to making a quality product." She glanced at her manager, who was smiling and unsuccessfully secretively mouthing encouraging words.

The presentation took almost forty minutes, and the Q&A session went for another ten minutes after that. Then Josh came in to refresh the coffee and snacks while the group casually met with Mrs. Davenport and her posse.

"We want them to believe they can turn their lives around even after they've left an abusive situation. We want them to embrace their ability to find healthy relationships again," Aileen was saying to Fortune, Tracey, and some of the other members on the seminar creation team. "That's hard for women to believe after being in abusive situations. Especially when they're single and in their forties."

"Don't I know it," Fortune mumbled before she could stop herself. She coughed to divert everyone's attention, but Aileen had heard her.

"How old are you?" Mrs. Davenport asked.

Wasn't it rude to ask someone's age? Not that it mattered who knew. "Thirty-nine."

Aileen Davenport squinted and gave Fortune a once-over, as if she were looking for a flaw. "Are you divorced?"

"Single," Fortune corrected. Where was this going? she wondered.

"Really? You look more divorced to me."

What the heck did that mean? *Don't snap back. She's the client. Stay calm.* "How so?"

"I don't know, you're just ... shaped like a divorcée. You know, flabby arms, a little round in the middle, like you've had a couple of kids and weekly Stouffer's lasagnas. You seem a little like you've settled for wowing them with your personality." Mrs. Davenport held her head high and looked up her nose at Fortune while absentmindedly twirling her wedding ring on her bony finger. The set was encrusted with diamonds of different sizes, and as she twirled it, the biggest diamond caught the light and reflected it into Fortune's face.

Fortune was stunned, but worked at keeping her face blank. She'd never been insulted like this by anyone after a client meeting, least of all the client. Was this woman out of her mind? Who said stuff like that in a professional setting? The woman had no filter or couth. Pebbles of rage were gathering and rising from Fortune's gut into her chest, ready to blast forth some well-deserved vitriol at Aileen, client be damned.

Then Fortune saw a flash of pink out of the corner of her eye and shifted to see the arm of Tracey's pink jacket as she signaled Fortune from behind Aileen. Despite the sympathetic frown on her face, Tracey mouthed, *You've got this*, behind and above the client's slicked-back bun. Ugh. Tracey had heard Davenport's ignorant offense! How embarrassing! Now, Fortune wanted to slide down to the floor and slink out of the room.

Get it together, Edwards. She could spin this so it wouldn't turn into blows, criminal charges, and her termination. "Seeing as over half the country is divorced, I'm sure divorcées come in many shapes and sizes. And, not to brag, but my personality is pretty wow-worthy." She chuckled softly to keep the raw edge out of her tone. "But the greater takeaway here is that I can speak effectively to those you help. Our videos and workshops will significantly help them because they'll come from a reference of truth."

Tracey gave Fortune a thumbs-up as the corners of Davenport's mouth turned up in a fake but apparent smile.

Fortune exhaled slowly. Another precarious meeting saved by a few moments of quick thinking and letting go of her pride. The more the customer mattered, the less she did. It was part of the job. A part she hated, but what the heck, she still got paid.

The meeting had worn her spirits down so much, Fortune just wanted to stay home and never go back out again. Forget going out to a new club on Friday with Elaheh. She could just sit and binge-watch all thirty-five seasons of *Soul Train*. She'd need some more wine. And possibly some chocolate chip cookies. She dialed her work bestie when she got home.

"Elaheh, I don't think I can go to a new place Friday. This new client just made me want to smack her into next week. Let's go back to Sly Foxes."

"Sure, if that's what you want. But we're having drinks tomorrow night at Jack's, and you're going to tell me about this new client."

A Kamikaze and a vent session with Elaheh sounded better than watching people in 1970s fashion doing dances that most folks in the 1970s couldn't do. Plus, it would get the bad news out of the way, so she could go to Sly Foxes free of the Debbie Downer vibe. "Fine. Have a nice night with Geronimo. See you tomorrow."

Four

LUCKILY, THE CLIENT-FROM-HELL INCIDENT was the only drama from the workweek, because who could afford cocktails in Uptown on Wednesday and Friday nights? Apparently, Elaheh, who had an Amex black card. On Wednesday, they had gone to Jack's just up the block from Sly Foxes.

Jack's was an English-style pub on the corner of a crowded block of bars and pubs. After an NFL player posted a selfie with half his team with the caption "New fave hangout" and tagged the bar, Jack's became almost impossible to get into on the weekend or a night the team was playing. What had once been an "everyman's bar" was now a trendy spot to be seen, and maybe even get a football husband, which was why Fortune had been to Jack's only on Wednesdays.

Husband, ugh. Now she was thinking about SwipeMatch and Graham and being single. Louis's "painfully single" comment crept to the front of her mind for the third or fourth time that week. Why did that observation bother her so much?

As Fortune pulled into a spot in the parking garage, her phone pinged.

Elaheh: In front of Sly Foxes.

The block's official moniker was the Epicenter, but Fortune called it Bling Alley. With a bowling alley and a dine-in movie theater as its biggest attractions, the self-contained block used to host everyone from college kids to middle-aged folks on date night. Now that more bars and clubs had moved in, everyone's goal for a good night out was to blind others with their bling or blindfold them with their stacks of money.

Sly Foxes hadn't changed its atmosphere, but because it was down the block from Jack's, everyone who didn't want to wait in line at Jack's simply turned around and waited in line at Sly Foxes.

Friday nights at the club were loud, pretentious, and packed with all the beautiful people Ed Sheeran sang about: semifamous locals, minor league sports players, and senior-level bank managers looking to get a moment away from their spouses and 2.5 kids. It was a great place to be seen ... if that's what someone wanted. If what a body wanted was to drink and dance without being bothered, then it was a great place for that, too. Unless that body walked in with the wife of a star minor league baseball player.

When Fortune arrived at the lounge, the line was already down the block. But Elaheh didn't do lines. She grabbed

Fortune's hand and strutted up to the bouncer holding the rope.

"Hey, Darius!" Elaheh leaned in and was immediately enveloped in one of Darius's famous hugs. When he hugged someone, he folded them into his being. Fortune could barely see the top of Elaheh's blond wig above Darius's huge arms. "You remember my friend Fortune?"

"Yeah. It's Ms. Delicious. How you doin'?" Darius did a spot-on imitation of Joey from *Friends*, even though he looked more like Deebo from the movie *Friday*. He gave Fortune a hug, then released the rope to let the ladies through.

Fortune let a giggle escape. "Hey, Darius." She smiled shyly. Why was this as flirty as she could get? Probably because she knew Darius was just being nice. Though she was cute in her shiny navy halter jumpsuit and silver medallion earrings, she was frumpy compared to Elaheh in her body-hugging gold dress, the hem of it an inch shorter than the platinum-blond wig she was wearing. Plus, Darius was married.

The line behind them moved slightly when they spotted the rope dropping. But when Darius put the rope back up behind the ladies, the group at the front of the line groaned. Being this close to entering one of the hottest clubs in town was akin to teetering in the middle of a rickety drawbridge. Fortune knew the situation well.

"Hey! Why does the whale get in before us?" a male voice yelled behind the ladies.

Fortune stiffened and inhaled a shaky breath. Why did jerks always have to stomp on her good time? And that hadn't even been a creative insult. What a jackass.

Elaheh turned. Platinum locks whipped around her body with the motion.

"No." Fortune patted Elaheh on the shoulder. "Don't engage. Let's just go in, okay?"

"If you say so. But you know we could shut that down." Elaheh balled up a fist and hit her other palm.

Fortune laughed. "Not worth it."

They ignored the heckler and entered the club. As soon as they stepped over the threshold, they were awash in neon blue, green, and purple strobe lights. Fortune took in the familiar sights—people on the dance floor in the center of the room, huddled around the three bars against the walls, and draped over sofas or seated at tables around the dance floor, upstairs in the semicircular VIP balcony, and in the cigar lounge in the back corner.

The DJ hyped the crowd from a booth suspended above the dance floor. The lights cast shadows over the booth, making it seem to float in midair. The air conditioning was on full blast to combat the heat from the crush of bodies dancing or huddling around every bar and made the atmosphere comfortable. Smells of alcohol and cigar smoke mingled with a sweet fresh scent that intensified every time the AC kicked on. The club seemed both familiar and strange every time she entered.

Elaheh pulled Fortune through the maze of people to get a drink, then to a booth near the floor. "I'm so glad it's Friday,"

Elaheh yelled over the music. "Work was kicking my butt all this week. Finally, some freedom! At least until the game tomorrow."

"Yeah. I'm so tired of this client. One more presentation on domestic abuse ..."

They finished their drinks while catching up on the gossip they hadn't already shared earlier in the week. A couple of guys asked Elaheh to dance. She declined. One group of guys sent a round of drinks over to them. Elaheh looked their way, waving at them with her ring hand. The platinum band glinted off the neon lights and dimmed the guys' hopes.

She went back to the gossip, intent on continuing her conversation with Fortune. If Fortune got as much attention as Elaheh, Louis wouldn't be forcing her to make a profile on SwipeMatch. But they had been at the club for a couple of hours, and the only attention directed at Fortune had been Darius's compliment and Line Stranger's insult.

At the sound of Ed Sheeran's voice over the speakers, Elaheh jumped up. "This is my song! Come on!" She grabbed Fortune's hand and dragged her through the gyrating bodies to the middle of the dance floor.

Fortune shook her head and laughed, dancing with her friend. It took only seconds for a group of guys to move in behind Elaheh. Predictable, Fortune thought. But near the end of the song, someone squeezed Fortune's forearm. Elaheh threw her an excited nod, so she turned, mustering the courage to talk to a potential new suitor.

The voice that greeted her wasn't flirty or even friendly. "The only reason you got in here was her." Line Stranger gestured to Elaheh, who was talking with the group of guys.

Fortune peered into angry, light green eyes and a hard, pale face halfway shrouded in darkness and blue neon lights. His blond hair was cut severely short and spiked all over, his T-shirt and chinos hung loosely on his thin frame, and his shoes looked as if he had rinsed them off after stomping through the mud. How did he even get in here? she wondered. Everyone else was dressed with crispness and a nod toward trendy that he lacked. He was no match for her finesse.

"Well, obviously, she's friends with the bouncer." Fortune rolled her eyes.

"If she wasn't she'd be here, and you'd still be in line, whale."

This kind of thing she was used to. Black-and-white plain-as-day rudeness. Filled with adrenaline tinged with rage, her response was inevitable and easy. "You mean the line which you'd be banished to the back of, douchebag? Let go of me." She yanked at her arm, but he held fast, his fingers digging into her flesh.

So she kneed him squarely in the groin.

He doubled over, wincing in pain, and dropped her arm.

"Whales don't have knees, asshole." Fortune stomped off the floor toward the bathroom, forcing the crowd to part and let her through.

Elaheh followed, leaving her group of admirers behind. "What happened back there?"

Fortune pushed the bathroom door open, and it banged against the back wall. "That ... that ..." She banged her fists on the sink and took a deep breath to expel some of the fire in her chest and calm the churning in her gut. Why was this getting to her? Fortune already had such low expectations of men. Still, she shook her head and blinked back tears.

Elaheh rubbed Fortune's back in small circles. "What's going on? I thought he was into you."

Fortune met Elaheh's concerned gaze in the mirror. "He was the heckler from outside. From the line?"

Her eyes widened. "Oh no! Fortune, I'm sorry, girl. Kneeing him was the least you could do."

"That's what I thought, too." Fortune's mouth twisted into a wry smile.

A young woman emerged from a bathroom stall and washed her hands at the sink beside them. The woman wore an impossibly tight sleeveless red sheath dress, and her makeup and hair were overdone. "Girl, I hope you aren't crying over that tired show out there. Some guy introduced himself and then asked me if my breasts were real. What the hell? I mean, they're not, but what kind of question is that to ask a woman you don't know?" She waved her index finger up and down in front of Fortune. "That jumpsuit is everything, girl." Then she snatched a paper towel from the dispenser and walked out.

Fortune and Elaheh stared at each other and broke into hysterical laughter.

"That jumpsuit *is* everything, though," Elaheh said.

"Thanks." Fortune dabbed her eyes with a damp towel. "Can we go now?"

Going toe-to-toe with scumbags like Line Stranger, dealing with impossible clients, these were easy social obstacles to overcome. She could do this in her sleep.

Talking to a certain store manager she had a crush on? Impossible.

But being out in a social setting like tonight with no one noticing her except to denigrate her in front of others meant that she wasn't going to be booed up any time soon, much less find a date for Louis's ball.

Ugh, the ball. It was only three months away, and she hadn't even had a meaningful conversation with Graham, forget asking him out. She also hadn't opened the SwipeMatch app Louis had loaded on her phone. Louis would be so disappointed.

She plugged in her phone, crawled into bed, and waited while the app loaded. But her mind swirled with the memories of tonight, and she couldn't stop herself from crying. The energy drain from work, getting ready for the evening, and dealing with Line Stranger pulled her farther down in bed and into sleep.

Five

THE NEXT DAY, FORTUNE awoke to a headache and mascara smeared on her pillow. Her phone was wedged under her arm and tangled in the sheets.

The SwipeMatch app was up when she unlocked her phone. It stared at her, taunting her. But she'd promised Louis she would at least try to find someone for his ball. And she had less than three months to do it.

Swiping mostly left through a bunch of photos, she almost gave up when she saw a profile for someone named JR4019. She stared at the photo.

It was him. Graham.

On SwipeMatch? Well, at least he was okay with the curvy chicks. She looked harder at the photo, mouth open, practically drooling.

But it wasn't just Graham. The photo showed a group of four guys, and Graham was one of them. It was an obvious buddy photo taken on vacation—someplace tropical, nothing like Charlotte—but it had been taken before the festivities and possible debauchery four guys in their early-to-mid-thirties could have. They looked like a group of preppy frat boys, all fresh-faced, wearing button-down, short-sleeved shirts and khaki shorts that came to their knees. There was an Indian guy with short crew-cut curly black hair. To his left was a taller guy with sandy-brown hair and a bit of scruff, then Graham with his obviously gelled, almost-black hair a la Neo from *The Matrix* and his body a la Jax from *Sons of Anarchy*, and at the far right of the picture, a tall, lean, blond guy with his hair pulled back in a man bun. Something about him looked familiar, but she couldn't figure out what.

In any case, Graham was here, within reach. She could right-swipe now, and they might match. Her hand was shaking as she hovered over the "like." But what if he didn't match her? She'd be devastated. No, she couldn't take any more ego bashing this weekend. Left swipe. Which one was left again—toward the left or starting on the left? How did she lose all knowledge about this app in seconds? Her hands shook, and the phone tumbled off her fingers. She lunged to regain control of it before it fell. Clumsy a—

She stared at the screen. A right swipe. And a match.

JR4019 instantly answered.

JR4019: Hey, gorgeous. Love your profile.

Gorgeous? Funny. She looked at her profile pictures again. Louis had some great face shots up there, but that full-body pic? Ugh, no. Her legs weren't visible, and her boobs looked like covered melons sitting on a shelf, the shelf better known as her big stomach. Her best assets looked their worst, and her worst assets were displayed in their fullest. Why had she agreed to this?

But this could be Graham. And he'd said she was gorgeous. Why not play along at least?

Diva3000: Hey, yourself. What brings you to this side of the internet?

OMG. How corny was that?

JR4019: You mean the seedy underbelly of ... the seedy underbelly of society? ;)

She snickered. This might turn out to be fun.

If she hadn't seen this guy in real life, she would be asking him a barrage of questions to determine if he was a Russian bot. The whole group in his profile photo looked like Gap models. They could have been cut-and-pasted right from the website. But Graham was a real guy she knew existed. She went back and read his profile.

Single by choice. Until now. Now, I'm looking for a woman that can appreciate a nerdy guy with a penchant for home improvement and desire to impart to the next generation that working with your hands IS a valuable vocation. Must love to laugh, trade barbs about random TV and movie characters, and coffee. Habitat for Humanity is my weekend workout spot, but I also love a good hike or kayaking adventure. Would love it if you did, too, but it's not required.

She'd known none of this about Graham, but then, they'd never talked about their personal lives. Maybe this was what he did when he wasn't at the store. Everyone had a side hustle or venture these days. Hers was crafting. But his extracurricular activities would explain the muscles.

The profile was so well-written. It was no surprise that he could produce a witty comeback. But none of this answered what she'd tried to coyly imply with her first question. She had to be more direct.

> **Diva3000:** Seriously, though, why this dating app? Why not Tinder or Hinge?

It was several minutes of bubbles popping up and disappearing before he answered.

> **JR4019:** I find the women on here are less about the hookup and more about a potential relationship.

> **Diva3000:** Really?

JR4019: Yeah. Plus, I don't do the Barbie thing. I'm against plastic and fakery.

Diva3000: LOL. Fakery? Explain it to me.

JR4019: The whole stripper-turned-reality-star look. Long blond extensions, silicone boobs, injected lips, injected butt. I want curves that occur in nature.

Diva3000: Unfortunately, mine occurred in fast-food drive-thrus.

JR4019: American nature at its finest.

Diva3000: LOL! Whatever you say.

She really was laughing out loud and was already falling for him, and she'd been talking to him for only … ten minutes? This must be a record.

JR4019: Okay, TV Nerd. Five favorite shows in five seconds. Go!

Diva3000: *Stranger Things, The Golden Girls, Mad Men, MacGyver,* and

She tapped the edge of her phone, stymied by picking a fifth favorite show out of all the possibilities. Was she secretly trying to impress him?

JR4019: Time's up! Oh, so close. Wow, you're stuck in the '70s and '80s, aren't you? Even now. *Stranger Things.*

Diva3000: The '80s were my best years!

JR4019: Who's to say your best years aren't ahead of you? I mean, you still haven't met me yet. :)

Jeez, this guy was confident. It was kind of sexy, but also kind of fear-inducing. Because she was categorically not confident, at least not around men. When it came to business, dealing with jerks, and TV show selections, she was a monument to self-assurance. Where dating and relationships were concerned, her insides turned into a jiggly, unsure mess. What if he met her and didn't like her?

What was she saying? He'd love her! Well, he'd love her personality.

Fortune stumbled out of bed, phone in hand, and went into the bathroom and stared in the mirror. "This is why you're not confident around men," she said to her reflection. What she saw and what she was sure that guys saw were different. When Fortune looked in the mirror, she saw a curvy, cute Black woman with gorgeous eyes and a smile that lit up a room. Sure, she had bad skin days and days where the curse of the Edwards wide, flat butt bothered her. But good concealer and tight boot-cut jeans could remedy that. She was attractive.

But most guys didn't see her that way. They saw a flabby, overweight chick with a big rack, no butt, and better-than-average legs. Doable, but not long term. A standby plus-one if you needed to show up at a function (because she looked good in a ball gown), a booty call if you needed to get laid. A solid four-and-a-half. At least that's what Marshall had told her.

Dang it, she was doing it again, going back to high school and using the way one guy had seen her then to categorize how men approached her now. Any guy who was only attracted enough to get what he wanted from her—which was usually sex—she called a Marshall, named after a high school crush who turned into a jackass in one night. She should stop naming guys that, but the description was apt for most of the men she'd met over the years.

Half of those ODating4U guys were Marshalls, and that's why they'd rarely made it past the first date. She'd had eight first dates that summer ... and no second ones, because she hadn't wanted to deal with any more Marshalls. Every Marshall she'd dated had broken her heart and hurt her spirit, her sense of who she was. And there had been more of them than there were good guys.

JR4019: Did I scare you off?

She hurriedly typed an excuse.

Diva3000: No. Something was about to burn. On the stove, I mean.

JR4019: Got it. I guess it is lunchtime.

What? She minimized the app to check the time, then leaned over to look at her bedside clock for confirmation. Jeez, it was almost twelve thirty, and she had just awakened twenty minutes ago from sleeping off the club humiliation.

Diva3000: Yeah. It's fine now. What about you? What are your favorite five shows in five?

JR4019: Hmm. Everything *Law & Order*. Can I do that?

Diva3000: It's your game.

JR4019: Well, I'm going to do that. Everything *Law & Order*, *Justice League*, *This Old House*, *Property Brothers*, and *Vikings*.

Diva3000: Interesting. I'm surprised you didn't say *This Is Us* or *A Million Little Things*. You seem like a crier to me.

JR4019: What gave it away? The Habitat for Humanity bit or the kayaking?

She laughed.

Diva3000: Do I detect a little salty in that response?

JR4019: Salty? Me? Nah. You haven't met me yet. I'm all about the sweet.

Fortune had nothing to say that wouldn't go into flirting territory. And she was so bad at flirting, even online. She put her phone down, stymied for a clever retort.

JR4019: Speaking of sweet, which Golden Girl do you think you would be? I bet you'd be sweet, naïve Rose. :)

Oh good, a subject change. Wow, he was good. But her answer—

Diva3000: Oh no. I'm a total Blanche.

—led right into a flirt trap again. Blanche the Southern sexpot. She should have said Dorothy. She usually said Dorothy.

JR4019: Blanche, huh? Does this mean I'm going to have to fight for time with you?

She couldn't initiate a flirt, but she could play along.

Diva3000: Possibly. I'm a real catch.

JR4019: That's evident. A great conversationalist that knows her '80s television? I need to stake my claim straightaway.

She giggled.

Diva3000: Why do I hear a British accent when I read that?

JR4019: Not sure. Maybe because you're imagining Prince Harry while reading.

Diva3000: Prince Harry is married. I don't fantasize that I'm talking to married men online.

It sounded a little harsh when she read it back, but Fortune was so into the rhythm of back-and-forth with him, and she felt comfortable saying it.

JR4019: Good to know. On both the Prince Harry and married-men fronts. And no, I don't have a wife or a British accent. If I got your number, I could prove it to you. At least the accent part.

Whoa. They were there? Exchanging numbers? That was fast. Her pulse throbbed furiously in her throat, and tiny beads of sweat popped out on her forehead. The bedroom was becoming too overwhelming, so she hopped out of bed and went into the bathroom. She sat on the toilet, phone in one hand, running the nails of her other hand back and forth across her knee. The all-too-familiar social anxiety attack began to overtake her. Her towel hung on a silver rack on the wall directly in front of her, and she stopped scratching her knee for a minute to dab at her forehead with the corner of the plush royal blue bath sheet.

This was ridiculous. They couldn't talk on the phone! She'd be a wreck, stumbling and stuttering over what to say, big pauses in the conversation while she thought about it, and turning him off in the process. Perhaps this would placate him, she thought as her thumbs pecked a response.

Diva3000: I can give you my number, but we'll probably end up texting. I'm better in person and over text than I am on the phone.

JR4019: In person, huh? Sounds like a meet is in order.

Yikes. What had she just done?

Elaheh called at midafternoon to ask if Fortune was okay. By then, she had almost forgotten the events of the night before. And even though she'd gotten out of giving this virtual stranger her number ("Too soon," she'd told him), she was riding on a conversation high from her back-and-forth with JR4019 and imagining how their first date would be, only half listening to whatever Elaheh was saying.

Each time Fortune's mind went there, she saw Graham—with slicked-back hair from the picture and his body from now, with a casual smile and a glint of delight in his eyes when he spotted her—sauntering into a dimly lit restaurant. She would have miraculously lost forty pounds and dared to wear a belted dress with an A-line skirt that stopped midthigh. When she stood, an invisible fan would blow on her from the side, moving the tips of her freshly colored auburn curls and the bottom of her dress to reveal even more moisturized thigh while "Uptown Funk" by Bruno Mars played in the background. It was a nice daydream.

"Fortune? Did you hear what I said?" Elaheh's concerned tone teetered on the edge of annoyance.

"Nope, sure didn't," Fortune answered.

Elaheh snorted. "Well, at least you're honest. I've been asking you if you needed anything."

"No. I'm fine, honest."

"Last night was crazy, right? I was telling Geronimo about it, and he said we should have reported the guy. Got him banned from the club."

"No need for all that. It was just a bad night, that's all." Fortune thought back to the meeting with the client. "It's been a bad week. People suck sometimes." Thankfully, Mrs. Davenport still wanted to do business with the company, but why the woman had been so nasty was beyond Fortune. Maybe Mrs. Davenport had her own problems.

Everyone had their own problems. For instance, hers—according to Louis—was being "painfully single." She flipped her phone around and checked the time. And she was twenty minutes late to see him. "Elaheh, I've got to go. I'm late to meet a friend."

Freshly showered and still emotionally boosted enough to take any of his trademarked "Louis antics," Fortune reached Louis's house just as the streetlights flickered on. At least she would have something good to report about this SwipeMatch venture.

Actually, she didn't want to tell him anything about SwipeMatch or JR4019. Louis could be judgmental and re-alistic, and she wanted to float on a cloud today. Especially after the night before.

Louis flung open the door before she could knock. "Where have you been? I should know better than to expect you to be on time, even to your own party."

"How is this my party? It's your house!" She swished past him to the kitchen and poured herself a Moscato.

He plopped down on the sofa and played musical remote controls for a few seconds. "Sweetie, *California Cowboys* is your show. You're the one who wants to watch it in real time!"

He was right of course, as soon as she learned they were making a TV show out of her favorite Rebekah Weatherspoon romance series, she'd begged Louis to DVR the first episode. They watched, and she was hooked, talking in double-time while bouncing on Louis couch, about the excellent casting, writing, and setting. No waiting for the end of the season to binge this one. She needed her weekly cowboy fix.

Louis clicked through a mountain of recorded shows until a still frame of three handsome Black cowboys lit the top third of the screen, and they sat back to watch for a few minutes in silence. "So, what's up with you?"

After decades of friendship, she decoded he was actually asking why she was late. "Elaheh was checking on me." Ugh, why did she say it like that? It sounded too much like something bad had happened, and Louis would want a rehash. Well, it was better than having him dog her about her conversation with JR.

"Ah, the Persian princess. Why would she need to check on you? You're grown. Or did something happen when you two went out last night?"

Fortune pointed in the air. "That. It was kind of a wild night, and she wanted to make sure I got home okay. I didn't even call her when I got home."

"Did you hook up? Please tell me you hooked up." He was bouncing up and down on the couch like a small child begging for a toy with his whole body.

"I did not hook up."

"Dammit!" He stilled; his shoulders rounded with defeat.

Why was he so invested in her love life? Oh yeah, she needed an escort to his ball. "Everyone can't be a maneater like you. Some of us have to settle for just dancing and having a good time with the friends they came with."

"Well, if you were having a good time with the princess, why did she have to call you?"

She sighed. "Can I please watch my Cali cowboys?"

"Fine." They went back to watching the program, Louis staying silent until the end. He looked as if it physically hurt him to keep from talking. "Okay. That was torture."

Fortune huffed. "I love this show!"

"Not the show, silly. Why did Elaheh need to call you?"

"It wasn't a big deal. Some guy shouted out some nasty stuff to me when we cut the line at Sly Foxes, and when he saw me inside, he grabbed me and kept talking crap. I kneed him in the groin."

Louis laughed and clapped his hands. "Yes, honey! Handling thangs!"

Fortune stared at him blankly, but she couldn't hold back the laughter building in her chest.

Louis stood and started dancing to some random commercial jingle, a wineglass in one hand and an empty bowl in the other. "I'm going to get some more popcorn. After this, we need to finally finish *How to Get Away with Murder*. You are Annalise Keating fierce right now. Yes!"

This was better than telling him about JR. She just needed to keep that to herself for the time being.

Six

OVER THE NEXT WEEK, her email inbox had been piled high with work requests, and her phone had pinged nonstop with new message notifications from JR4019 on SwipeMatch. Pretty soon, she was going to have to forgo this app and just text. One day, she was going to get caught using it.

Elaheh sank into a conference room chair beside Fortune, iced coffee in one hand, tablet computer in the other. The dreaded four o'clock department meeting—where everyone wanted to talk, but no one wanted to listen—was about to get underway.

"How's Devilport?" Elaheh asked. They had come up with the nickname after two—or was it three?—Kamikazes the Wednesday before. "I haven't seen you for our three-thirty coffee klatch in over a week."

"Yeah, sorry. It's been nonstop with this client. And it hasn't been just seminars. They want us to present how we could revamp all of their marketing, and Davenport wants me to head it up. You're going to get roped into this, just wait."

"Thanks for the warning. Be glad I don't have my gun, because shooting the messenger sounds like a great idea right now."

Fortune chuckled, but it came out as a yawn and a grunt. "I'm so tired." She didn't want to tell Elaheh that the tired part was mainly from staying up late at night chatting with JR4019 until they couldn't keep their eyes open.

Fortune peeked at her phone and thrilled inside when she saw the SwipeMatch notification from him.

JR4019: How's the day going for the lovely Ms. Diva3000?

Diva3000: Boring. I'm stuck in another meeting. I really need a vacation.

JR4019: If you could leave that meeting right now and go anywhere, where would you go?

Fortune didn't need to think about this answer.

Diva3000: Amalfi Coast. Hands down. What about you?

JR4019's answer came just as swiftly.

> **JR4019:** Anywhere where I can see you in a swimsuit. This time of year, I think the Amalfi Coast qualifies.

A blush warmed her face, and she bit back a smile.

Elaheh peered over Fortune's shoulder and whispered, "What's up?"

Hopefully, no one was paying attention to Fortune and Elaheh.

"Ladies, more pressing business, I take it?" Gary asked the two.

Ugh, spotted. Gary and his self-important a—genda.

Fortune straightened in her seat and cleared her throat.

Elaheh sighed and addressed the room. "I think we all have more pressing business than listening to you blather on about colors in your brochure for one of your old-folks-home clients." She looked to Tracey. "Can we adjourn this meeting, Tracey?"

Tracey's eyebrows raised in a moment of shock, but quickly registered her calm. This hadn't been the first time someone attempted to cut Gary's updates short. And usually, that someone was Elaheh. "Sure. Let's get back to work." Tracey rose, and the rest of the attendees followed suit.

The conference room cleared except for Elaheh and Fortune. "So, what did I go toe-to-toe with Gary for? Let's see."

Elaheh snatched the phone away and turned from Fortune's grabbing hands to view the screen. "What's SwipeMatch?"

"It's like Tinder," Fortune whispered, though no one was within earshot. A brief moment of panic swept through her. While they were close friends, Elaheh and Fortune maintained a professional air at work ever since they'd met at the first departmental meeting. Online dating seemed like too personal a discussion to have at the office where others could hear. Fortune reached for her phone and successfully snatched it back.

"You're doing the online dating thing? Why? That seems kind of sad."

Fortune held in a sigh and attempted a smile for her work buddy. Leave it to a married, modelesque woman to blurt the obvious and embarrassing. How did you explain going online to find a plus-one to a woman who could literally walk out the door and have several men begging her for dates in seconds? *You just tell her, silly. Who has never been alone?* "I need a date for Louis's ball."

"Finding a casual-sex partner online? Yes. But finding someone for an event that requires dressing up and meeting people you know? You'd be better off using an escort service." She headed to the door. "Good luck."

Fortune followed, the pair ending up in the break room. Today, it smelled like yeasty dough and marinara. Red and white pizza boxes were stacked in and around the trash can like a half-played Jenga game, and open pizza boxes containing random slices lay on the table. It was a miracle they didn't have a pest problem. "How would you know, Mrs.

Santos? Have you even seen an online dating site before today?"

Elaheh waved dismissively. "Oh, honey, you don't even know. Just because I look like me now doesn't mean they were always lining up at the door. Plus, who hasn't ever been alone?" She headed out to find the intern, Josh, to clean up.

Fortune nodded at hearing her thoughts spoken aloud. Still, this JR4019 guy could possibly be in it for more than some casual sex. He had used the word *relationship* in their first text conversation. In any case, she needed to get off this app. This had been the most uncomfortable conversation she'd ever had with Elaheh, and Fortune did not want a repeat of it.

Diva3000: Let's text each other from now on.

JR4019: Sure. Here's my number.

She glanced at her computer's calendar while she read Tracey's email confirmation. Only a week and a half after meeting the team, Aileen Davenport—"call me Mrs. Davenport"—was signing with Davies Marketing as a client. It turned out that she liked all the marketing material and wanted Fortune to manage the entire account.

Fortune liked to think that it was because she had kept her cool and had been on top of her game in the proposal pitch. But honestly, their company was one of the few local marketing firms that worked with nonprofits. Everyone wanted to work with companies that made the big bucks, that could afford splashy ads, celebrity endorsements, and social media managers. Imagine having one person to monitor your Facebook and Instagram accounts all day. It had been hard enough to remember to look at her SwipeMatch app after Louis had made her profile.

Boy, was she glad she had. She loved talking to this JR4019 dude.

Once the discussion went off-app, JR4019 texted more during work than he had before. Maybe he hadn't wanted anyone to see him using the app, either. Funny how he hadn't pressed Fortune for her number. In fact, after the first conversation, he hadn't even mentioned it again, and when she'd suggested texting, he'd given her his number instead of asking for hers. Just the thought of that made everything more comfortable. Everything about talking with him was just relaxing and fun. When was the last time that happened? She hummed a few notes of Jill Scott's "Easy Conversation" as she made her way to the afternoon department meeting.

The good news about the new client went over so well at the department meeting that even Gary couldn't drone on. Tracey ended the meeting early, which meant more time Fortune could use to get to know JR4019.

It took only a couple of days of texting before she and JR had a routine. Or rather, like Elaheh, Fortune had her own midafternoon fix: start or continue a chat with JR4019. He was in major chat mode around four, and with a few stops and starts—her hasty "going into a meeting" or his "headed home now" followed by thirty minutes or so of silence—it continued into late evening. She couldn't figure out if that was Graham's schedule, because she saw him only on the occasional weekend when she went grocery shopping, and she hadn't been to that store since they met online, opting to go to the one near Davies Marketing instead. Had that been on purpose? Was she hiding because she didn't want him to put one and one together and get ... her?

What they chatted about was so interesting, she didn't even think that he hadn't mentioned seeing her in the store. She was cute, that was a fact, but she'd long gotten over the fact she wasn't a stunner whose beauty seared a memory in men's minds. It was her personality that they remembered, her wit and her effervescence. And that's why JR was so captivated. When they'd meet he would be so attracted to her words, their previous association would just be a darling anecdote—it took SwipeMatch to see what was right in front of us!—and all that jazz.

Today's conversation had started off about what each one had majored in during college—he'd majored in construction science; she'd majored in marketing—but had somehow ended up as a debate about the merit of comic books as reading selections.

Fortune: Please tell me you read more than just comic books.

JR4019: I do. But a man needs some wind-down time every now and then. Comics are my wind-down.

She laughed aloud at his retort.

Fortune: Fair enough.

JR4019: Well, I need food now. Talk to you later?

OMG. What time was it? She focused on the time above their conversation. Yikes, she would be late to meet Louis. Again.

Fortune: Sure. I have to go, too. Talk to you later!

JR4019: Maybe in person? Next weekend?

She hastily typed, "Sure!" and locked her phone before realizing what she'd done.

"I haven't seen you in a week! And you're late on top of that. Where have you been?" Louis stood in his doorway, his arms folded across his chest, blocking Fortune's entry. He reminded her of one of her mother's sisters, overly dramatic and overly motherly.

"We got a new account. Hey, do you know an Aileen Davenport?"

He stepped away from the door just enough to let her in. "Yep. Director of SEW Foundation—Saving and Empowering Women. Rich husband."

Fortune made a beeline for the kitchen for Moscato and then to the living room. "You would know that. Anyway, we're revamping all their marketing and external communications material. Total rebrand."

"They've been on the gala guest list for years! And with good reason." Louis grabbed a handful of popcorn from the bowl on his coffee table.

Great. So, she'll have to make nice with Aileen at the gala. Fortune breathed deeply. "About that ..." She poured a generous glass. "I think I might have a plus-one."

Louis's eyebrows rose a mile, and his mouth formed a small O. "Let me see."

Fortune showed him JR4019's profile and the most recent texts that she was okay with sharing. "Wait ... you've already agreed to go out with this guy! You realize this is a group picture, right?" He snatched her phone away and scrolled through a few more texts while Fortune huffed with annoyance. Then he gave his best friend a hard gaze. "You haven't even asked him which one he is."

Fortune sighed and rolled her eyes. At this point, who cared which one he was? She was falling for him on wonderful conversation alone. Truthfully, she was so sure he was Graham, she hadn't even thought to ask. "Fine." She took her phone back.

> **Fortune:** I forgot to ask, which one are you in your profile photo, BTW?

A few minutes passed before JR4019 typed back.

> **JR4019:** I'm the one in the middle with the blue shirt.

Fortune and Louis looked at the profile photo again. Both Graham and the taller guy to his right wore blue shirts. The other guy's shirt was a solid blue, but Graham's shirt was a blue-checked print. So technically, they could both be the guy "in the middle with the blue shirt."

"Well, that was not helpful." Louis huffed, irritated.

"It eliminated half the possibilities! Who cares? It's going to be Graham." Fortune smiled, pulling her legs under her. "But if it isn't him, the other guy is cute, too."

"Cute? Do you have cataracts? That's a tall drink of water right there!"

Fortune looked back at her phone. This was the first time she'd really looked at anyone other than Graham in the photo. The taller guy had been caught in midlaugh, showing off impeccably white teeth. He had a medium build, obviously in great shape, but unlike the rest of his long and lean friends, he was bigger. He looked strong, like he used that degree in construction science and could swing a sledgehammer or lift a bag of cement ... or her. Possibly. She gaped dreamily at the picture and grinned. "Yeah, he kind of is."

JR4019: So, about next weekend. How's dinner Friday night sound?

She held the phone in midair, staring at the screen. Was she breathing? Doubtful. Was her heart beating with jackhammer speed and strength? Definitely. When was the last time she'd been asked out? Who knew? Oh, that's right, she did. Visions of jerks who'd stood her up, dudes in board shorts, and guys who had left her in crowded bars because they hadn't wanted to be seen with the fat chick popped into her thoughts. She willed away the visions, but she still couldn't move.

Louis nudged Fortune. "Are you going to answer him?"

She shook out of her daze.

Fortune: Sure. Where should we meet?

Louis jumped from the sofa and clapped, grinning like a Cheshire cat. "Yes, honey! I get to dress you for a date again. Finally!"

Evidently, Louis knew, too. "It hasn't been that long ago. And I'm not a doll!"

"Yes, it has, and I get that!" he snapped. "But you know you can't dress for dates. You don't have anything else to do this afternoon. Let's go shopping!" Giddy, he ran back to his bedroom.

"Um ... now?" she asked, sighing heavily.

She hated shopping for clothes. Hated everything about it. Somehow, though, Louis made it tolerable, and sometimes even, dare she say, fun? At the mall, they went from one plus-size store to the other and even hit the big department stores' plus-size departments before they found an outfit they agreed on. Correction: two outfits. Louis dragged her to "one last store," because he swore she needed three complete looks.

"Am I hosting the Emmys or what?" Fortune asked, a smidge of irritation coloring the words.

Louis rolled his eyes at her. "As long as we've been friends, you should know better. We need choices! And you have none at home."

"But—"

He held up his hand to stop her. "Don't argue with me. I've memorized your closet inside and out, sweetie."

"That's because you came out of it when we were in high school." She raised her eyebrows. She could give as good as she got with Louis. Most of the time. They'd done this a lot over the years, throwing shade back and forth like hitting a volleyball over a net.

"And I looked damn good doing it, too. So, time to catch up, hon."

Touché. "Fine." She flipped through a rack of clothes marked Clearance halfway between Women and Maternity. The rack had a hodgepodge of items, and most of them weren't in her size. Louis was predictably at the front of the department, no doubt grabbing hundred-dollar tunics that she would have to fight with him to put back. Who spent that kind of money on a blouse for one date?

The strap of a dress in her favorite color peeked out from between two pairs of maternity jeans. She wriggled it back and forth, wedging it free of the other clothes on the stuffed carousel. "This is the one!" she said in an excited whisper, falling in love as each part of the dress was revealed: keyhole cutout in the back at the most optimal spot, A-line skirt. She freed the garment and turned it around, spotting the size. A maternity large, which was not nearly large enough for her. She sighed and pushed the dress back into the heap of fabric.

She hated when she found the right garment in the wrong size on the clearance rack. It was like finding fool's gold after weeks of panning.

Fool's gold. What if JR4019 wasn't the guy she thought he was? Would she hate him, too?

Seven

AFTER THE SHOPPING TRIP, and subsequent trips to the nail salon, hair salon, and her aesthetician during her free moments of the next week, it was Friday night, and Fortune stood in her bedroom in front of Louis, smoothing the flowery and forgiving A-line skirt that hit her just above the knee.

"Wear those cute strappy sandals you have, the ones with the chunky heel," Louis instructed as he walked around her.

She nodded. She did as Louis directed, grateful for having one less item to worry about. Louis would never let her go out looking a mess. "What do you think?"

"Masterpiece, as always."

"You do good work!" She laughed and held up her hand for a high five.

Instead of slapping her a high five, he grabbed her hand and pulled it to his heart. "Thanks, but you know that's only half me, right? You're a ten, sweetie!"

She gave him a quick hug, then headed downstairs. "Thanks, Louis. Let yourself out whenever. And don't eat all of my cheesecake!" With one last look in the downstairs bathroom mirror, she applied a little more lipstick, then walked out the door to meet JR4019.

The parking lot of Diamond Steak Co. was packed on Friday, but that was usual. It was the hottest fine dining in town, reservations only, and they had to be made days in advance. Graham had gone all out, Fortune thought. She was getting out her phone when he texted.

> **JR4019:** Heading into the restaurant. Meet you at the hostess stand?

She was already in the door texting back when some-one behind her called her by her screen name, startling her. She juggled her phone and whipped around to come face-to-face with ... not Graham.

JR was the other guy in the blue shirt. She bit her lip to keep her face from showing shock. His eyes went straight to her mouth, then back to meet her gaze. Her arms peppered with gooseflesh, and she pulled in both her lips to muffle the coy smile creeping out. It emerged anyway.

"JR?"

"Hi. Everyone calls me Jason." He stuck out his hand.

She shook it. Yep, his accent definitely was not British. More like Californian. But who cared? His voice was deep and rumbly, befitting his big, tall frame. "I'm Fortune." The handshake was turning into just holding hands, his grip warm and scratchy.

"Weird that we didn't exchange real names." He slowly let go of her hand and went to the hostess stand to inquire about the reservations. "But then, not weird."

He was right. Their conversations had started off so fun and witty, who cared about exchanging names? Plus, it wasn't like he was Sexgod24. JR was a respectable thing to call someone in public; it could have been his nickname.

Although Sexgod24 wouldn't have been far off. Louis had been right. Jason was a tall drink of water! Next to a bunch of the other guys in the picture, he'd seemed only slightly taller than them. Standing next to her, he seemed like a giant. Even in chunky heels, she only came up to his shoulder. And while he wasn't Graham, he was swoon-worthy. The profile picture had been taken a few years ago, because Graham looked less baby-faced now, but Jason had gained ... what was the word? Swagger. Grown-man masculinity.

Her stomach fluttered with butterflies.

Jason's eyes were a deep blue, reminding her of the last cruise she took to the Bahamas. He wore his hair messy and spiky, like in the picture, and his five-o'clock shadow was still in place. But his body seemed bigger. In front of her now, Jason looked more like Jax in *Sons of Anarchy*, not Graham. Maybe it was just time and perspective.

The hostess gestured them to a booth next to the hostess stand. "Have a seat. We need a few minutes to get your table ready." The booth had just enough room for them to squeeze in beside other waiting patrons.

They sat together in silence while they waited for their table. Fortune felt too awkward to talk about SwipeMatch so close to almost silent strangers. Jason must have felt that way, too. Instead, she took in his lower half sprawled out next to her. His at-least-size-twelve feet were clad in expensive loafers with khaki-and-navy-striped socks. His legs, inside khaki dress pants, were long and massive, like the rest of him. Suddenly, she felt okay that she was a plus-size woman. Sitting beside this man, she felt almost dwarfed by him. Sure, her waist was bigger than his. She would probably never be able to sleep in one of his T-shirts like skinny girls did in every romantic comedy she'd ever seen. But between his height and stature, she felt that small cute-girl rom-com feeling. Nothing like the Aunt Jemima way she imagined guys saw her at work.

"Reed, party of two," the hostess called.

Jason stood.

Fortune hurriedly stood as well. Really? How did she not even know this guy's last name? Usually, she was super paranoid about knowing all a guy's vitals—his full name, his license plate number (or at least the kind of car he drove)—so she'd have a clear picture of who he was. After she'd gotten all the information she could without seeming crazy, she would text it to Louis just in case she came up missing. But since Fortune had assumed JR4019 was Graham, she hadn't done any of that stuff. But then again, what was Graham's last name? She knew only that it started with R, according to his name badge. Gosh, she was lovestruck in the dumbest way.

They were seated and given menus, and Jason immediately put his aside.

"Come here often, do you?" Fortune asked.

"This is my favorite restaurant. Plus, it's close to my place."

Did he think she was going back to his place after only one date? Wouldn't be the first time a guy thought that. Guys probably always thought that. "Where's your place?"

"Around the corner and about five minutes down Gentry."

She looked over the menu, picturing the area in her mind. She'd last been in this neighborhood several months ago, meeting Elaheh for something, she couldn't remember what. All Fortune could remember were acres of freshly unearthed red clay, apartment and condo buildings with no siding, and a sign at the entrance of one development that advertised townhomes starting at $350K. That was over twice what Fortune had paid for her house. Impressive. But all she said was, "That's a lot of new construction."

"Yeah, my company did most of it. I got a good price on one of the units."

"So that explains the degree in construction science." She'd passed off that tidbit as a dream deferred when she'd thought he was Graham. People rarely had a job in their major these days.

"Yep. I have a multiresidential and commercial construction business. And when I'm not doing that, I like to teach kids about the trades. I commit to substituting at least once a month at one of the neighborhood schools. I need someone to swing a sledgehammer for me when I get too old to do it myself."

"That's pretty awesome." Fortune imagined him demoing drywall in a high-rise office building, his muscles bulging, mouth set in a determined line, hair slicked back and darkened with sweat. She wished she could afford a renovation on her house so she could watch him work.

She blinked away the daydream and changed the subject. "You know, we never did the 'vitals rundown'—job, school, whatever. We focused on the fun stuff."

"No, we didn't do the rundown." Jason leaned in, ready to talk.

She was suddenly aware of how handsome his face was. Those ocean-blue eyes were deep set and framed by gorgeous long lashes. His nose was exactly right for his face, and his lips were a shade of pink and probably the only thing soft on him. His five-o'clock shadow was barely there, but still noticeable along his strong, angled jaw. So noticeable that she wanted to reach out and touch it, to experience the contrast between his soft lips and his hard, scratchy jaw.

"Where do you work?" he asked.

The waitress interrupted them. "Have you made a decision?" she asked.

Boy, have I ever, she thought. "Not yet. May we have a few more minutes?"

"Sure." The waitress scrutinized them with squinty eyes, as if she was trying to figure something out, then left to wait on another table.

Fortune leaned in and beckoned Jason to do the same. "Did you see the way the waitress looked at us?"

"No, I missed it."

"It was like she was trying to figure us out." She swiveled to see if she was in hearing distance. When she spotted the waitress across the room, Fortune turned back and continued. "Like what we are to each other."

Jason beamed. "Let's give her something more concrete so she can get the picture." He took her hand across the table, surprising her.

Instantly, the warmth of his hand coursed through her body. The pads of his fingers had calluses and scratched against the back of her hand, but his palm was smooth against hers. It was a comfortable hold, a protective grip, which made her want his arms around her, surrounding her whole body in a protective hug. Was she swooning over him already? This was fast—too fast, if she thought about it. Especially considering she'd thought she was meeting someone else. She hadn't even gotten over that internally awkward moment yet, and here she was ... feeling stuff.

When the waitress came back to the table, she smiled, but it didn't reach her eyes. Obviously, she'd gotten the hint. *Yep, this one's taken.*

"Ready now?" she asked.

"Sure," Jason piped up. "I'm having the filet, medium well, with the whole green beans and the riced cauliflower." He looked at Fortune. "Sweetie, what are you leaning toward? The chicken again? Live a little. Order a steak! I mean, it is a steakhouse."

Fortune pursed her lips to keep from laughing. This guy was hilarious. She met his gaze. And so handsome. Did he call her *sweetie*? For a few seconds, she forgot the menu and imagined running her fingers through his sandy-brown locks, messing up the already messy look he had, and feeling his scruff against her cheek as he called her sweetie.

"Sweetie?" Jason bent his head to look into her eyes and flashed a cheesy, squinty grin.

He did it again! *Calm down, it's only pretend.* "Yeah, I'll have the chicken with the beans and the riced cauliflower," she said, not looking away, instead throwing Jason an all-knowing smirk and rolling her eyes.

"Sure thing. We'll get that right out for you." The waitress hurried away.

When she left, Jason let go of Fortune's hand. Instantly, she felt a little lost, less sure of their connection. But when he gave her a mischievous wink, she couldn't help but giggle.

"Your laugh is amazing," he said, his hypnotic blue eyes daring her to look away.

Thank goodness he couldn't see her blush. God bless brown skin. "Thanks. That was pretty funny, huh?"

"Yeah. And nice." He was still intent on her, his look curious and pleasant.

She cleared her throat and shifted in her seat. Had they turned down the air conditioning? Heat was inching from her cheeks all the way through her face. "My BFF calls me sweetie. But it sounds better when you say it."

"Really?"

"Yep. But it's probably because he's usually following it up with some admonishment. 'Sweetie, those heels don't go with that skirt.' 'Sweetie, no more wine, you've got work tomorrow.' 'Sweetie, we can't spend all weekend binge-watching *The Handmaid's Tale*.'" Yikes. She wished she had stopped before that last one. It made her sound like a lonely spinster with no weekend plans.

But he seemed not to care. "Sounds more like a mother than a best friend." The word *mother* came out closer to *muvah*. It made her think about drag queens, which Louis was not, not even at the balls he hosted. "But I'm sure he means well."

"He's not a mother, but he does mean well. He's the best."

Jason nodded, a thoughtful expression crossing his face.

Plates of food were delivered by one of the chefs, who instructed them to enjoy. Jason immediately cut into his steak and popped a piece into his mouth without checking to see whether it was done to his liking. He chewed and grunted a little, clearly taking the chef's words to heart. "This is good stuff."

Fortune casually laughed, but inside her nerves were pinging with arousal at his grunts. "Clearly."

His eyes lit at her laugh, and the look made her warm deep inside.

This guy was so open, so blunt, so confident. There was no question that he enjoyed her company, at least enough to make it through dinner. When they continued the vitals rundown, she learned his immediate family consisted of parents, a younger sister, brother-in-law, and a niece, he'd graduated from Arizona State University, and he still wished to this day he'd researched more before starting a business.

She told him about her job at Davies Marketing and her mother and older brother back home, only mentioning her dad by talking about his futile battle with cancer when she was twenty-six. His phone vibrated on the table mid-conversation, but he hit the power button and shoved it in his pants pocket before going back to his steak and listening to her.

All the joy rolling off him made her feel like a fraud. She had come here set on meeting Graham. And in the first seconds after spotting Jason, she had to admit that she was briefly disappointed that he wasn't Graham. But that disappointment faded rapidly, replaced by genuine like—and a healthy dose of sexual attraction—for the guy sitting across from her, devouring a steak with pure bliss.

Still, Fortune couldn't reconcile not telling him about Graham. Jason and Graham were obviously friends, and friends talked. "Um, I have to be totally honest."

"About what?" He swallowed a bit of steak. "Was I chewing with my mouth open? This steak is like buttah!"

She giggled at his attempt at a New York City accent. "No. You're fine." She leaned in. "I have a confession about my SwipeMatch intentions." Unconsciously, a horrible English accent emerged.

"My good lady," he retorted in an equally horrible British lilt, leaning forward to meet her. "Might you have ... debauched thoughts on the brain?"

"More like traitorous thoughts. But not anymore, I swear." She cleared her throat, changing back to her regular dialect. "I thought I was meeting one of the other guys in your profile picture tonight."

Jason reared back in his chair, chewing while contemplating. "Seriously?"

"Um, yeah." She pulled up the photo, flipped her phone so he could see the screen, and quoted him. "'I'm the guy in the middle with the blue shirt'?"

"But I am ... Oh yeah, Graham's checks are blue. And there's four of us—no one person in the exact middle. I swear I'm not this oblivious. I am humbler than I come off." He peered at her. "And this isn't going to sound vain and egotistical at all ... but do you think he's better looking?"

"No! It's just that ... I, um, I kind of know him from the grocery store where he works?" This was harder than she'd thought. "As in, we talk sometimes, and I might have had a crush on him?"

He sat silently for a moment, his face devoid of emotion.

Her neck and cheeks flamed in embarrassment. She wanted to hide under the table. Really, she wanted to walk out of the restaurant and go home and never come back out on a date again. But sitting here, enjoying his company when she hadn't even planned to, had felt like living a lie. And what if he'd wanted a second date? Or for her to meet his friends? She couldn't survive that without having told Jason the truth.

"So is the operative word 'crush' or 'had'?"

Her eyes lit up. "Had, of course. I'm having a great time right now. And now that I know it's you I've been having those awesome conversations with, the Graham thing is in the past."

"Okay, then." He smiled. "No harm done. Unless you're planning to go out with him."

She shook her head. "No. I'm not planning to go out with him."

"I'm not saying never. If this doesn't work out, maybe like ten years after that ..." He gave her a knowing look.

Fortune laughed. "Who's to say that this isn't going to work out?"

"Not me. He can settle for 'best man' at this point." His tone was flat and even, which caused her to look up.

His face was as blank as his tone.

She met his gaze with a wide, incredulous stare. No way was he serious. Was he?

Then he smiled and waggled his eyebrows before going back to his steak.

Heat rose from her chest over her face. Was this dude for real? She hadn't expected this ... whatever this was. Usually, guys were looking for an exit by now, which reminded her of that episode of *Friends* where Chandler kept telling his date, "Let's do this again soon," when he actually didn't want to see her again. Hot guys like Jason certainly never hinted at marriage.

The waitress grabbed their empty dinner plates, interrupting the seductive staring match. "What'll you have for dessert?"

Jason answered without looking away from Fortune. "Just the check, please. Thanks."

When the waitress left, he leaned across the table. "Have you ever been to Beans & Bread? Best place for dessert."

She had heard of the coffeehouse, but had never been there.

"Better-than-average decaf and great pastries. Want to walk there?"

She looked at her watch in an attempt to break the stare that was going on forever. "Um, okay, sure." She caught him grinning, and the look reminded her of when Louis would suggest something devious. It was only hanging out over coffee. Maybe a cinnamon roll. Now, she was thinking about cinnamon rolls.

He paid the check, and they left, headed to the coffeehouse at the end of the block. Everything here was less than five years old—the buildings, the sidewalk, the old-fashioned-style streetlights giving off a muted glow. Even the strategically planted trees had the spindly newness of saplings.

They had made it halfway down the block when he grabbed her hand. It was a swift gesture, like she had dropped something, and he'd picked it up. It startled her out of her cinnamon roll fantasy. He swung their clasped hands up, almost into view.

"Hmm," she said. "We're doing the holding-hand thing?"

"We're doing the holding-hand thing."

"So, that's why you've got that sneaky grin plastered on your face?" Before she could take back the words, they were out there. Too far for a first date? *Stupid SwipeMatch, making you think you know a person for months and—*

"No, that's not why I've got the sneaky grin." He intertwined his fingers with hers. "The sneaky comes later." He flipped their hands over and glanced at her nails. "Neon green?"

They didn't match her outfit, but at the salon the day she'd gotten them done, neon green had called out to her. The wilder the color, the more she liked it. Louis had told her she needed to get a professional manicure before this date, and she had. It wasn't the French manicure he'd suggested, but after decades of friendship, he should know better. Now, she wanted to hide them, but she couldn't pull her hand away. How rude and insecure would that look?

"Yeah. I love wild colors." She laughed nervously. *Don't say anything negative, Fortune. Don't apologize. Don't—*

"They're cute. A little of you peeking out." Jason lifted their hands and pressed his lips against the back of hers. His kiss was like a whisper on her skin and made her feel special and as cute as he said. He let go of her hand and spread his palm across the middle of her back. A shot of heat surged up her spine then pooled in her belly. "We're here," he said, ushering her inside.

As Jason opened the door, the familiar aroma of freshly brewed coffee wafted over her, followed by syrupy sweet and nutty smells. The air was thick enough to taste, and she wanted everything. "Sweets and coffee are my weaknesses," she said.

She sighed a little, but it came out more like a moan of pleasure.

He chuckled. "I love them, too. This place has the best cinnamon rolls ever created. You want to try one?"

How had he known she was thinking about cinnamon rolls? The cinnamon-sugar aroma wafted to her nose as they walked to the counter. The rolls looked like sin, huge and gooey and covered in a frosted glaze that had a dash of cinnamon in it. She did want one, but she didn't want him to know. Especially after that huge piece of chicken at dinner. "I'm just going to have a decaf latte. I'm stuffed."

"Okay." He turned to the barista. "We'll have a decaf latte, a decaf black coffee, and two cinnamon rolls, one to go."

He put his hand on the small of her back again. "You will love these, trust me." Then he leaned down to her ear, pulling her closer to his side. "I love sweet things," he said so close to her ear that the tip of his nose brushed the outer edge of it. His breath warmed her ear, down her neck and down her back. Being this close to him was sweeter than any cinnamon roll.

That casual touch sparked something inside her low in her core, and her mind crowded with thoughts. When was the last time a man had been this close to her? Was he hinting that she was the sweet thing he wanted? Was her deodorant still working? She was attracted to him, but up until now, she hadn't felt a sexual vibe between them. Now, it was evident. Graham would have to take a back seat to this tall drink of masculinity.

The barista handed them the coffees, a plated pastry, and a brown and pink bag with the other delectable treat boxed inside.

"Here." He handed the plate to Fortune. "You find a seat; I'll get napkins and condiments. Sugar?"

"Two packets of the yellow stuff." She found a table in a corner of the shop, away from the rest of the occupants, almost grateful when she set the plate down. The decadent, sugary smell mixed with the coffee's nutty aroma was going to do her in. She might have to eat hers in the car.

Jason sat across from her and handed her a fork. "You're going to want to try this." He pushed the plate to the middle of their little table and pulled off a piece of the roll with his fork. He licked the icing before tasting his bite. "Mmm. Yep, still amazing."

Fortune hesitated, but couldn't resist and dug in. The roll might have looked like sin, but it tasted like heaven. She closed her eyes and chewed, savoring every morsel of carb-loaded cinnamon goodness. When it was over, she licked her lips so as not to miss a taste. She felt his gaze on her, and she opened her eyes to his smile.

"Oh, Blanche. You look totally hot right now," he said. "We're definitely doing this again."

Yeah, Mr. Lumberjack, we sure are, she thought and smiled.

Eight

Jason

L AST NIGHT HAD BEEN amazing. He'd suspected it would be, based on their chats since they'd matched. But he'd feared that she wouldn't be that witty, fiery vixen from online. That fear had quickly dissipated as soon as they'd been seated. Sure, she'd been nervous—hell, he had been, too—but she'd gotten over that once the conversation started. They'd easily fallen into the witty banter they'd had online—banter he loved.

Talking to her had been easy and, with that throaty alto of hers, exciting. Her normal talking voice was smooth and bedroom-y, but when she got excited about something, it went up an octave. Every time he heard it, he wondered if that's what she sounded like in the throes of passion, or if it even went higher. He'd always liked screamers. And her moans when she was eating that cinnamon roll ...

Fortune looked exactly like her photo. Scratch that—even better. With all the curves that occur in nature that he craved—hips, thighs, boobs. Her rack was next level—each breast had to be more than a handful, an assumption he'd prefer to test sooner rather than later. Even her calves were smooth and shapely, he recalled as he mentally followed them down to gorgeous feet with toenails painted the same neon green as her fingernails. She was like an Amazon—hard but soft, substantial but womanly. Real. Real enough to touch.

It had been all he could do to stop himself from touching Fortune's gorgeous skin. It was a velvety medium brown with undertones of red, the color of a rich, antique cherrywood, and made him long to be a carpenter again. But he hadn't wanted to come off as a lech. Cherry was not a cheap, practice wood. You had to plan everything about your project before you started creating with it. You cared for it. And you did not screw it up. From what he could tell, Fortune was more like an antique cherry than her skin tone.

He hadn't expected to like her so much, to feel so much so fast. She was a world away from the line of vapid single-minded women he'd dated recently.

His last few dates had been setups by well-meaning family and friends. A school coworker had set him up with Janey, one of her friends, and they had double-dated with the coworker and her husband—dinner with almost strangers at a stuffy restaurant where you had to wear a blazer. Janey was extremely quiet, and anytime Jason had engaged her in conversation, she'd looked on the verge of tears. It had been the most boring, most awkward date ever. He suspected the coworker had been trying to do the good deed so she could drag her husband out to dinner.

When he'd told Graham about it, Graham had sworn he knew someone who was available and completely opposite Janey. And boy, was she. When he'd opened the restaurant's door for Tina at the start of the date, she'd grabbed his arm and tucked hers into his elbow until they were seated. When he'd made a suggestion about the menu, she'd gushed to the waiter, "Isn't he sweet for remembering what I like?" *Umm. What?* And when they'd gotten back in the car, her advances and her venomous smile had made him more than a little uncomfortable; he'd been a tiny bit frightened at her volatility.

Fortune's smile had the opposite effect. It was like a ray of sun beaming into a dark room, and those beams pulled him in like a tether. He seemed calmer when she smiled. He wanted to tell someone about Fortune, someone who would understand how awesome it felt to find this woman.

Usually, that someone would be Graham. They had been best friends since freshman year of college when they'd played on the golf team together. Graham had been in school on a golf scholarship, and Jason had needed an extracurricular activity. From there, their group had grown to a foursome, adding Graham's roommate Seth and Jason's RA partner senior year, Ranjan. Graham was Jason's confidant, though. They would hang out all day talking about each other's lives, no doubt practicing for when they would be old men together sitting on some porch at an old-folks' home.

However, Graham couldn't find out about this. Fortune's crush made that impossible, even though she'd said it was in the past. Jason would have to stay clear of all the guys' favorite hangout spots. So, no drinks at The Graveyard. Surely a city as big as Charlotte was big enough for the three of them to coexist. Right?

But he had to tell one of the guys about Fortune. Especially after they'd dared him to sign up for SwipeMatch in the first place. He would call Seth.

"Yeah?" Seth answered on the first ring.

"Still at work?" Jason asked. He remembered Seth saying he'd be working weekends for the foreseeable future because he was up for a promotion. Why working weekends would help Seth get the promotion, though, Jason wasn't sure.

"I was about to head home. What's up?"

"So, there's this girl—"

"There's always a girl."

Jason ignored him. "She's amazing. I mean, the way she eats a cinnamon roll is so ..."

"So she's a fat chick. Are you still on that app? The Hinge-for-fat-chicks one? I thought that was a dare."

Jason remembered meeting his friends at The Graveyard after the Tina incident. And now, he was tolerating jabs after the same friend had dared him to go on SwipeMatch. He knew Seth was finicky about the women he dated, but when had he started making fun of Jason's choices? "Seth, you're a jackass. Why am I even talking to you?"

"Why *are* you talking to me? You and Graham are the ones in the bromance. I'm the keg guy."

"I can't tell Graham."

Seth lowered his voice in a conspiratorial whisper. "Why? Are you secretly dating Dani?"

Dani was Danielle, Graham's off-again, on-again girlfriend since college. Right now, they were off, but to the friends, she was permanently off—off-limits. Jason had never been attracted to her anyway. She was like a little sister to him. "No. My date had a crush on Graham."

"Why would she tell you that?"

"Doesn't matter. I don't need his ego on this. I need some objectivity."

"I am that. The objective keg guy with no filter." Horns honked in the background. "Watch it, moron! Charlotte drivers. How many dates have you been on?"

"One, but I—"

Seth interrupted. "You're just talking out of your dick, then."

"Don't you mean ..."

"I said it correctly. You're letting your little head think for you. You really need to get laid. Work that crap out of your system. When was the last time you got some?"

"That's not the issue."

"It is. You haven't slept with anyone in a while. Even Tina, and she was hot." He tsked Jason like a disapproving mother. "Go on another date or two and get some before gushing about this chick being so amazing. God, you're such a girl sometimes."

"Why are we even friends?"

"Because I'm—"

"The keg guy, I remember. Bye."

"You're welcome!" Seth sang out as Jason pulled the phone away from his ear.

Seth was wrong. Jason was thinking with his sound mind and not just his genitals, even though they were part of the equation. Fortune was something different. From Tina, from Janey, from every other girl out there. Still, he wouldn't mind seeing her eat another cinnamon roll.

Nine

Fortune

LOUIS WASN'T BEING SLICK by asking Fortune to meet him at the UICC offices and help him with gala preparations. This would be a gossip session, plain and simple. She knew it, and he had to know that she knew it, because he'd promised coffee and pastry.

Pastry. Her mind flashed back to the night before to Jason's awe at her eating a cinnamon roll. He'd called her Blanche, for goodness' sake. Her cheeks heated as she remembered how he'd looked at her in that moment. It was almost like he'd wanted to devour her the way she'd been devouring the roll. Did he really want her that way? Surely, a guy that fine had no trouble finding a bedmate whenever he wanted.

Their whole date had been amazing. There'd been in-person chemistry, no real lag in the conversation ... hints at a second date. And later, after she'd been home in bed, there had been dreams. Wonderfully sexy dreams. She hadn't had those in a while. It was nice. She would keep that part to herself, though. Louis's need for gossip be damned.

As wonderful as the date and the dreams were, though, she was really in this for an escort to the ALZ gala. Past experience had told her that hoping for a relationship with a guy this perfect on paper was a disappointment waiting to happen. Knowing that guys saw you as a four-and-a-half meant lowering your expectations of an actual relationship.

Fortune texted, then waited outside Louis's office for him to let her in. The building was ten stories—with floors six and seven occupied by UICC—had a security desk, and required an employee to sign in guests. And while it wasn't a weekday, there was sparse but steady traffic in and out of the building. *We work too much*, Fortune thought wryly.

She thought about Jason and both of his jobs, one in construction and the other substitute teaching. He still had time to date her, though. She was getting sidetracked. *Mooning over this guy already? Yikes.*

Louis was his work self: serene, calm, poised, but his dark brown eyes glinted with mischief. "I need some help putting these swag bags and thank-you gifts for the auction participants together. It shouldn't be more than a few hours."

"A few hours! I do have a life, you know."

He leveled his gaze at her. "We're the only ones working on this, and I've already got three hundred tickets sold. Just because you had one date does not mean you have a life now, missy."

"I've always had a life. Even if that life includes a day of binge-watching *Golden Girls* reruns." She followed him into his office, where boxes of party goods were stacked on and around his assistant's desk.

Louis's office was tucked into the corner of UICC's upper floor of office space, with the front and back walls made of windows trimmed in stainless steel. Louis had chosen mahogany furniture to accompany the light gray walls and gray-flecked carpet. It warmed the space in a way the black and silver furniture of her office didn't. Fortune wondered what Jason would think about Louis's design choices. And then she was thinking about his lips on her fingers and his palm on her back.

"You are such a Dorothy." Louis pointed at her, then handed her a box of shiny gift bags from behind him. His desktop was clean except for a computer, a pastry box, and a cardboard tray with two coffees. But in the back corner on her side of the desk were colorful bags of ribbons, tissue paper, and wrapping materials.

"He called me Blanche last night." Dang it, she'd spilled the beans before Louis had even asked. He was a gossip voodoo priest. She was sure of it. She set the box of bags on the floor beside the gift wrap and plopped in a guest chair.

"Oh! What did you do to become a Blanche?" Louis asked, beaming from ear to ear. He wriggled a cup free from the holder and set it in front of her. "Cheesecake doughnut? You know you love them." He opened the box of pastries and showcased them like they were a prize.

"And *you* know I see through all of this." Fortune waved her hand over the spread of goodies.

"Okay, you've got me. So, how was it?"

Wow, he'd caved fast. Was he that starved for gossip? "How was what?" Fortune batted her eyelashes.

"Don't tease me like that." Louis tapped her shoulder to emphasize each syllable. "I want every last detail. Down to the color of socks he wore."

Fortune looked at him with one eyebrow raised. "His socks were khaki and navy striped. He was dressed like a straight-up yuppie."

Louis tilted his head, settling himself behind his desk to face her with the death glare if necessary. "There's something you're not telling me."

She crossed her arms. "I'm not telling you a whole lot of things. You gossip too much." She pursed her lips and played with the beginnings of a smirk.

He waved his hand as if he were showering her with glitter.

She was briefly taken aback, because one time he actually had. Of course, that had been years ago. Still, there were a few bottles of glitter in the decorations supplies.

"No, no. There's something big you're not telling me, besides the fact that he has questionable fashion sense. What happened?"

She sighed, and her shoulders slumped. "He wasn't Graham. He was the other guy."

"What did I tell you?" Louis jumped up and threw his hands in the air as if the Holy Ghost had taken hold of him. "I told you! What did I tell you?"

"Please sit down. You sound like a scratched record."

Her deadpan glare prompted him to sit, but he was still animated, shaking and clapping because the Holy Ghost obviously hadn't let him go. "You should have asked him to specify. Specify!" He breathed, and his body stilled. Possession over apparently. "So, what happened? Did you leave?"

"No."

"Did he leave?"

"Why would he?" She made a flourish over her body with her hands as if to say, *Who would want to leave all this?*

"Right. I dressed you well." Louis drummed his fingertips on the desk and hummed. "Well, if you didn't leave, how was the date?"

Fortune sighed, mentally giving herself permission to tell him ... almost everything. He was her best friend, and he seemed so invested. "Let's actually get started on this task before we talk for hours and get nothing done."

He nodded. "I've already separated the items. We can assembly-line this." He produced a finished swag bag from one of his desk drawers. "Note the finished product, please, ma'am. I don't need you going off book."

It was all glittery and adorned, but the crafter in her could do better if she had her way. "Of course, I will."

"They all have to look the same! Don't mess with me." His mouth widened in a sneaky grin. "Blanche."

She blushed, the name instantly flashing her back to last night. "Yeah, okay."

Between bites of cheesecake doughnut and sips of coffee, they unpacked the boxes and arranged a makeshift assembly line, each of them filling the gift bags. Fortune kept quiet about last night until Louis couldn't stand it, which was all of five minutes.

"You've got to give me something here. At least tell me if he was as fine in person as he was in that photo," Louis begged.

"He pretty much oozes gorgeousness. The man is built like a lumberjack." Fortune conjured memories of Jason's lower half stretched out from the banquette in front of the hostess stand. Everything on him was big. At least all the parts she could see. Jason's ruggedness and his build were arousing and comforting at the same time. He could wrap his arms all the way around her, bend his head, and she would be wrapped up in him. Literally. The thought of it made her warm and tingly. He was like a suburban Paul Bunyan, a magnificent combination of city and outdoorsman gorgeousness.

"We went to his favorite restaurant and his favorite coffee shop." She put down her gift bag to stare into space and cup her cheeks. "He loves their cinnamon rolls. We ate one. That's when he called me Blanche."

"You and pastry. He was probably jealous of the cinnamon roll." He laughed and rolled his eyes.

She snapped out of her memory and threw a ball of ribbon at him. "Shut up!"

He ducked, and the ribbon went into an open box behind him. "So, we like this guy?" Louis's Cheshire grin almost caused Fortune to burst with laughter.

Instead, she held her face blank. "We might like this guy."

"Great! I wonder what a lumberjack looks like in a tux? I'm thinking delicious. I'll need to remember to pack the selfie light for my phone." He gaped at the ceiling with soft eyes and probably faraway dreams of being with a lumberjack.

Hey, who could blame him when they came packaged like Jason? But all of this was pie-in-the-sky thinking. She'd have to bring Louis back to reality. One good date didn't indicate future happiness.

So, instead of feeding into his lumberjacks-in-suits fantasy, she made a futile joke. She gave him a forlorn expression and praying hands. "Please don't turn him gay."

"You know that's not a thing. No one can turn anyone gay or straight." He rolled his eyes again.

Fortune got up and hugged him, flattening his arms against his body.

Louis let go of the bag he was stuffing with tissue paper and sighed, but smiled.

"I know it's not a thing, but you're quite a compelling case for your team." She blew a raspberry on his cheek and grinned.

He playfully nudged her away. "Don't do that to him ever, or he *will* be on my team." They laughed. "Now, get back to work. I do need actual assistance here."

Ten

Jason

AFTER SOME THOUGHT AND even creating a list of places where Graham wouldn't be caught dead, he decided to call Fortune and broach the idea of another date. "I have to take you to my favorite ramen joint. Are you okay with Japanese food?" Jason asked.

"Food you can slurp? Yes. I will always be down for messy food."

He laughed, happy to see she had varied tastes and relieved she wanted to go to a restaurant that Graham hated. "How about Friday?"

"Friday sounds good." There was some shuffling on the other end, and then a woman said something about "cold caffeine" and "the meeting." Fortune came back to the phone. "I've got to go. The dreaded department meeting begins in five minutes."

"I probably should go, too, or these people will have me making something akin to Stonehenge in the middle of Uptown."

She laughed. "Well, you don't have to call me all the time. You can text."

"When we text, I don't get to hear your laugh. Or that sexy voice of yours." God, he loved that alto. It coursed through him like smooth brandy. And her laugh was like a hit of some powerful drug. When he heard it, everything was right in the world. Damn, he was an emo. Or seriously hung up on this woman.

"You're going to get me fired. Bye," she whispered with a giggle.

The week had been an endless blur of meetings with architects and designers, then a demo for an office renovation in the middle of the city, or as residents called it, Uptown. He hated working there. There was nowhere to park, they could demo only during certain hours, and he had to hold his crew and contractors to their schedules—which was nearly impossible to do when they had other jobs or items weren't ready for installation.

Friday couldn't get here fast enough.

As soon as Jason pulled into her driveway, Fortune opened the front door. When she stepped onto her porch, he did a double take. Could she have gotten more beautiful since he'd last seen her? The woman was stunning, and she was stunning him. Her top was a low V neck, her ample cleavage peeking out. She wore a pair of fire-engine-red dressy shorts that stopped midthigh and strappy heels that showed off her shapely legs. A flash of her wrapping those gorgeous legs around his waist went through his mind. Her toenails were painted neon yellow. She was flirty, alluring, and sexy wrapped in a neon yellow bow, and he couldn't wait to open her up like a kid with gifts on Christmas morning.

He got out and opened the passenger side door. "I've been looking forward to this all week," he blurted before he could rein himself in.

Her breath quickened, and her lips quirked into a half smile. "And hello to you, too."

"Ready for RamenHouse?" He hopped back under the steering wheel, staring at her as she buckled her seat belt. His pants grew tight just looking at her. *Calm down, Reed,* he admonished. *You haven't even kissed her yet.*

"So ready. I'm starving!"

"Me, too," he answered. Although he wasn't sure if he was craving ramen or Fortune.

RamenHouse was so crowded, they were forced to sit at the bar and eat. Fortune watched with rapture as the three cooks made ramen by the bowlful, each one passing their bowl to the next chef in the process, until the noodle guy had to stop for more noodles. The whole kitchen waited for the Master Chef—since he was the only one allowed to make the noodles—to finish.

After twenty minutes of watching the ramen-making spectacle, they got their food. Fortune took a huge slurp of ramen, then stopped, eyes wide. A sheen of perspiration on her forehead glistened. "OMG. My mouth is on fire!" She fanned her face futilely with her hands.

"Wow. That sounds kind of sexy."

She continued, avoiding looking at him. "Do you realize what you ordered?"

"Yeah! It's chicken miso. What's the big deal?" He slurped a spoonful. It was as if he'd lit a match inside his mouth. His lips were slick with oily broth and searing with heat. Even the back of his throat burned. He coughed and reached for his drink.

"See?" She braved another slurp. "OMG," she repeated. "I don't think I can eat this." She gulped her drink and ice.

He agreed the ramen was hotter than usual. But Fortune was hotter than the ramen, fanning her neck with her hands and her napkin as she recovered from eating the miso. Her head was thrown back, her eyes closed, and she was rolling a piece of ice around in her slightly open mouth. He wondered if that's what she looked like in bed. He secretly smiled at the thought of her on top of him, lost in the moment, her body as hot as the ramen.

"I'm sorry." She was still flushed, but somewhat recovered. "I'll pay for my share, but I can't eat any more of this." The waiter brought her a refill of water, and she downed that one, too, giving him another show of her sucking on ice.

"No, no. It's cool, really." He laughed at the unintended pun. "Not cool, I mean, it's fine. It *is* a tad spicier than normal. How about a DQ milkshake?"

She turned to him and smiled, tears streaming down her face. "Best idea ever."

He chuckled, then cupped her face and wiped the tears from her cheeks with his thumbs. For a moment, they sat like that, staring at each other. He should kiss her, but he couldn't move, afraid if he started, he wouldn't stop until they were sprawled out on the floor of the restaurant, her pinning him down between her thighs. The heat deep in his core was beginning to match the chili pepper heat of the shichimi togarashi on his lips.

But then she blinked and glanced toward the waiter taking their bowls, and the moment passed. "You really do like sweet things, don't you?" She giggled and hopped off the barstool, heading for the door.

He paid the check and followed her, appreciating the view as she walked in front of him.

They arrived at her doorstep, milkshakes in hand, joking at how clumsy the DQ guy had been when he'd dipped the ice cream for their milkshakes.

"He shouldn't have leaned over that far!" she said through bouts of laughter.

He loved hearing her laugh. It reminded him of Julia Roberts in *Pretty Woman*, hearty and unashamed. He stared into her eyes, content to stand and listen to her mirth. "I had a great time tonight. Spicy miso and all."

"Me, too. My lips are still tingling!" When she met his gaze, she stopped laughing and stared at him the same way she had at RamenHouse. Her chest rose in a brief gasp, and the smooth skin there darkened with a flush in the porch light.

"Let me see." He cupped her face and softly brushed his lips against hers. Her lips were like pillows, full and soft and plush, and tasted strongly of vanilla milkshake and faintly of chili peppers. She went rigid at first, so he moved his hands from her face to her neck and into her hair and deepened the kiss, licking the sweet-hot taste from her lips.

She yielded then—her body melting against him, her lips parting for him, her arms winding around the middle of his back. Even her soft hair curled around his fingers. It was as if her whole being were embracing him, inviting him in.

If anything was tingling, it was his own skin because of being this close to her. The heat from her lips coursed through him, setting fire from his insides to his toes to ... other areas. The vision of her on top of him invaded his thoughts again, and he was wishing like hell it would become reality. He admitted he needed to get laid, as Seth had said, but he wanted only her. He felt this hunger only around her. There had to be something to that. Something more than just hormones.

He trailed his hands down her back as his arms skimmed her sides and hugged her waist and pulled her in closer to savor every morsel of her mouth, her taste, her heat.

She broke the kiss, and he instantly missed her lips. But then she asked, "Do you want to come in for a drink?" and his hopes were buoyed again.

"Sure." He was grinning so hard he was showing teeth. *Man, you have got to be cooler than this.*

Fortune's house was a modest two-story with a semiopen floor plan on the first floor. He followed her down the hallway, past the formal dining area on the right and the half bath on the left to a living room and kitchen with a breakfast nook. In one corner of the living room, a set of stairs led to the bedrooms. The light green and beige color scheme and lack of clutter gave the first floor a hotel vibe, until he spotted the touches that made it hers—pictures and artistic photos of Black women and colorful unusual landscapes in every room, colorful throws and pillows on all the living room seating, and a wall of family photos above the fireplace.

Her house was set up for individual comfort: Her sofa was a gray-blue dual recliner with a console between the seats. Her breakfast nook had a two-seater bistro table that had one side piled high with disposable plates and kitchenware and unopened mail. Even her dining room table, though it looked like she was in the middle of polishing it, had one place setting at one end. She was very comfortable here, but very ... alone.

"Do you want some Moscato?" she asked. "That's the only thing I have for a true nightcap."

He refocused on her. "Doesn't have to be alcohol. What else do you have?"

"Not much." She opened the side-by-side and searched inside. "How about a ginger beer?"

"I'll have water, but may I?" He went to her refrigerator and peered inside over her shoulder. The fridge was filled with all kinds of food and drinks. Two shelves were dedicated to various home-cooked items in plastic containers. The vegetable bin had fresh vegetables in it. And he thought he saw a whole cheesecake in the snack tray. A fully stocked fridge—this was amazing. "Is that a cheesecake?"

She sighed heavily and frowned. "Yeah. I baked it yesterday. Two of my vices—baking and cheesecake." She emerged with a bottle of Moscato and a filtered-water jug. "And here's my other vice." She held up the bottle before setting it aside to pour him a glass of water.

"You really are a Golden Girl," he mused, coaxing a giggle out of her. "My vice is a woman who can cook. Such a rare find these days."

Fortune shook her head. "Oh, no, I can't cook. Well, not really. Now, my grandmothers? They could cook. They threw things into a pot or a skillet, and out came something so delicious you'd want to slap your mama. I can't come close to that. I can bake, though. With measuring cups and recipes, of course." She smiled.

That smile and laugh would undo him. It was musical and somehow comforting. It calmed him. How was she having this effect on him after only two dates? The women he usually dated didn't do this to him. He hadn't even had a second date with a woman in several months, but he was thinking about a third date with her.

Fortune acted nothing like any of those women. She didn't look like any of those women, either. Her brown irises were rimmed in gray, hypnotizing him every time she stared at him. Her curves made him think of the whirl and rush of riding a roller coaster, from the swells of her breasts, to the slope of her torso, to the curve of her hip. He could see himself holding her there, his thumb rubbing her waist in that notch on her side above her hip. And her lips ... he wanted to kiss her again, to feel them quiver against his own ... or somewhere else on him.

But right now, she was saying something. "Hey, you. You here?"

"Yeah, yeah." He ran a hand through his hair. Jeez, he was getting messed up over this woman.

"I was asking if you wanted to sit?" She pointed to the left recliner. The pillows and throw hanging over the top of the headrest meant that the right side was obviously where she spent most of her living room time.

"Oh, sure." He followed her to the sofa.

"My dad was a recliner connoisseur. We always had two recliners in our living room growing up. He always used to yell at us kids for playing who could recline the fastest. 'You break that chair, and I'm going to break your butt,' he'd always say." She snickered and shook her head in nostalgia. "I couldn't pass up an opportunity to get this baby on sale." She looked off with a wry smile. "Now, I realize how impractical a choice this was."

"Why?"

"This is in the way." She patted the console between them.

It had a cup holder and a hidden storage area for remote controls or whatever. It was a great place to stash condoms, and the way she'd hinted, it could be used for that in the future. He tried to think of a witty retort. "I think it's pretty practical, actually." He took her glass and set both their glasses in the cup holders. "See? Now, recline yours a little."

She did.

He reclined as well, but farther back than she had. Then he leaned across the console and kissed her cheek.

She giggled, so he backed away. "What did I do?"

"Nothing," she said between bouts of laughter. "Nothing! It was ... cute!"

"Well, you're cute." He straightened and sat up. "But yeah. That was a lot for a kiss."

"How about we just talk and drink our drinks?" She smiled as she righted her seat.

His heart soared at her smile. This woman was more than he'd hoped for when he'd made the SwipeMatch profile. This might even become a relationship. Could that happen? Wait a minute, she was talking again.

"... and with Javier Firestone there, all the volunteer spots are gone."

"Javier Firestone's where?"

"At my best friend's charity gala. I knew you weren't listening!" she admonished, slapping his shoulder and laughing.

"Okay. So why is Javier Firestone at the gala a problem? You can't go unless you volunteer?"

"No, I can go. But I need an escort." She cleared her throat and preoccupied herself with adjusting her chair and balancing her wine to avoid looking at him.

Was she asking him to this gala? They weren't at that place, yet. Surely, she had other prospects. "Are you asking me?"

She turned to him, but wasn't looking him directly in the eye. "Sure. But only if you want to—I mean, we haven't known each other long ... I shouldn't have asked. It's on Saturday, about eight weeks from now, and I ... Forget I asked."

"No! Um ..." He raked a hand through his hair. A part of him was telling him to say yes. *Say yes to whatever she wants so you don't lose her,* it said. Another part of him—one that sounded a lot like Seth—was telling him to say no. Neither of these voices was clear or compelling.

What he was really waiting for were his gut warnings—the creepiness up his spine, the clanging alarms in the back of his mind telling him something was wrong. He'd felt the creepiness and heard the alarms with Lily, his last long-term relationship, and he'd ignored them. What a mess that had turned out to be.

Now, he waited and listened for that internal warning. Sure, the warning had him venting to his friends like a petty teenager about the lack of prospective partners, but it kept him out of a lot of bad dates that could have turned into bad relationships.

He waited for the uneasiness to build at her escort invitation. Nothing. The only thing building inside him was a craving to kiss her again, to peel off those fancy red-hot shorts of hers. But he'd better be cautious; his lust could be blocking his senses. He'd decline her invite the easiest way he could—by echoing what she'd said. It made sense. And Gabi's reminder to sync his calendars because she'd added the city's Chamber of Commerce's spring small business mixer popped in his head at that moment. The truth sometimes made a great scapegoat.

He coughed and swallowed the lump of regret building in his throat. "I think I have another event that night. I'll have to check. But you're right. I'm not sure we've known each other long enough that you'd want to hear my boring formal-event jokes." He half chuckled. "But I have time to think about it, right?" He grabbed her hand. "Possibly get a few more dates with you?"

She smiled, but the smile didn't reach her eyes. "Sure," she said. "Actually ... forget I asked."

Way to go, jerk. Clearly, she saw this as a brush-off. Or she could be embarrassed. Either way, this wasn't going well. The sexy vision of her head thrown back above him was dissipating. He had to figure out a way to get it back. To get *her* back.

"No, I won't forget. Just give me some time, okay?" He leaned in closer to her, gliding his knuckles over her cheek. "You have to see how bad my dancing is first. You may not even want to take me after that. How about next Friday?" He chuckled softly.

She didn't respond. Instead, she gazed at the cup holders.

Why had he said that? He liked her company, and there was nothing wrong with his dancing, at least that he knew of. Why was he being so hesitant? "I don't want to embarrass you in front of your best friend," he added. *Crap.*

With a severely pinched expression, she looked as if she were calculating the square root of 427 in her head. Or she could be crafting the most vicious way to tell him off. "Hmm.

Okay," she said finally. She met his gaze again and attempted a tiny smile. "Next Friday."

After a couple hours more of chatting, leaning over the console to kiss, and watching a couple of *The Golden Girls* episodes, Jason reluctantly said good night to Fortune. She had seemed as happy to be with him as before the gala disinvite, but her eyes had a little less sparkle in them.

The mixer he had that night wasn't a must-attend. It was more casual than he'd let on. He could have changed his plans. Something in the back of his mind was telling him he should be cautious. Had it really been too fast, though?

He thought about Lily. Memories of her were messing with his mind, sabotaging another relationship. *Just focus on next Friday*, he thought. *Forget about Lily.*

He needed to plan the best date in the history of the world for next Friday.

Eleven

Fortune

AILEEN DAVENPORT WOULD UNDO Fortune after only a month. She was as sure of that as she was that night followed day. Fortune and her team, cross-departmental and created only for Aileen's specific requests, had been working late evenings for the past week to prepare for a "check-in" meeting Aileen had requested to go over their progress. They'd commandeered the big conference room, which was always stocked with fresh coffee and pastries on the side table and a bottle of water at each seat at the main table. Great, Fortune thought, as she passed up the tray of sweets for the third time that week. *Why not put doughnuts in front of the stressed-out fat chick? It's not like she has a handsome lumberjack to keep interested or anything.*

"You're doing it again," Elaheh commented as she entered, her iced coffee and tablet in hand, as always.

"Doing what?" Fortune set up three easels for the graphic designers on the team, then took her place at the table. She'd informed the team that each member would present their own work to showcase their contribution. Truthfully, she didn't want to be scrutinized by Devilport in front of her colleagues again.

"You're giving the doughnuts the evil eye."

Fortune dipped her head in embarrassment, but then shook it off. She met Elaheh's gaze. "Well, they are evil. Some of us have our waistlines to think about." She picked up her bottle of water and took a few sips.

"Oh please. Give me a break." Elaheh waved her hand dismissively at Fortune.

The rest of the team came in, and shortly after, the receptionist led Aileen and two of her employees into the room.

The meeting started on time, with each team member presenting. Some of the team worked collaboratively and presented their contributions as a group, but everyone had some time in Aileen's hot seat.

Fortune sat back, and for the first time since she'd been working for Davies Marketing, she felt relaxed at a client meeting. Usually, she was a bundle of nerves, worried that whatever they had done would be rejected by the client. But not today. Today, Fortune was confident Aileen would love this, even though she was putting the screws to everyone who presented.

Elaheh was last to display her department's work—a volunteer recruitment video and accompanying social media ads. Fortune remembered the first meeting with the social media department, and how on board they had been with her ideas. She knew it wouldn't take much effort to execute her vision, but the skill of the team and the fact they'd created the campaign exactly how she'd outlined it with such flawless results amazed her.

It amazed Aileen as well. She sat, rapt, during the presentation. When Elaheh asked for questions, instead of barking out critiques at her seat, Aileen stood and addressed the room. "I must say, I'm impressed with what you've put together here. This is top-notch work. Elaheh, you've created an amazing social media campaign here. I can't wait to see the end product. Fortune, you've got some impressive thinkers here coming up with such unique ideas."

Fortune peered over her laptop at Aileen, hoping her eyes didn't betray the frustration churning in her gut. This woman was not going to give her an inch, a morsel of direct praise. Well, if she liked the work, and the check cleared, it didn't matter. *It's all about the client.* "They are the best!" she said, letting a tad of the bitterness slip into her words.

Elaheh cleared her throat. "Mrs. Davenport, that was Fortune's idea. Actually, most of the campaign's themes and directions were Fortune's ideas. We just fleshed them out. She even came up with the color scheme you commented on earlier."

Fortune stretched above her laptop to show Aileen her smile. "We're glad you approve, Mrs. Davenport."

After the client left, Fortune stood and addressed the team. "How about we get out of here on time for once? Good job, everyone."

Gary spoke up. "Good job to you, Fortune. We don't say it often enough—you're the idea person here. We follow your lead. You're the boss when it comes to big visions and creating out of thin air. Aileen will come around. Like all of our other clients." He patted her on the shoulder as he walked out.

Wow, Gary had complimented her? As the rest of the team left, most of them voiced agreement with Gary, and a few more patted her on the shoulder. Elaheh even threw her arm around Fortune's back and leaned in for a brief hug. Fortune was finally being recognized for what she brought to the table.

She was so sure of her value at the office. She was an asset there: She was awesome at her job, a great coworker, and even her most uptight client to date was singing her praises. Never mind the Aunt Jemima comments or the fat-girl jokes she imagined her coworkers made behind her back. Those put-downs didn't matter anyway. What mattered was who she was as an employee, a worker, a valuable member of the team. And she was. She knew it, and now she knew they knew it, too.

But then, her value at work was never an uncertainty. Her value as a potential girlfriend, however—she always had to guess at that. And even then, it wasn't her assessment. She *was* a great girlfriend. Attentive, loving, giving. She brought so much to the table. Unfortunately, most guys wanted to keep their distance, keep it casual. Most men she'd dated would string her along until they found someone they thought was better. Why couldn't they see that better wasn't white and size two? Why couldn't they see that better could also be brown and plus-size?

For some reason, they couldn't. And at that point, Fortune would usually shut down. She would not put herself out there and possibly be hurt again. She'd learned her lesson the hard way. Whenever guys said they wanted to keep their distance, it meant they'd already written her off. Maybe one of their friends had made fun of him with the chubby chick, or they'd found out what sleeping with a Black woman was like, and now they were ready for a "serious relationship." Whatever their excuse, the outcome was always the same: push the issue, and get your feelings hurt.

That was what had happened with Marshall.

High school, senior year. She'd been playing in the powder-puff flag football tournament with most of the girls in her senior class. There was a series of three games every year between the junior and senior class girls, coached by a few guys from the varsity football team, with the final game played like a regular varsity Friday night under the stadium lights—except in the middle of spring semester.

The only reason she had agreed to play: Marshall Li-Schneider. He was the perfect guy: smart, charming, and so handsome she'd been afraid to look directly at him for fear of blurting, *Wow, you're hot*, to his face.

Fortune had learned everything she could about him, preparing for the day when she'd trip and fall into his arms, and he'd ask her out, like characters did in every romantic comedy she'd seen. His father was a stereotypical hedge fund manager—wealthy, arrogant, and white. His mother was a strong-willed, slight, Chinese woman and a second-generation immigrant. Marshall was the oldest sibling, an honors student, and right guard on the varsity football team.

That year, Marshall had also been co-captain of the seniors' powder-puff team and worked with the offense. She'd been a guard on the offensive line. Perfect line of sight, perfect position to ogle until her heart's content with him being none the wiser.

But after a few practices, he'd caught her staring, and he'd stared back. Sometimes he'd smiled. For a few practices, he'd taken only the guards and tackles aside to work with them. Never the other positions. Surely, that had been to get closer to her!

During one of the games, Fortune had been illegally tackled by a junior and busted her lip.

Marshall raced out onto the field to her aid. He brought her to the sidelines and pressed some ice wrapped in a towel to her lip. "Chin up, all right? We're gonna win this. Then you can give her an elbow to the face." Then he winked.

Fortune thought, *This must be love.*

The seniors won that game and the tournament, 2-1. After the last game, varsity took the powder-puff team out for fast food. Riding the endorphin high from the win and thinking she'd picked up on a vibe from him, she flirted her way into the back seat of his car while everyone else was making a ruckus in the restaurant.

He'd parked near the back of the parking lot away from lights and halfway hidden behind a dumpster. Had he planned this?

"Let's celebrate this win." Marshall leaned over and planted sloppy kisses around her lips, but only a few landed on their targets.

He couldn't kiss, but hopefully he could do other things, she thought.

In a few minutes, both of their shirts were off, and Marshall was unhooking the clasp of her bra.

"Maybe we should stop." Fortune straightened in the seat. They had already gone further than she'd been with any other guy, and she didn't want her first time to be in the back seat of a car with a guy she hadn't been out on a date with yet. "They might wonder where we went."

"Oh, it's okay. Kylie doesn't care if I'm with other girls." Marshall leaned back into her neck, reaching around her.

Fortune reared back. *Kylie Porter? The powder-puff quarterback?* Kylie was the marching band's hottest solo flutist, and that year, one of only two girls in AP calculus. With a perfect size zero, long red hair, and piercing blue eyes, Kylie was not a girl Fortune could compete with. "Why would Kylie care about us?"

"You know Kylie's my girlfriend, right?"

"I thought she was with Draymond Faison."

"Not since spring break."

"Oh, okay. Whoa ...Wait a minute ..." Her eyes went wide with recognition and shock. "Why are you making out with me, then?"

"Wanted to see what it was like to kiss a Black girl. And I heard the big ones are always up for it."

"What?" Her body shook with rage.

Marshall seemed indifferent. "I told you Kylie doesn't care—"

She slapped him. "Asshole! I thought you liked me!"

He covered his cheek already growing red from the hit. "Bitch! Have you seen Kylie? She's a ten! You're like a four-and-a-half. Why would I like you?"

She threw a punch, but he blocked it. So she scrambled out of his car and got in her own, speeding away from the fast-food place and from being that vulnerable in front of a guy ever again. She cried the whole way home.

If Fortune dwelled on that memory too long, she'd hate every guy she'd ever met.

That memory was why she already doubted Jason's motives.

From afar, Marshall had seemed like the perfect guy. So did Jason. From the first time they'd talked online, she was sure of it. With Jason, the connection was so easy. Their conversation was witty and fun, but they'd learned so much about each other's personality. And then there were the little flirty remarks that made her hope for a relationship.

Meeting him had only solidified that hope. He was exactly who he'd been online and more. She was looking for a gala date—and perhaps a little validation—but what she'd gotten was so much more.

And their kiss on her porch? That'd been amazing. Her arms and legs raised with goose bumps as she thought about it. His lips were smooth and slick as they glided against hers, his mouth pulling at hers as if he were coaxing her heartstrings to mingle with his. He kissed her from his soul, there was no mistaking that.

At that kiss, Fortune's imagination conjured scenes of them at the gala, trading barbs and laughing at inside jokes while sipping wine and making other guests jealous. He would happily hand her the bread because she'd asked. They'd leave right after dessert, hopped up on sugar and building sexual tension, for a hotel room upstairs because there was no way they'd be able to make it back to one or the other's house.

So, him turning down the gala invite had felt like a slap of reality in the face of her dreams. Like he was checking her, correcting what she thought was a connection. And her mind went right back to that seventeen-year-old girl being called a four-and-a-half by a guy she'd hoped would fall in love with her.

But she wasn't a four-and-a-half, even if Jason was acting like a Marshall. And she still needed a date to the gala—a date was the only way to avoid a mess like last year, since she couldn't make herself busy working the event as a volunteer.

Graham's face flashed through her thoughts. Could she really ask him out? She had snagged Jason, after all, and he was gorgeous. Then again, talking with a guy online when neither of you was sure what the other looked like and going up to a guy you knew was out of your league were two different things.

Jason wouldn't like this, especially since she'd told him her crush on Graham was past tense. But it was only a charity gala. It could barely be called a date. Besides, it was obvious Jason didn't want to go.

And it's not like they were boyfriend and girlfriend. She was going to ask out Graham.

Fortune scrawled a list of grocery items she needed, and after work, she headed for Graham's store. After a brief but enthusiastic pep talk in the car, Fortune went in and began shopping.

She spotted him behind the customer service desk, training a new associate to dispense and ring up lottery tickets. The girl had to be no more than eighteen, the minimum age the law allowed to handle lottery tickets. There was no way Fortune would be able to ask him out now.

Graham looked up and spotted Fortune. They locked gazes for a moment, and he smiled. She smiled back, but skirted off down an aisle. Nope, she couldn't do it. Instead, she scanned the crumpled list in her hand and finished getting the things on it.

After Fortune loaded her groceries in the trunk, her phone rang.

"I was dreaming of cheesecake, so I thought I'd call you." Jason's smug laugh caressed her ear through the phone.

A pang of guilt shot through her, but it was gone as quickly as it came. "Is that your way of asking to come over and eat my cheesecake?"

"Are you saying yes? And if so, is there a double entendre in your question?" he bantered back.

"I—uh ..." Her cheeks filled with warmth, and she was stymied for a clever response. Had she misjudged him? Perhaps he wasn't being a Marshall. But then, *being a Marshall* didn't mean he didn't want her. He just didn't want others to know about it.

"I'm joking. That's not why I called," Jason said.

She exhaled. "Oh. What, then?"

"Are you still free Friday? I want to see you again. Now, I need to get these dirty cheesecake dreams out of my mind." He chuckled.

Fortune stilled in the driver's seat. She hadn't thought that Jason would stop seeing her, but she hadn't expected him to make good on his suggestion. Instead, he was making sexual innuendos about cheesecake and asking her out again. She forgot all about Graham and wondered what Jason had planned for this date. "Where are we headed this time?"

"Not going to tell, but here's a hint. Two words: playing and dancing."

"Okay, so dancing with you would probably also require a few drinks. So, a club?"

"Yep."

"And the playing ... I don't know. Mini golf?"

"Nope. You're not going to guess correctly, and I'm not going to tell you. It's a surprise. So, Friday at seven? My place?"

"Sure." Fortune's face ached from her smile. She hoped it sounded in her voice.

"Great. Oh, and in case you do the chick thing and wear heels to a club, you'll want to bring sneakers or something else for the play part."

"Why are you trying to make me as unattractive as you?" Fortune teased.

"You know I look good. Stop hatin'."

Fortune doubled over in laughter. But dang it if he wasn't right.

Jason was different from any other online guy she'd dated. Fortune wasn't a conquest to him, she was a person, and he seemed to like that person.

The gala brush-off was rubbing her the wrong way, though.

Twelve

FORTUNE SWUNG HER SHOES in one hand and rang Jason's doorbell with the other. In the end, she'd chosen an outfit that she thought would work with heels and sneakers—her favorite *The Golden Girls* T-shirt and an extra frilly tulle miniskirt.

Jason pounced with innuendo the minute he saw the shirt, which had all four ladies' profiles encircled by the chorus lyrics from the show's theme song.

"So, are we hinting at something, Blanche?" He locked his house, and they headed to the car.

She flashed a coy smile. "If you mean, am I hinting at you taking me to the cinnamon roll place again, the answer is yes. Anything else is ... inference." She moved to open the car door, but he reached around her and opened it for her.

She stepped out of the way and clumsily backed into his arms—one of his hands gripped the door from behind her, the other held her at her waist, steadying her. With his chest solid against her back and his fingers caressing her side, she felt ten degrees hotter. He smelled delicious, his aftershave like a fresh rainfall. Forget the cinnamon rolls, she'd nibble on him instead. She wanted to lean her head back, stick out her tongue, and get a taste.

"Inference, huh?" His voice was low and deep in her ear. "So, what am I to infer from your head on my shoulder?" He chortled.

"What?" She straightened. Had she leaned her head back? Yikes. Well, at least she hadn't stuck out her tongue. *Way to go, Hornball.* "Oh wow, sorry, I ..."

He dipped his head and brushed his lips against her cheek, silencing her. His lips were so soft; the kiss felt more like the most intimate touch she'd ever had. A touch that she wished hadn't ended so quickly.

She looked up into his eyes. "That's probably what I meant," she whispered.

They stood, staring at each other for a long minute. Fortune imagined he was kissing her like that, but they were in his bed and wore a lot less clothes. She imagined his hands on her breasts, in her hair, not gripping the edge of his car door. Could he sense what she was thinking? His heartbeat had sped up, hammering through her back. If he wasn't thinking the same thing, he was close.

Jason cleared his throat. "We'd better go. Our first stop closes at midnight."

She scrambled out of his arms and into the car, the ghost of his lips still on her cheek, the warmth of him on her back. This was already turning out to be a good night.

When Jason pulled into the parking garage attached to the Epicenter, Fortune silently wondered where they were going for the "play" part of the date. She knew about most of the bars and clubs—there were plenty of dancing places—but the only playing places she knew about were for families and closed at nine.

"Where are we going?" She hopped out of the car and fluffed her skirt. "Is it the bowling alley inside the—"

"Nope." He grabbed her hand, and they exited the garage and walked away from the Epicenter down the street.

They headed to a low row of white nondescript buildings that used to be … she couldn't remember what. She thought they had been abandoned, but these exteriors sported newly repointed, white-painted brick. Lights shone from every window—most of them fluorescent, some blue, green, and purple neon. And all the doors had Gen-Xers, Millennials, and Gen-Zers spilling out of them, looking down at the screens in their palms.

Jason steered her through the closest doorway and into a room alive with the chaotic clicks and clacks of dozens of video games. The arcade was packed with young adults, laughing, pushing one another, and huddled around the machines. There was even a DJ spinning hits from ten years ago in the right back corner.

She turned to her date, staring at him with wide eyes. "An arcade?"

He smiled. "What do you think?"

"I didn't even know this was a thing! An adult arcade with old-school games? So awesome!" She surveyed the room, looking for some of her favorites and spotting them.

"Pretty cool, right? And some of the best nachos and mini egg rolls I've ever had at a bar." He steered her toward the left half of the arcade, where there were two fully stocked bars in front of a kitchen and several pub-style tables where patrons were eating, drinking, and playing a bar trivia game.

"What the heck is a cotton candy cocktail?" she asked, standing in line and squinting at the menu. She leaned into him so only he could hear, despite all the competing noise.

"I think it's a vodka drink." He let go of her hand and snaked his arm around her back.

"Oh. Yuck." She scrunched up her face.

He shook beside her, laughing silently.

She looked up and met his stare. His blue eyes were alive with mischief and something darker that stirred something deep in her core.

"You are so adorable right now." He pulled her close and pressed his lips to hers.

The high school version of her was mentally jumping up and down and screaming at the top of her lungs. A scorching-hot guy was kissing her in public! Woo hoo! This was not something Marshall Li-Schneider would have ever done. Jason's feather-soft lips were rendering her pliant and loose in his arms, and her insides were chanting, *More*.

When he broke the kiss, she sighed a little in resignation. No need to come up for air, she could kiss him all night. She turned away from him and looked into the face of the bartender, who was grinning from ear-to-ear. Were they at the front of the line already?

Jason tugged at the fluffy tulle of her skirt and winked. "Shall we order?"

After sharing a plate of nachos and mini egg rolls—of course you could get a plate of appetizers as dinner—and two rounds of trivia, they decided to check out the arcade games. Fortune made a beeline for *Ms. Pac-Man*, then half turned toward him with her hand out, like a little kid begging her parents for money.

"So now I'm just an ATM to you, huh?" He chuckled under his breath and pressed a dollar's worth of quarters into her palm.

She playfully punched his arm. "No! Not at all." Wow, he was solid. Her knuckles stung a little after punching his bicep.

He laughed harder.

"No, seriously, you're playing, too. Right? I mean, I've got to beat you at my favorite games before I beat you at yours." She put two quarters into the game and waited.

He raised an eyebrow and sidled up to the machine. "Oh, a challenge? Oh yeah, it's on." He nudged her out of the way and grabbed the joystick, choosing to be player one.

"You don't play fair!" She nudged him right back and caused him to miss two cherries.

Despite his cheat tactics—pinching her cheek, tickling her side, and once blocking her vision by maneuvering in front of her for a kiss—she still beat him twice on *Ms. Pac-Man*. He looked sullen for all of three seconds before he had a good-natured laugh with her. And she didn't miss the way he checked out her boobs as she jumped up and down, cheering.

They moved on to one of his favorites, *Super Mario Bros.*, then back to two games she loved, *Frogger* and *Donkey Kong*. While she laughed and shoved him during their four rounds of *Donkey Kong*, she forgot about him not wanting to go to the ball and how insecure he'd made her. She forgot about how after he'd left her house that night, she'd thought about Marshall Li-Schneider and how much it had stung to put Jason in that category.

Since their first two dates had been to Jason's favorite restaurants, he'd listened to her and planned a date doing what she liked. She was so happy that he understood her love of everything '80s and had found this place for their date. And he'd kissed her in the middle of it. In front of people. He might not be a Marshall after all. Maybe he did need time to come around to the gala idea.

After a couple more hours and several handfuls of quarters, Jason asked if she was ready to go to the "dancing" part of the date.

"How far is it from here?"

"Not far. In fact, we can walk to it from the car." He glanced at her sneakers. "I assume you want to change your shoes."

"For any club in this area? Definitely!"

They went back to the car. He stood in the doorway while she slipped off her sneakers without untying them and put on strappy-heeled sandals that matched her skirt. "So why are we going dancing?" she asked. "The arcade was more than enough."

"I told you that I wanted you to see how I dance before you commit to going to a gala with me. So, here's me doing that."

They took the elevator down to the ground level, exited the parking garage, and turned the corner where Jack's pub was. In front of them was the end of an exceptionally long line. A line that she knew well.

"Sly Foxes?"

Suddenly, memories of her night clubbing with Elaheh a month ago came to the surface, unbidden and unwanted. Her encounter with Line Stranger was almost visceral as she remembered him grabbing her arm on the dance floor. She looked down, ready to knock it away. But Jason's hand was there instead. She wanted to turn and run in the opposite direction. From this club. From him.

"Have you been here?" he asked.

"Yeah." Fortune sighed heavily. She should have told him not to bring her here. They weren't even in the club, and she was already edgy. But how would she explain if he asked her why?

Hopefully, there would be no Line Strangers tonight; she didn't want to embarrass her date. Elaheh knew about jerks, but Jason? He didn't seem like the type to walk into a place like this with a girl like her. An arcade where everyone was an oddball was one thing; a velvet-rope club where everyone tried to impress was another. He was more like this crowd than she was; he could leave her, blend in with the crowd if someone taunted her, act like he wasn't with "that girl." But he wouldn't. *Would he?*

Drowning in indecisiveness, she hadn't realized Jason was even talking. "Hey, you okay?"

"Yeah." She shook her head and blinked away the thoughts. "Yeah, I'm fine. And yes, I've been here." Her lips went up into a shaky but devilish smile. "Don't be jealous if the bouncer recognizes me."

"So, you're that girl?"

This time, she outright cheesed. Clearly, he was thinking about a different "that girl" than she was. It was so cute, and kind of refreshing, to be the fun girl and not the oddball. "I have no idea what you mean."

He laughed. "Well, maybe you can get us in." Jason by-passed the line and walked up to Darius.

"What?" Panic shook through her. While she knew Darius, she didn't have the clout Elaheh did to pass the line. Her breath caught in her throat, and she frantically tugged on Jason's shirt. "I can't get us in! I was joking!" she whispered loudly.

Darius spotted the two coming toward the rope and broke out into a grin. "How y'all doing tonight?"

"Pretty good, now that I've got this lovely lady with me. She says she knows you and can get us in," Jason said. He slung his arm around her and gave her a quick squeeze.

Darius looked over at Fortune. "Ah, Ms. Delicious. Looking very lovely this evening. Come on through, guys."

"Thanks, Darius." If she could have turned beet red, she would have. As it was, her hands were sweating, and she was flushed with embarrassment. She clasped her hands in front of her and walked in.

Behind her, she heard Jason greet Darius as if they were old friends. She turned as they clasped hands and gave each other what could only be described as the one-armed bro-hug.

"Jason, good to see you, man. Been a while," Darius said.

Fortune stared at Jason, flabbergasted. "You know Darius?"

He joined her, and they walked in together. "Ms. Delicious?" Jason grinned.

"I mean ... I—it's only a nickname! Answer my question!"

They wound their way around the crowd by the closest bar. "Yeah. Darius and I go way back. He's married to one of my school coworkers."

Fortune narrowed her gaze at him. "You know him better than I do. So, I pretty much made a fool of myself back there."

"I wouldn't say that. It was a joy to watch you work your 'charm' back there." He sidled up to the bar and pulled her along. With his back to the bar, Jason yelled to the bartender, "An IPA, whatever you have, and a Moscato."

Jason's stare never left her, the blue of his irises dark and stormy, his mouth a straight line. She squirmed under his gaze, like she could almost feel him mentally peeling her clothes off. Why did she need to see his dance moves? His bedroom maneuvers had to be more exciting.

Except her memories of the last time she'd been at Sly Foxes with Elaheh, and the reason she and Jason were there now, kept getting in the way of her feeling sexy, and the squirmy feeling became uncomfortable again. Should she tell him about Line Stranger? Maybe to stave off two bad nights at the club and help him understand why she was on edge?

Obviously, he hadn't brought her here to humiliate her. But something about the way Jason had said, "I wanted you to see how I dance," made her feel ... What was the term? Set up.

Fortune turned and looked around the room, needing a break from his stare. The bar patrons surrounding her were glancing and nodding in her direction. Her skirt, which had been so adorable while they'd been at the arcade, seemed to be a nuisance at the crowded bar with people pushing the tulle out of their way. The skirt wasn't even that big!

"People are staring at us," she said.

"No, they're not."

"Yes, they are!" Her back was to him and the bar as her glance darted around the room. "Do you think it's because of the race thing?" Charlotte was a tolerant place, but still ...

"Nah, that's not it. If they are staring, it's at you."

She whipped around to face him, forcing herself to remain calm. "Why? Do I have something in my teeth?" She reached for her purse.

He laughed, stilling her hand. "Of course not. They're staring at your beauty. Fortune, you're gorgeous." There went that intense look. What was he really thinking?

"For a chubby girl, you mean. The whole 'you have a cute face or hot legs even though you should be grotesque due to your weight' thing. That's not exactly a compliment, you know."

"No." His stare was shaded with concern. "Not the 'you have a beautiful face,' or 'hot legs,' or whatever else ignorant dudes say. You're beautiful, period. Although, your rack ... wow. That's a whole different level of beauty."

She calmed and giggled. "You're silly."

"But honestly ..." He squeezed her hand and leaned close to her ear. "Don't ever think you're not a goddess."

"Okay." Fortune shivered, though her face—and other parts of her—were warming by degrees. She exhaled. "Okay."

After they downed their drinks, they went out on the dance floor, Jason determined to showcase his dance skills. And while he spun her around a few too many times and had the very unpopular 1990s "Urkel dance" as his signature move, he didn't once step on her toes or throw her off balance. Each spin out, he hauled her back in. And he did not attempt to twerk. Then again, a twerk for an over-six-foot man built like a lumberjack would be overselling.

After a few more songs, they revisited the bar for another drink. Jason grabbed a bottle of water; Fortune had another glass of wine.

"Anyway, so now you've seen how awful a dancer I am. If this gala involves any dancing, I'm probably not the best escort." He shrugged.

Yep. Setup. "A plan B, perhaps?" she suggested.

He visibly calmed. "Yeah." This whole dancing display was akin to him screaming, *Please, take someone else. For the love of God.*

Which meant she still needed a date for Louis's gala. She couldn't go back to SwipeMatch for round two. What if Jason was still there? Oh, Fortune would be genuinely mad, but then again, they weren't committed to each other. Jeez, this was too confusing.

Jason upended his water and swung her back onto the dance floor. "Let's go again. This is fun."

No. It wasn't. Well, maybe a little.

Thirteen

T HEY DANCED TO A couple more dance hits, him being generally silly and obnoxious, her laughing and no longer caring who was watching. He'd proved his point, even though it seemed a little overzealous to keep on taking up space on an already crowded floor.

Then a slow song came on. Time to really exit. She unfolded out of his grasp, thinking he was ready to be off the floor, but he caught her hand and pulled her back to him. He pressed her against his body and began to sway—in time—to the music. How was he doing it? He was so bad at fast dancing. She wound her arms around his waist, and he two-stepped her in a circle—and still ... no accidental toe-smashing.

Her mind struggled to take note of his contrary behavior, but her body wanted to do away with all the nitpicking and enjoy. She was so warm against him. His chest felt hard and strong against her cheek. And he smelled like rainfall and beer. Who knew those scents together would be so inviting? She closed her eyes and danced with him, ignoring her common sense and savoring him instead.

"I like having you this close." Jason gave her a brief squeeze as the current song faded, and another slow tune took its place. "I also like doing this." He dipped his head and kissed her softly.

She liked when he did that, too. His lips were like a drug when they touched hers, and a flood of heady lust flowed through her that she couldn't get enough of. For a moment, they danced and kissed, but after only a few seconds, they had ceased dancing and were just kissing in the shadow of the DJ booth, with other couples swaying and grinding around them.

He wound his arms around her and pressed the full length of her body against his, and she hugged him, thrilled at the heavy flatness of his palms against her back and the strong solidness against her front. The chaos from the club fell away until the only thing left was the thump of the music and her heartbeat thudding fast in her ears. Fortune wasn't giddy and proud to be kissed in public anymore. She was just needy and hungry for his lips.

He moved from her mouth, kissing along her jaw to a spot behind her ear, and sniffed. "You smell so good. Edible."

She felt the rumble of his words deep in her core, shaking the butterflies in her belly. What did you say to that? Thanks? How could she form a coherent thought when her brain was mush, and her body was a slow-burning fire? "Uh ... we probably should get out of the way." Dancers were brushing against them and nudging them as they stood still.

He took both her hands in his and led them to one of the semicircular booths in the back corner of the club. Almost under the floating DJ booth, the seat was shrouded in shadows. Because there were no speakers here, the bass rumbled through her less. Instead, Jason's closeness caused her body to pulse.

As soon as she sat, his hands were framing her face, pulling her in for another kiss under the shadowed darkness. He took her mouth with a controlled urgency, as if he had to have her, but he was still aware of where they were. His hands moved from the sides of her face down her body to her waist, and he dragged her into his lap.

Her mind flashed back to Line Stranger calling her a whale, and she seized up, hyperawareness of her size invading her thoughts. She wasn't a whale, but surely her full weight on him would be an instant turnoff. *He can't have all my weight on him, not now.* She whimpered in protest.

He leaned back. "What is it?"

"I ... I'm too heavy." She looked down to avoid his stare as she slid off his lap.

He held fast to her with one arm braced to keep her still, then tilted her chin up, forcing her to meet his gaze. "I'm not made of glass. You can't break my lap. You're not too heavy. You're too self-conscious. In fact, you've been this way ever since we got here. What's going on?"

She didn't want to tell him about Line Stranger or even point out how vigorously he wanted to prove he would be a bad gala escort. She just wanted to be out of here. "I think I'm done with the club scene tonight."

"Are you sure? Something I did?" Jason asked.

"No!" She'd said it a little too loudly and at a low sound point in the music. It caught the attention of a few people surrounding them, and she was reminded that she was straddling Jason's lap wearing a short skirt with her butt in the air. She quickly righted herself on her feet and leaned her backside against the table behind her. "It's not you. You've been great. The arcade was totally awesome. And I don't think I've ever laughed so much on a dance floor. It's ... I'm ready to go."

Jason was motionless for a few moments, his stare hard on her as if he were looking inside her skull and searching for real truth behind her prettied-up words. "Sure. If that's what you want."

"Yep." She headed toward the exit before he got up so she could be a few steps ahead to hide the sadness in her eyes.

The ride back to his place was silent and awkward. Until now, she'd only ever felt uneasy once—at Diamond Steak Co. while they'd waited for their table. She remembered wondering why he was even on a plus-size dating app when he could have gotten anyone he wanted. She had already compartmentalized him, putting him in that box with the Marshalls—the guys who kept her a secret, as if society would trash them if they were caught dating a fat chick.

But since that first meeting, Jason hadn't been like that, especially during the first part of tonight's date. Taking her to an arcade, remembering that she loved '80s pop culture

... that was not typical Marshall behavior. But at Sly Foxes, he'd been goofy and just friends in the spotlight of the dance floor, while in the shadows away from others, he'd had his hands all over her. Some of his actions and words were drawing her in, and some were pushing her into the friend zone. Correction, she thought as she remembered their club make-out session—friends-with-benefits zone. That was classic Marshall behavior.

Maybe he was cleverly distancing himself, ensuring he was safely out of gala-escort territory ... and miles away from boyfriend town.

It wasn't until Jason had cut the engine that she realized they were back at his townhouse.

"Do you want to come in?" He rubbed his hands together like he was unsure what to do with them.

"Sure." She grabbed her sneakers and purse and reached for the door.

"Let me get that." He jumped out of the car like he was being chased and opened her door before she could. And she was thrown for a loop yet again. Being chivalrous, calling her beautiful ... Why was he complimenting her and being so nice and at the same time being so adamant about not going to the gala? This was confusing.

A mental light went off. *He wants to get laid!*

Fortune had been down this road before, so she didn't understand why she hadn't realized it until now. A hot guy wanting a good time and wanting to get out quickly: Why not go for the overweight Black girl? From all those years ago, Marshall's words came back to her: *I wanted to see what it was like to kiss a Black girl. And I heard the big ones are always up for it.* It stung now almost as much as when he'd said them.

She eyed Jason as he fumbled with his keys. He was a little nervous. Dang it. It was a sex thing. Well, he was hot, and she was attracted. More than attracted, she thought, remembering his lips on hers, his warm, rough touch. But instead of getting more excited by the prospect of getting more of him, Fortune was disappointed. She'd secretly been hoping for more than a gala escort; she'd been conversing and falling and hoping for a relationship. She'd thought he was, too. But it looked like while she dreamed about #couplegoals, he was dreaming only about casual sex.

Jason cleared his throat as he led her to the door. "So, this is it. I may or may not have some dirty laundry lying around." He chuckled as he let them in.

She wanted to make a witty comeback, but her brain was crammed with so many thoughts, doubts, and admonishments, she couldn't express any. Afraid to blurt out something that would make her seem insecure or unhinged, she mutely followed him inside.

The entryway was almost nonexistent and blended to a set of stairs against the left wall and a living room and kitchen in front of her and to the right. Underneath the stairs, a door to the powder room was slightly ajar, and two sconces reflected light off the bathroom's mirror.

Jason's house was the antithesis of everything she'd imagined. It was mostly modern, but with rustic accents here and there. She would have pegged the industrial metal and wood coffee table and the humongous mahogany leather sofa as his style, but the gleaming white kitchen with gray concrete countertop, gray tile backsplash, and stainless-steel pendant lighting were surprises. From what she could tell, those additions weren't mere upgrades—they were custom picks. Jason was more than a construction worker. He was a bit of a designer, too.

"Have a seat," he offered. "Or would you rather have the tour?"

"Maybe later." She sank into the squeaky plushness of the sofa, which looked back toward the front door, and briefly wondered how many other women had sat here. The sofa faced the TV and was flanked on its right by matching club chairs and on its left by an expansive kitchen island with industrial barstools with leather seats. All the furniture went together, but in a unique way. A way that had been planned, instead of her way, which had been to buy it as she could afford it. This was his sanctuary, not his bachelor pad. He wouldn't have invited every girl here.

Maybe she was viewing this whole situation in the wrong way. And now, she was confused again.

But wait, he was saying something.

"... beer and water. Oh, and Gatorade, but I'm sure you don't want that."

"Did you say Moscato? I wasn't listening." She shouldn't have another drink. She was reaching her safe limit. But something forming in her gut was not sitting right with her. The glass of Moscato after that plate of nachos at the arcade could have been the culprit. Or maybe she was ... feeling things. Emotions. Ugh. They ruined everything. They wanted more from a relationship than a good time. They wanted to be acknowledged, to form deeper connections, to be taken to galas and shown off to best friends. And that was keeping her from having some good old-fashioned casual sex with him. Barely, but still.

She fiddled with the remotes on the coffee table, trying to find the one that turned on the TV. There were, like, four of these things here. Shouldn't he have a tablet that did all of this?

"Yes, I have Moscato. Why weren't you listening? I could have been pouring my heart out there!"

"Well, you can pour me a drink instead," she said flatly.

When he laughed, it echoed through the whole house and through her. This was where they worked. Playful banter. Her mind went back to how much fun they'd had at the arcade, laughing, playing, and being generally rowdy. But the kissing at the club hadn't been bad, either. In fact, the kissing had been wonderfully good.

He brought over the uncorked bottle and a glass, while he had a beer. He poured her some wine, set the bottle on the table, and plopped down beside her, his grin spreading across his face, his heat warming her side. "Ahh, so this is why you were ignoring me. Figured it out yet?"

"Figured out what?"

Jason nodded toward her lap.

She held a remote control in each hand and had another two on her lap. "Um, yeah ... No. This is the definition of rocket science."

Jason laughed. "It's really not."

He took the two remotes out of her hands, and their fingers brushed.

She looked up, and a pair of blue eyes stared into hers. His jaw ticked. His scent was an intoxicating mix of the beer, his aftershave, which smelled like outdoors after a rain shower, and him. It was curling around her like a comforting hug, drawing her closer. An intense bloom of heat radiated over her neck and cheeks. Nope, she wasn't going to sort out any emotions other than the lust stirring inside her that was so powerful she wanted to dive at him like a hyena.

He reached up and brushed his thumb across her slightly parted lips, breaking their gazes to focus on her mouth. Her heart was beating as if it wanted to be free of her chest. *Don't just look at them, kiss them,* she silently begged. She dropped the biggest remote into her lap, her muscles loosening from his touch.

Jason brushed the remote from her lap, dragging his other hand across her thigh.

Her skin seemed to vibrate, and she wanted more of his touch. It was like a shot of adrenaline through her torso. She breathed sharply, her breath sounding like a gasp.

"Fortune?" His thumb was still gliding back and forth along her bottom lip, making it hard for her to breathe.

"Yes?" she whispered.

"I want this." He squeezed her thigh, right above the knee. "Do you?"

"Yes." This was going to happen. Heck, it was already happening. How long had it been since anything like this had happened to her? "Jason? Um ... It's been a while since ..." How did she say this gracefully?

"Yeah, me, too." He crushed his lips against hers. She opened to him, and he took the invitation hungrily, searching for her tongue to intertwine with his. He kissed with wild abandon, moving his arms to fully embrace her and pull the tail of her shirt free from her waistband. His hands groped frantically under the shirt, cupping her lace-covered breasts, then slid past the lace and tweaked a nipple.

She moaned into his mouth.

His other hand skimmed down her side, down to her knee, then up the inside of her thigh.

She knew where he was headed, and he was going to be disappointed with what he found, or rather, what he wouldn't find when he got there. Her mind was in full arousal mode, but her lady parts ... weren't. Well, she wasn't twenty-one anymore. A combustible reaction couldn't happen from ten seconds of fierce making out and a little groping.

Even if she were twenty-one, her body wouldn't respond if her mind was somewhere else. And her mind was still imagining a Jason and Fortune couple at the gala and wondering why he couldn't see what she saw.

She clamped her thighs together, trapping his hand.

He let up on the kiss. "Everything okay?" he asked.

Don't stop, just give me some more time, she thought. "Yeah. Can we slow down a little?"

He took his hand out of her shirt and leaned over to kiss her behind her ear instead. It was one of his magical lip caresses, and she melted under their touch.

"That more your speed?" he whispered, his breath tickling her ear.

"Yeah. Do more of that," she answered, low and throaty.

Her arms went around his waist and under the hem of his shirt, her hands touching smooth skin over hardened muscle. His body was so solid. She'd have sex with him for no other reason than to get a glimpse of his body. If he looked as great as he felt underneath clothes ... Jiminy Christmas.

He slowly kissed a path from her ear down her neck to the hollow of her throat.

She released the thigh-hold on his hand, and he continued up her leg, slower this time and caressing along the way. Everything hummed, and arousal ran through her again, from his tweaking her nipple, licking her throat, tugging her skirt.

Wait, why was he tugging her skirt? She looked down at him pushing and pulling tulle out of the way to get to her. She held in a barrage of giggles.

He swore as he fumbled with the layers of fabric. "Never wear this again, okay?"

She giggled. "But you said I was adorable."

"Lie back," he ordered.

She did, and the skirt puffed up in the air. A whoosh of air rushed over the tops of her thighs.

"Better," he said, a smug grin surfacing. He leaned over her, nudging her legs apart with his knee. She felt the weight of him on one side, his fingers moving from her breast to cup her chin. His other hand resumed its journey southward while he took her mouth in a rough kiss. Everything was humming again. Except something was painfully digging into her kidney. She rolled away and reached under her, grabbing whatever it was and flinging it above her head out of the way.

Loud moans from the TV speakers echoed through the townhouse.

Fortune's eyelids flew open and caught an eyeful of a couple on the Playboy channel displaying a heck of a lot better coordination than they were. *How did that guy get that woman's legs to do that?*

Jason clambered for the remote to turn off the TV, and Fortune scrambled out of his way. Limbs flailed, clothes twisted and rode up, and Jason's hand went from twisted in Fortune's skirt to inside her underwear.

"Stop moving. I see it!" Jason reached past her with one hand, the other between Fortune's lower stomach and tangled in her lacy panties that might have been a little too tight and, right now, weren't doing her any favors. She promised herself to throw them away when she got home.

His fingers were heavenly. Heavenly if he had them in the right place, she thought as he lovingly caressed her stomach. It didn't matter anyway, because she was still drier than the Mojave Desert ... down there. It was like her vagina had gone on strike.

"Almost there," he said.

"Not hardly," she mumbled, squirming out of the way despite his warning to stop moving.

"What?" He leaned back toward her. "Got it!" He shifted his body to point the remote.

Then one of his trapped fingers slipped lower and curled ... She yelped like a wounded animal.

He jumped off her like she was a live wire, hurtling to the remote and turning off the TV, landing on the floor between the sofa and the coffee table. "Are you all right?" he asked, panting as he used the arm of the sofa and edge of the table to help himself stand.

Fortune straightened, but couldn't say anything because she was breathing so hard. Her face was hot with embarrassment.

His chest rose and fell with heavy, deep breaths that slowed as minutes ticked by. He sat beside her and held her hand. "Fortune?"

"Yeah, yeah. Totally okay ... but maybe we should stop," she said, her breath evening out with his. She looked at their clasped hands to avoid his gaze. She couldn't decide whether to laugh like a crazy person or cry like a petulant child who wasn't getting her way. A flash of the old show *The Three Stooges* went through her mind, and she burst with laughter. This had been right up there with the Stooges' best slapstick moments, if they had been rated PG-13.

"Yeah, of course. Oh boy, this was silly, right? Like *Three Stooges* funny," he said.

She gazed at him. "That's what I was thinking!"

She stood, and he stood with her, not letting go of her hand.

"I think I'd better go. We've done enough damage for one night." Her laugh came out like a small whimper.

He walked her to the door. "If you scratch this last part, you had a good time, right?"

"Yeah, actually I did." She stretched up on her toes and planted a kiss on his cheek. Even though the last part had been crazy awkward and more than a little confusing, she wanted to say but didn't. "One question, though. Um ... the Playboy Channel?"

"Had to do something to stop dreaming about you covered in cheesecake." He winked and took advantage of her gaped-open mouth by covering it with his.

As she rode home, the hilarity wore off, and the flood of whys and what-ifs crowded Fortune's thoughts. What had started off as the best date ever had devolved into a comedy skit worthy of *Saturday Night Live*. The cliché about things going downhill felt right for this whole night. If their date had ended after the arcade, it wouldn't have become a confused mixed-signals mess. Did he only want sex, or did he want a relationship? The more she thought about it, though, the more she was convinced that he was acting like a Marshall. Her vagina knew it, even if her heart had trouble processing it.

However, one thing was clear. Jason did not want to be her date to Louis's ball.

She could ask Graham. It would be so much easier than going back to SwipeMatch. But would he turn her down? Just because the guys were friends didn't mean they liked the same type of woman. Graham and Fortune were going to have to go out on at least one date to find out. In any case, she and Jason weren't exclusive yet. If his gala refusal and tonight's dancing disaster told her anything, it was that he wanted to keep her at a distance.

Only six weeks remained before the gala. She needed to act now. It was settled. She would ask Graham out.

Fourteen

FIVE DAYS LATER, FORTUNE found herself back at her old haunt. Graham's store. She had a list of eleven items, but she really had one goal to reach before leaving—to ask Graham out and get him to escort her to the gala.

The UICC ball was one of the highlights of her year. After attending seminar after seminar and evaluating them, it was a refreshing change of pace to attend an event and do nothing except the occasional volunteer duty. The only dreaded things now were her need for a date and the memory of last year's ball without one.

Last year's gala had been themed "The Days We Forgot" with the ballroom decked out in '50s decor. She'd thought it would be cute to go in sort of a costume. She'd binge-watched a couple of seasons of *Happy Days* and decided on a cocktail dress with a hoop skirt and had even grown her hair long enough to wear ribbons in it. She'd looked good. And Louis, in his infinite wisdom, had sat her at a table with mostly people her age who had obviously bought single tickets.

The woman to her right, Veda, had been dreadfully boring. The guy on her left had had a weight lifter's body and had been polite but extremely standoffish. For some reason, he hadn't wanted to pass her the bread or the butter, ignoring her whenever she'd asked for it. She'd asked Louis later about the guy and found out that he was a personal trainer at the big "meat market" fitness center near Uptown. It made sense then. He hadn't wanted her to get fatter with carbs and fat. And she'd been going on and on about how much she loved bread with Veda because Veda had talked endlessly about avocado-toast recipes.

Thinking about that night made Fortune want to shed tears again. She shook her head and mentally pepped herself up. *You can't ask Graham out in tears.* She composed herself and continued down the aisle, but lingering too long in the aisles was a no-go because she would look suspicious ... or like she was stealing. In a sense, she had been stealing—glances at Graham, time with Graham, views of him for her fantasies. Since Jason, though, the Graham-stalking sessions weren't as appealing as they'd been before.

A conversation on the next aisle caused her to stop.

"Has this been finalized?" Graham's whisper coursed with helplessness. A shuffling sound like someone shaking boxes of dry pasta played intermittently in the background.

"Yes. We've monitored the situation for six months since the new Trader Saver went in down the block. With that and the Superstore a mile down the road, there's not enough potential revenue to make this location viable," a woman's voice whispered back at him with the bland detachment of upper-level management.

"Some of these people have families to feed!" Graham's urgent whisper couldn't contain his exasperation at what the woman was telling him.

Was the store really closing? Fortune was devastated! All these people would be out of work—including Graham! She eavesdropped a bit more.

"We're making sure everyone displaced can be accommodated at another store in the area. Minimal job loss." The woman was silent for a few moments. "Can't you get someone to finish this? This is not the best place for this conversation."

"Let's go back to my office." Graham and the woman shuffled out of the adjacent aisle and toward the front of the store, where the manager's office was.

At least he wouldn't lose his job, but where would Graham go? The next-closest store was clear across town! Why had she had that double espresso before heading to the store? Now, she was flushed, nervous, and jittery. The combination gave her a rush of energy and panic that probably overinflated the moment. Comparing it to how Jason had reacted to her escort request, her reaction wasn't any more overkill than that.

If Jason in all his gorgeousness didn't mind being seen in public with her, she couldn't be as undatable as she thought. And since Jason didn't want to go to the gala with her, why not swing for the fences and ask out her crush? Sounded like he could use a pick-me-up as much as she needed a date to this gala. She could do this!

She meandered around the store, periodically looking up at the manager's office until Graham came out. When he finally appeared, dragging behind the store chain's director, Fortune walked toward him, mentally pepping herself up for what she was about to do, assuring herself that asking him for a date would get his spirits soaring. After a moment, she realized she was giving the same pep talk she gave herself before every big presentation at work. Whatever, she *could* do this.

"Lane four is open for checkout, miss." Graham motioned to the lane in front of her.

Jeez Louise, she probably looked like she was staring into space like a confused hamster. At least she'd gotten his attention.

"Thanks, but actually I wanted to ask you something first."

"About the store?"

"No. About your plans for Saturday night."

He sucked in a breath and put his hand on his hip.

Suddenly, every brush-off that she'd ever heard—personally, from others, on TV—went through her mind. What if he was gay, or had a girlfriend, or was otherwise occupied with a nightly ritual of trying to take over the world? Her mouth started spouting explanations for her behavior. "We ... we talk sometimes, and I thought I sensed a vibe between us and wondered if you felt it, too. Anyway, you seem like you could use a break from this. Perhaps a night out?"

What the hell was that? A few customers gave her side glances, but thankfully no one was staring right at her. Warmth crept into her cheeks.

Graham stared at her and blinked. Then he looked off to the side and chuckled softly.

OMG, I humiliated myself! And for nothing. She forced her feet to move, but they refused.

"Yeah, I felt something, too." He blew out a heavy sigh. "And I could use a night out. Now more than ever. How about next Saturday?"

"Sure. I should be free then." She looked toward lane four, which was now lined with customers, some obviously eavesdropping. "But it looks like lane four isn't anymore. Off to lane seven."

They exchanged numbers and awkward smiles and waves before departing.

He'd said yes! It took all her composure not to break out into a happy dance on the way to the car. Or maybe crumple in a faint. For the first time since Friday, she felt relieved that she'd had a plan B, even if that plan was shaky at best. But even better was that tiny ego boost that only a *yes* from a guy she'd been crushing on could give. Surely, a woman who could get *two* gorgeous guys wasn't a four-and-a-half, right?

On Saturday, Fortune met Louis at Party Supplies Warehouse to help him pick out some items he needed for the gala. Usually, Louis would go shopping with his assistant, but she was very pregnant and very useless in a store with no customer restrooms.

Party Supplies Warehouse was exactly what it said in its name, a warehouse with endless racks of party supplies. It was a big brick end cap of an abandoned strip mall on the edge of town, claiming the space from a bankrupt electronics chain. Though the big, gray, metal interior always had its loud HVAC system running, it was constantly a tad too hot in the summer and too cold in the winter. The only thing inviting about the space was all the bright colors in the back half of the store—the décor department.

But the store didn't need to be flashy, because it was the only warehouse of its kind in Charlotte, a city that had a party every other weekend nine months out of the year. And as a Davies Marketing employee with a bestie in nonprofit, she felt like she'd been to most of those parties.

However, this year's UICC gala was set up to be unique, at least for her. With Javier Firestone and possibly having a date instead of volunteer duty, it could happen. Graham seemed like a nice enough escort, considering he was an almost stranger she had a crush on.

Louis met Fortune at the sliding-door entrance. "Thanks for coming. Funny how none of the volunteers on the wait-list want to help before the event date." He rolled his eyes. "Remind me never to announce a celebrity guest to volunteers before they get placed. Have you asked Jason to the ball yet?"

She stopped. In all the craziness, she had forgotten to fill Louis in. He wasn't going to see a lumberjack in a tux this time. "Yeah ... about that ..."

He wrangled a shopping cart free and steered it around Fortune into aisles of table décor.

She followed, summarizing what had happened between her and Jason since their first date, her eyes glued to her phone screen to distract her from getting emotional or facing Louis. "So, since he didn't want to go, I asked out Graham ..." she blurted without thinking.

He stopped in the middle of an aisle, staring at placecard holders.

She mentally cursed herself for the overshare. He was sure to make fun of her. He'd probably call her a player and laugh.

Louis picked up a tall silver holder, flipping it over in his hands.

Fortune wondered if he was still listening, he'd been silent for so long. Then he turned to her.

"The Graham thing? Not a good idea," Louis warned, the worry in his voice making the words sound shaky. He put two boxes of the holders in the cart and walked away.

Oh crap.

Fifteen

G RAHAM WAS LATE. FORTUNE had been standing outside of the golf venue for fifteen minutes, watching people enter and leave and becoming increasingly uncomfortable each time they did so.

The venue was fairly new—part driving range, part entertainment space, and all bar—and on a Saturday night, it was filled with pretty, pretentious Millennials who were new to the city. Immediately inside the doors, the atmosphere was loud, dark, and hyped, not conducive to first meeting someone. Fortune felt like a mediocre racehorse who had been put out to pasture, right beside the stable of the newest Triple Crown winners. This was not her first choice for a date.

This had been Graham's idea. She wanted to be accommodating, since he was her crush. But the fact that she'd felt she had to was a symptom of the "Marshall syndrome." She really needed to stop thinking every guy saw her as a pathetic four-and-a-half and act like the ten she was. Jason had liked her, and he seemed to be sane.

And now she was worrying about Jason. This probably had crossed a line. *Stop being stupid, Fortune. This definitely crossed a line.* Just because he didn't want to go to the gala didn't mean that he would be okay with her going with a buddy of his. Maybe Graham would stand her up, and she wouldn't have to even think about—

"Hey, Fortune. Sorry I'm late." Graham sauntered up to her with a sheepish grin.

"I've only been standing here for"—she checked her watch as dramatically as she could (complete with arm flails)—"twenty minutes. No big."

Obviously not taking the sarcastic hint, his face relaxed. "Oh good. Not long." He reached for the door, held it open, and puffed out his chest, proud of his chivalrous door-opening act.

Was he for real? She scrunched her nose up in a confused frown while he peered over the parking lot, distracted by a loud group of Gen Zers. *Shake it off, Fortune.* When he directed his attention back to her, she was all smiles.

They entered the venue. The room was nearly filled with patrons, the gigantic neon-lighted logo painting everyone blue.

"I've never been here before. What should we do first?" She took inventory of the crowd, concluding that she wasn't the biggest, most overdressed person in the room in a short-sleeved shirt, knee-length skirt, and wedges, but she'd bet money she was close. Great.

He steered her to the closest bar. "First, we get a drink. Then we go pitch a few wedges. Are you a Cosmo girl?"

"Gross, no." She leaned against the bar to see the selection. "Do you have Moscato?" she asked the bartender.

"Yeah, sure. Pink or regular?" The bartender brought up a wineglass.

"Pink." She caught a glimpse of Graham. His eyebrows were raised as if he'd learned something new about women. *Congrats for finding out we're not all exactly like Carrie Bradshaw.*

"Done." The bartender looked at Graham. "Do you want to start a tab?"

"Um, no. I'll have a Sam Adams Pale Ale." Graham shifted uncomfortably from one foot to the other.

She wondered if he thought she'd read something into not starting a tab. Did he want to cut the evening short? Honestly, she'd rather have a sober, slightly nervous date than a sloppy, ugly, drunk date, anyway.

The bartender also rented a driving lane for them, and the two were out of the bar area and onto the patio. Finally, Fortune thought, a little breathing room. Until a group of guys in business suits got a lane beside them. The guys looked like they were around Fortune's age or a little older, and all were Big Finance types from Uptown. The very snobby, very douchebag types.

Graham shifted again and turned his back to them while he was instructing Fortune on how to hit a golf ball. "Now, here's how you pitch a wedge."

He performed the motion first, making sure he was standing opposite her and far away. Was that so she could see what he was doing, or so he wouldn't be seen as her date?

Her douchebag-defense system went from mere detection into overdrive.

The guys glanced over one or two at a time, as if they were trying to figure out Fortune and Graham, probably wondering what they were doing there together. She fought to concentrate on Graham's lesson, but when she caught a few of them snickering, her focus was gone, replaced by the desire to punch all of them in their throats. It was almost as bad as Line Stranger at Sly Foxes calling her a whale.

"Think you can do it?" Graham asked.

"Sure!" Fortune lied, a little too loudly and brightly. She stepped up to the tee and hit the ball far short of the target. And another one, closer but still missing the mark.

The douchebags laughed.

Graham turned. Instead of standing up for her, like she'd assumed, he pointed at one of the guys. "Hank? Hank Stolarz, is that you?"

"Graham? Graham Reynolds?" The guy laughed as he pushed his friends out of the way to say hello.

They crossed the lanes and did the bro-hug thing. Graham and Hank took a few minutes to catch up before Hank started introducing Graham to his friends. Then they went back to talking about what sounded like work. No one acknowledged Fortune was even there.

Fortune stood politely by, sipping her wine and sending vent-texts to Elaheh. She didn't dare text Louis for fear he would text back, *I told you so*, and she would have to race to the bathroom so no one would see her tears.

Elaheh sent back sympathetic smiling and hugging emojis, but gave little advice on how to deal with the blatant ignore situation.

The dude-bro conference lasted only a few minutes, but they were the most uncomfortable few minutes of Fortune's life. She was a pariah, complete with hunchback, chin hair, and nose wart. Graham was one of "those" guys, or at least he wanted to be. She looked at the group, and Marshall Li-Schneider's face appeared on every guy's body as they laughed. And Graham fit right in. Why was he even out with her?

"... and we're thinking of expanding that division in two or three months, so send me your résumé," Hank was saying to Graham, who seemed to be lapping up every word like a thirsty dog. Hank glanced over Graham's shoulder and smiled at Fortune. "Who's your friend?"

Graham twisted briefly, startled, then turned all the way around. His cheeks reddened as the realization that Fortune was still there registered in his eyes. *At least he has the common sense to feel guilty.*

"Oh man, I'm sorry. Fortune, this is Hank Stolarz. We interned at the same company in college. Hank, this is Fortune."

"Pleasure," Hank said, offering his hand.

She shook it and smiled as if Graham's lack of manners hadn't bothered her at all. "Nice to meet you, Hank. How're your driving skills?"

"They need some work, I'm afraid. To be honest, we only come here for the booze and the"—he paused and looked pointedly away from Fortune—"atmosphere. It's nice to meet you, as well." He slid his hand from her grasp and smoothly turned back to the rest of the Marshalls.

Hank furtively glanced back at Fortune, panning down to her bare legs and gazing for a moment before rejoining his friends. She quickly looked away, half grinning. He was pompous, but at least he could recognize beauty in front of him. Fortune laughed triumphantly inside.

Graham focused on Fortune. "Having fun?"

Yep, he didn't miss that.

"Considering I have yet to hit a ball anywhere close to a target, I'd say that 'fun' is a little hyperbolic at this point." She pasted on a sweet smile.

"Let me help." He placed a ball on the tee and came up behind her. His cologne surrounded her in a heady fog of trees and lemongrass. Mixed with the pale ale breath he breathed down the side of her face, it was overwhelmingly masculine. But all his smells were wrong. It was like he was trying to bulldoze her with his manliness.

His arms encircled her as he reached around her to guide her swing. He was radiating warmth, and she had to resist the urge to lean back into him and focus on swinging the wedge instead. A handsome man all over her? Her body couldn't help but respond.

"You're really cute, you know," Graham whispered in her ear. "Nice legs."

Ugh, no. The spell of lust he'd cast over her was broken. It was all she could do not to cringe at what he thought was a compliment. Well, at least he hadn't added *for a chubby girl.* "Thanks." She forced her lips to form a smile.

For the second time that night, her thoughts flashed back to Jason—the moment at Sly Foxes when he'd bluntly told her why people were staring at her. *You're beautiful, period.* Why had she chosen a guy who called her *cute* when she could have a man who called her *beautiful?*

They did some practice swings before Graham stepped back to let her try again. She swung the wedge, and the ball soared over the target into the netting.

Graham faced her. "Why don't we get something to eat?" he suggested. "I know this bar with some great wings and chili pepper poppers."

Two food items she hated. But anywhere would be better than here, she thought. And she was getting hungry. "Sure! I don't think golf is my sport."

They pulled into the parking lot of a bar called The Graveyard at almost the same time, Fortune following closely behind Graham even though he had given her the address to map the route.

"Have you ever been here?" Graham asked as they made their way inside.

"Actually, no. Is this new?"

"Not really. It's about five years old? Six?"

Fortune counted the new places she'd been in the past several weeks, and a thought occurred to her: The city had been changing and growing, but she hadn't. In fact, her world had gotten smaller. Maybe this was what Louis had meant by *painfully single*. She had been limiting her world one binge-watch weekend at a time.

They sat at an available table near the front corner of the room and ordered drinks. She thought she'd lead with some innocuous small talk. "What do you think of the date so far?"

Graham took the question and rambled for several minutes.

"... was so good to run into Hank. I might actually get a job. The store is going to close, and relocating would be such a pain. You know, they told me about it the day you asked me out."

"Mm-hm." She took in the laidback atmosphere of the bar, the patrons—mostly guys—laughing and drinking, and hoped their good spirits would infect her or at least distract her for the rest of the date.

"So, you're like a good-luck charm. With a cute face."

"Thanks," Fortune replied absentmindedly. One of the guys sitting at the main bar to the left and behind Graham looked familiar. Of course, she was seeing him only from the back. But the way he stood, a smidge taller than the people around him, mussed-up sandy-brown hair, and a commanding, broad-shouldered build, made her think about lumberjacks ... Oh no.

And then he turned and met her gaze, confusion furrowing his brow.

Jason.

Dammit.

Then she realized this was the guys' hangout spot. Perfect. Why would Graham bring her here? The only reason she could think of was to show off. How douche-y was that?

Another guy sidled up to Jason and gave him the infamous bro-hug. They talked for a few minutes. When Graham wasn't looking, Jason pointed toward their table. Oh no! They were coming over.

When the other guy headed toward them, Fortune caught a glimpse of his face. Without the man bun to prevent it, and standing beside Jason to enhance it, recognition filled her brain. This was Line Stranger from Sly Foxes. And Man Bun in Jason's SwipeMatch photo.

Double dammit.

They were friends with him? Did he even know Jason liked curvy girls? Did either of them know she and Jason had dated?

They walked over. "Graham, hey," Jason drawled. "What's up?"

Graham grinned and puffed out his chest. "Just a little get-to-know-you date. Guys, this is Fortune. Fortune, these are my buddies, Jason and Seth."

"Nice to meet you, Fortune." Jason stuck out his hand, giving her a genial but blank look. He was acting like they'd never met. Was he ashamed of her, or saving face in front of his boys?

Or was he somehow trying to save her from embarrassment?

She laid her hand in his, playing the role. "Nice to meet you, Jason."

"You look familiar," Seth said. He leaned across the table as if seeing her at a different angle would help his mind place her. Clearly, this guy didn't care about embarrassing anyone … or making polite conversation

She reared back, keeping her face blank to avoid showing disgust at his proximity. "I don't think so," Fortune lied. *Please don't recognize me. Please.* She turned back to Graham, Jason still holding her hand.

"Wait." Seth gave her a once-over, then righted himself to full height. Was he really trying to intimidate her? "This was the girl I told you about from the club! The one that kneed me!" He pointed, his body shaking with rage.

Jason looked from Seth to Fortune and back again as if he was struggling to understand. "What? When was this?" He paused, then gave her hand a squeeze. "Which club?" he asked, his voice quieter.

Fortune ignored Jason. He was obviously thinking about their last date, and she did not want to unpack that mess of emotions right now. "You called me a whale," Fortune blurted to Seth. "You deserved worse."

Graham tilted his head. "C'mon, Seth."

Jason let go of Fortune's hand and turned to Seth. "What did you call her?"

"Dude, come on. She's a fat, Black bi—"

Jason punched Seth in the mouth before he could get the curse out.

Fortune gasped.

"What the hell, dude?" Seth held the right side of his face and glared at Jason.

Graham stood and quickly worked his way between the friends and placated them. He frowned at Jason. "Man, you don't even know what happened. And you just met this woman."

"I don't need to know what happened. And no, I haven't. We went out a few times," Jason said.

"What?" Graham asked.

"This is the 'amazing girl' you couldn't talk to Graham about?" Seth used air quotes as he said *amazing girl*, then laughed as if it were a big joke. As if she were a big joke.

"What?" Graham breathed to maintain his composure. He looked at Fortune. "What are you playing at here?"

"I ..." She couldn't finish. What could she say? This date was going from a too-hot frying pan straight into hell-fire. Three men surrounded her—one she'd kneed in the groin, one she'd lied to, and one she'd spent a self-absorbed date with—and all of them stared at her with disappointed frowns and rage-filled eyes.

But rewind. Had Jason told his friend she was *amazing*?

"This is the woman you found in that dare!" Seth bowled over with laughter, causing other patrons to stare at the group.

"Dare?" Fortune asked, surveying the group, her lips pursed in a frown. She felt her eyes grow hot with tears, and she blinked rapidly to keep from crying. "You dared him?"

Graham stood to get some distance between himself and the rest of the group. "I didn't do anything."

"I kind of fudged the real reason I was on SwipeMatch." Jason rubbed his jaw. "I was ranting about a bad date, and

Seth dared me to find someone on there." His stare was pensive, maybe even worried. He pushed Seth hard in the shoulder, and Seth stumbled into the back of someone at a nearby table.

The bar manager came to the table. "Folks, I need to ask you to leave. Patrons are complaining about the noise."

"We're sorry," Fortune said to the manager and the patrons at the nearby table. She grabbed Jason's hand, determined to get to the bottom of this, and pulled him out of the bar.

"Yeah, we'll leave." Graham threw some bills on the table and left with the group.

As soon as they got outside, the battering began.

Seth swung at Jason, catching him on the chin.

Jason retaliated, punching Seth in the stomach.

Seth reached for Jason's neck, but Jason gave him another gut punch, doubling him over.

Fortune grabbed Jason's arm. "What the heck are you doing?"

Graham stepped in between the two to stop the pummeling. "Guys, cut it out."

"Fortune, get off me," Jason growled. His body shook, and his breaths came out in loud huffs like an agitated stallion.

She gripped his bicep with both hands, but neither was doing a particularly good job at restraining him. For once, a body part of hers seemed small.

"You probably need to go, Fortune." Graham faced away from her, keeping the friends apart. "I've got this."

Fortune hesitated, but reluctantly let go and turned away from the entanglement of male limbs and egos. What had she done?

The entire drive home, Fortune couldn't get the image of the guys fighting out of her mind. Oh God. What if she had caused friendships to end? She didn't know what it felt like to be a homewrecker, but it couldn't be worse than what she felt at that moment.

Fortune opened the door and seethed all the way upstairs straight to her bedroom, stripping off clothes as she went. When she got there, she threw her purse on the bed and all her date clothes in the laundry basket.

It wasn't the worst date she'd ever been on—that was still the guy who'd worn board shorts to Capital Grille—but it was a solid runner-up. Fortune thought it would be what Graham had said: an innocent get-to-know-you date. Well, she had gotten to know him, all right. He was a social-climbing wannabe, an opportunist, and a user.

Was there anything worse? A liar, that's what. The confused look on Jason's face as he'd recognized her on a date with the one person she'd said she wouldn't still stung as she replayed it in her thoughts.

But Jason had lied, too. He'd said he was on SwipeMatch because the women there were more real—because he "was against plastic and fakery" and "less about the hookup"—when he'd actually been following up on a dare. Had Seth picked her out and told Jason to date her? This was even more evidence that he wanted to keep his distance. Who fell in love with the fat girl anyway? It had all been an act, and she'd bought it.

And then, Seth and Jason had fought over … what, exactly? Her honor? What Seth had said was disrespectful, no doubt, but Jason fighting in a bar parking lot with a guy who's supposed to be his friend and was an obvious racist? What was the point? Ugh.

It had been such a horrible night that she wanted to crawl under her bed instead of in it. Instead, she stood in the middle of the room in her underwear and wedges and on the verge of tears. A plush, striped chair she'd dubbed her reading chair was draped in a thin T-shirt and a flimsy pair of jogging shorts Fortune had been wearing around the house earlier. She plopped down in the chair, unlaced her wedges, and slipped them off.

How had it all gone so wrong? Graham was nothing like she'd thought he would be. Hmm. That was why it went wrong. He was supposed to be like she'd imagined. If he had been, then all of this would have been worth it. Why hadn't he caught her hints? Why hadn't he vibed with her like Jason had?

And Jason had told Seth she was amazing. Ugh. Why couldn't Jason have told *her* that?

When Seth had made the comment, Fortune knew she'd made a mistake going out with Graham. She'd only wanted a date to the gala. He'd obviously wanted to beat his friend at a long game of Truth or Dare. So, how had all of this happened?

She had to talk to Jason, because he needed to hear her side. Graham was obviously going to spin things his way, which might or might not show her in a favorable light. She wasn't going to be the bad guy in all of this.

No, it wasn't about her. It was about them. She wanted to find out how a childish game of Truth or Dare had turned into three adventurous dates and Jason punching a guy to defend her. Was this all a game?

A wave of embarrassment and anger washed over her. Another man toying with her emotions. Again! She got up, redonned the tee and shorts, and reached for her phone, ready to text Jason.

Then the doorbell rang.

Sixteen

S HE OPENED THE DOOR to a mussed-up Jason. His shirt was untucked, his sneakers were scuffed, and his hair was ruffled. A small, bright red scrape marred his right cheek. Some of the anger churning in her gut subsided, replaced by concern that he'd been hurt.

"Jason! Are you okay? You're ..." She reached up to his face.

He leaned away, avoiding her touch. "It's just a scratch. That's not why I'm here." He barged his way in, backing her down the short hallway into the living room. His voice was calm, but tension rolled off him in waves. Clearly, he was still amped from his and Seth's fight in the parking lot. "Why were you out with Graham tonight?"

She faltered. Had he already talked to Graham? Part of her wanted to defend herself against whatever he might have said. Another part wanted to accuse Jason of toying with her emotions over some ridiculous game.

Deep down, though, a small part of her was thrilled that he might be upset with himself for not telling her he wanted to be exclusive. *Get your head out of the clouds, Fortune. This is serious.* "What did it look like? I was at a bar, drinking and having a conversation with him." Her top lip raised in a sneer.

"You said you weren't going to go out with him, remember? You said that on our first date! You remember it, right?" He kept clenching and unclenching his fists.

The scene from their first date flashed in her mind, and she was back there feeling all cute and special that this towering man was a tad jealous over a crush. But this was not a tad jealous. This was bothered and annoyed. Well, so was she! "Yeah, I remember."

"And you went out with him anyway! He's one of my closest friends!" Jason was pacing, his face and neck red, his chest rising and falling heavily.

"Some friend," she mumbled.

He stopped and stared at her. "Why were you out with him?" he demanded, his voice low and gravelly.

They were inches apart, so close that his breath heated her forehead. It was labored, heavy, and smelled like beer and spearmint. Being this close to his delicious maleness made her insides swirl with excitement. "I'm sorry, but—"

"You went out with him even though we had a connection. What about after the arcade?"

After the arcade, he'd made it clear that he didn't want to go to the gala with her. She remembered the fake bad dancing, the fumbling attempt at sex on his couch—

"Or do you make out in the back of clubs with anybody?"

So, that was what he remembered about the date after the arcade—her straddling him in the back of Sly Foxes. It was her most insecure moment of the night, with her butt in the air to keep from putting all her weight on him. His insinuation that she whored around jabbed her like a hot poker in the side. The nerve of this guy. "Now, wait a minute—"

"You can't see him. Ever." His blue irises were dark, and his mouth pursed in a tight, jagged line as he straightened to his full height.

What was his problem? They had been on only three dates; they weren't committed to each other. He must've thought he was making a power move. She wanted to laugh in his unbelievably gorgeous face. "You aren't my boyfriend!" she spat, hoping that revelation would sting. He wanted to keep his distance? Fine. This was what he got for agreeing to be plan B.

He didn't even flinch. "And you aren't my girlfriend. But you can't go out with him."

She folded her arms across her chest. *Okay. You want to pull out the big guns? We'll pull out the big guns.* "Clearly, I'm not. I'm not even your first choice. Seth had to dare you to go out with me!"

At that, he looked away from her gaze, but he didn't back down. "That's not how it went—"

Fortune cut him off, indignation regaining strength in her gut. "You want to know why I went out with him? Because I need a date for the gala. You know, the invite you turned down? I was trying to find someone who would actually want me enough to be my plus-one."

He reared back, something else hard in his gaze. "I want you."

"And you showed that how? By punching a guy in the face and getting us kicked out of a bar? What are you, a caveman?"

"You don't get it. When I saw you with Graham, something happened. I—"

"You realized your big, Black secret was out. Heaven forbid, you *liked* the woman they dared you to date!"

"No. That's not it at all!"

"Of course it was. Your friends didn't even know about us. You hid me from them because you're ashamed of me!"

"Dammit, woman! Will you let me talk?" He seized both her arms and pulled her to him, shaking loose her defensive pose.

Adrenaline and need surged through her at his closeness, matching his energy. "Fine! What?"

"I'm not ashamed! They can't have you! Because I want you!" he roared.

She peered at him, his face inches from hers, his blue eyes as dark and deep as ocean water. His mouth was right there, so close it was torture not to kiss him.

"I ... Me, too." She parted her lips, and he took the invitation with hearty lust and kissed her hard, his tongue pushing its way inside her mouth, seeking hungrily to claim hers. His kiss was insistent and ravenous, as if he were drinking from a trickling fountain in the middle of a desert. The need flowed into her, and she moaned into the kiss.

As he took her mouth, he loosened his hold on one of her arms, moved south, and held her side at her waist, settling at the notch above her hip. His hand curled around her side, and his thumb pressed into her pelvis like a brand, hot and heavy.

But instead of sinking deeper into the embrace, she worried about what he would think of the roll of flesh there. When she put her hands on her hips, the roll flopped over her fingers, and she felt the faint ridges of stretch marks that wouldn't go away no matter how much cocoa butter she applied. That had to be the most unsexy thing ever. Fortune didn't want him to think she wasn't sexy and stop what he was doing, especially since, she had to admit, she'd been wanting this since their first date.

He broke the kiss and leaned back, catching her gaze and holding it in a hard stare. "Did you just move my hand?" His tone was tinged with harsh incredulity, demanding a satisfactory answer.

She hadn't even realized she had reached for his hand and slid it to the middle—the smooth part—of her back. Moving his hand had been automatic, a deflection. Keep him away from the fleshy parts to keep him interested. No man had ever called her out on it. A flush of embarrassment warmed her chest and throat. "I ... uh ..."

"Is it because you want me to stop?" Jason asked.

No, she pleaded silently. *That wasn't* stop. *That was* please stay interested.

"No, don't stop." The words came out as a breathy moan. Everywhere her skin touched his was ablaze. She wanted more. She just wanted to ensure he wanted more, too.

He moved his hand back to her waist and grabbed her tighter, pulling her in closer. "Then I put my hands where I want," he said in a ragged whisper, his lips grazing her ear.

A delicious shiver of anticipation went through her. "Yes."

His other hand moved from her arm to under her T-shirt, groping her breast to make his point. His eyes widened at his discovery of soft flesh instead of fabric. "Fortune," he singsonged. "Are you not wearing a bra?" He smirked and pinched the tip of her breast between his thumb and forefinger, then rolled her nipple until it pebbled.

This had become a battle of wills to see who would succumb to desire first. Jason was taunting her, teasing her into submission, but Fortune wasn't giving in. She sucked in a breath, vainly holding in a moan, but then he yanked her shirt off and bent over her chest, taking her nipple in his mouth. The pull of his lips sent a bolt of lightning straight through her. She cried out, the sensation too overwhelming for words.

"Upstairs. Now," he rumbled as he kissed his way from her breasts to her neck.

Sidetracked by imagining them rolling around in her bed, Fortune was hesitant to move. The way they were at each other's throats, the sex might be ... rowdy, and she hadn't had any in a while. Then again, it might be incredibly good, and that wouldn't matter.

Jason straightened, looking down into her eyes with concern creasing his eyebrows and forehead. "I won't do anything you don't want. But I'm still upset that you were with him. This will not be gentle," he said, answering her unspoken thoughts.

Liquid heat pooled between her thighs at his declaration. How did he get even hotter? Her lips went up in the sexiest, most evil grin she could muster. "What do you think I am? Some delicate, fainting flower? You think I can't handle you?"

"Handling you is the least of what I want to do." He was on her again, his lips lighting a path of flames along her jawline and down her neck.

He hadn't answered her question, but his statement made her pause. Other guys always told her what they wanted from her—*please me, show me how a Black girl does it, give me what I want.* None of them had clued her in on what she was about to get, which would have been handy, because what she'd gotten had usually been lacking. Angry or not, she knew Jason wouldn't hurt her. But what he would do ... Her heart raced at the possibilities.

He nudged her up to her bedroom as he was kissing her, and it was all she could do not to fall as she clumsily backed up the stairs. Midway, she tripped, and he grabbed her, an arm securely around her waist, another cradling her backside.

In any other circumstance, she would have burst into laughter, but everything in her body screamed, *Not the time.* "I ... I'm going to fall. You've got to ... let me go." Her words were coming out clipped and hoarse between fevered panting.

"No, I don't." He heaved her over his shoulder like she weighed nothing and climbed the last few steps to her bedroom.

She squealed and held on to his shoulders and back. *Such a massive, muscular back.* She ran her fingers up and down his back and groaned.

He dropped her across the bed and toed out of his sneakers as if her touches hadn't affected him. "Are you waiting me out so I'll be less rough with you? You can't wait me out." His hand lingered on top of her sex before he yanked her shorts and underwear off in one fluid motion.

"You think I'm waiting you out?" Her lips pursed into a mocking smile, even though inside she was begging him to touch her. "I'm trying not to laugh. You're barely registering on my meter."

He slipped a finger into the heat between her legs. A growl rumbled low in his throat, the sound making her flush with need. "I think Little Fortune says differently."

The way he talked—so arrogant and conceited—would have annoyed her if she weren't so turned on at the same time. The truth was the whole caveman thing was hot. No guy had ever stood up for her like that. It was raw, primal, lust-worthy. Those hands, one of which was half inside her, probing and twisting until she was slick with desire, had defended her honor.

The friction of his callused fingers flooded her with sensation as he slid them in and out of her, teasing her. "So wet.

I'm getting everything I want tonight," Jason said, rubbing his thumb in harsh circles across her already-sensitive bud until she writhed and panted under him.

She couldn't get enough of him—his touch melted her sass into desire, his heady scent of masculinity and after-shave made her drunk with longing, and his muscular arms made her crave him more. She tugged at his shirt, so he left her long enough to take it off, dropping it on top of his shoes.

His chest was smooth, solid, defined. She remembered hugging him, dancing with him, and now she wanted to be pressed up against him, skin to skin. But doing that would send her right over the edge, especially now that he'd pushed a third finger in her.

"I told you you can't wait me out," he said. "Or are you afraid to let me see you come?"

It had been only a few minutes, but the orgasm was already building in her core. She closed her eyes, clutching the sheets and trying to will herself not to fall apart from his touch. "If you think a look and a couple of fingers is all you need to make me come, you're sorely mistaken," she said, the strain in her voice evident.

"You're really going to challenge me right now?" He leaned over her, his mouth next to her ear. "It's going to feel so good; you're going to beg me to come. And I'm not going to let you." He pressed his fingers deeper into her and took her mouth in a messy kiss.

His body was so close, she could feel his heart beating. With her eyes closed and his mouth on hers, everything felt more intense. She was more aware of his fingers inside, his thumb outside, and his tongue thrusting in and out of her mouth, all of it bringing her closer to shattering in front of him. Her insides were on fire, and she was about to be consumed. She moaned, high-pitched, into his mouth, and he broke the kiss.

"There she is," he said, as if he'd successfully coaxed a kitten out of a hiding spot.

She opened her eyes and saw him standing over her at the edge of the bed, one hand still inside her, the other unzipping his jeans.

Dammit! Now, he was preening. He was also rubbing that wonderful place between her thighs, causing her vision to blur. "Jason," she panted. "You pri—" A wave of orgasm turned her curse into a keen. Was the room shaking? No, that was her. She was shaking, vibrating with the power of the orgasm. "Jason!"

For a moment, he was tender, dragging his fingers in and out of her. "I'm here, baby. That's it. Keep coming for me." When the orgasm finally calmed, he licked those same fingers, and his wicked grin returned. "You really are edible, Fortune."

What was this man doing to her? In a fuzzy, orgasmic haze, she watched Jason step out of the rest of his clothes. Jeez Louise, he really was built like a lumberjack. From that smooth expanse of chest to his muscled, sun-striped arms to his legs like tree trunks.

When he briefly turned his back to her to reach into the pocket of his jeans, she saw a tattoo on his shoulder. It was of a hammer striking a piece of metal on an anvil.

Its symbolism caused her heart to speed up again, thinking about the strength it took to wield a sledgehammer. Jiminy Christmas, he was like Thor. She could play his Valkyrie, at least for the night.

Then he turned toward her, and that luscious V she'd only had glimpses of before arrowed down to a whole lot of manhood. The words came out before she could think them. "Oh God," she breathed, watching him roll a condom up his length.

"Think she's going to help you?"

Cocky jerk, she thought. *Cocky sexy jerk.* But she couldn't help but lean back as he climbed into bed, his hips nudging her knees apart. Could she handle all of that? Her inner voice was loudly calculating the years and months it had been since she'd last had sex. Over two and a half years? That couldn't be right.

He tilted his head to meet her gaze. "You sure you want to do this?" His voice was low and rough, but his expression flooded with concern.

However dickish he was being, it was all for show. In the end, Jason would respect whatever she wanted, and damn, that made her want him more. She scooted toward him. "Yes, I want this."

He grabbed behind her knees and tugged her closer, then spread her legs apart. Her fleshy, inner thighs bumped against his hard, muscular hips. "Then stop trying to get away from me. I'm not done with you."

With the remnants of her orgasm still coursing through her, she felt the pressure of Jason's erection against her opening, as if he demanded entry. She clutched his arms, the need for him overpowering any other thoughts.

He lowered his body on hers, his chest pressed against hers, his lips and then his teeth on her neck. He went to a spot, just above her collarbone, licked it, then clamped down in a prickling bite. When she gasped, still processing the sharp sting, he covered her mouth with his and slammed into her.

Her scream was taken by his tongue, her shudder absorbed by his body. The shock of him there stilled her, but only for a second before she arched against him, wanting more.

He understood her bodily ask, lifted, and thrust in her, giving back everything she gave him.

After only a few moments, she felt another orgasm building inside her. Under him, she was like a banshee, panting and moaning. But he didn't seem to be anywhere close. His jaw was clenched in determination, and his lust-filled eyes greedily devoured her even though the corners of them still crinkled with annoyance. But nothing in his expression signaled an orgasm was imminent. How could he not be close when she was about to explode? If she could just ... She snuck her hand in between them and stealthily moved southward.

He saw what she was doing and seized her wrist, pinning it above her head. "Uh-uh, Not yet."

His hold on her wrist sent a jolt of pleasure straight through her. It was obvious he'd won the willpower battle.

He controlled this show, and something about that made the pressure in her core build even more.

If he wouldn't let her grab him there, she'd find some of his other erogenous zones. She let go of his arm and slid her other hand all over his body to coax him to as feverish a pitch as she was. His stomach was a wall of muscle. His backside was perfectly round. She even dug her nails into his luscious, strong back to arouse him. But with one hand still pinned and every part she touched drool-worthy, she only aroused herself more.

"So, *now* you want me?" His voice was low and growly and thick with lust. When he looked down on her, his grin was as mocking as hers had been.

"Always ... want you," she said between breaths.

For a moment, he slowed, turning her chin toward him, forcing her to look him in the eyes. "Then no more dates with him."

"Okay," she whispered.

He slowed more. "You're mine, Fortune. Say you're mine."

She squirmed, frustrated that she was climbing a mountain, and he was blocking the way to the top. "Jason, I ..."

His deep-blue eyes were boring into her with the same intensity as his thrusts. "Say you're mine, or I'm going to stop."

She was already clenching on him, waves of ecstasy building deep in her, on the edge of a second orgasm. "Jason ... please!"

"Fortune." He let go of her chin and thumbed one of her pert nipples as he slowly stroked in her. "Say it."

She held his arm and tossed her head backward as the waves of climax crashed through her. "God, Jason! I'myoursI'myoursI'myours!" Her eyes shut tight as the orgasm radiated up her spine. It was the most powerful thing she'd ever experienced. Like being awakened suddenly from a deep sleep. Like coming back to life again.

"That's it, baby. Yeah, you're mine." He kissed the exposed hollow of her throat, then groaned loudly from his own release. Guess he'd been closer than she'd thought.

He collapsed beside her, making sure his full weight wasn't on her, and peppered her face with tiny kisses.

She breathed heavily and ran her hand up and down his side. They lay there for several minutes to catch their breaths before Jason got up and disposed of the condom.

Fortune's body felt limp, every muscle exhausted. She barely had enough energy to pull the covers over her, reaching blindly for them in the dark. What had just happened? He'd been angry. She'd been angry. And they'd had some of the most explosive sex she'd had since ... ever. What the ...?

When he came back to bed, Fortune lay on her back, staring at the white ceiling, the color reflecting the slivers of moonlight peeking through the upturned blinds onto his skin. "What the heck was that?" she asked, stealing another glimpse of his naked body.

He pulled back the covers. "Some pretty hot hate sex." The bed shifted under his weight as he crawled in beside her and laid his head on her shoulder. His breath was warm on her collarbone.

"Are we going to talk about it?" she asked.

"Yes."

"Now?"

"No."

They were silent for a few minutes—or a few hours; she couldn't tell.

Fortune thought Jason had gone to sleep, but then he mumbled, "God, you're beautiful when you come."

Seventeen

Jason

JASON HAD NO IDEA how long he'd been asleep, but when he awoke, light shone on him, and his back was sore. He gazed around the room. Pastel paisley sheets, a skirt hanging on a doorknob. This was Fortune's room. And then he turned and saw her sleeping form beside him.

Instantly, memories of last night flooded his consciousness. Betrayal, a fight with his friends, and later ... incredibly hot sex. He peered at Fortune turned away from him in deep slumber, her forearm on her forehead, and her fingers splayed across her face. This week's nail color was hot pink. He urged his body to stay calm as he remembered those hot-pink nails fisting the sheets while she'd vainly tried to force herself not to come apart in front of him. Her nails weren't the only thing hot about last night—just thinking about her moans, her skin, and being inside her aroused him. It was what he'd hoped; hell, it was more than he'd hoped.

But he couldn't do that again. She'd lied to him. She'd said she wouldn't date Graham, and there she'd been, on a date with him.

The anger built in Jason's chest again. Why would she betray him like this? They were perfect for each other, and why she couldn't understand that mystified him. She could have picked anyone else to go to that gala. But she *had* to pick Graham. He hated her and wanted her all over again.

She stirred. "Hey, you."

"Hey, you," he echoed. His mind was racing. What should he say first? Should he interrogate her about the date? Call her out on the lie? "Are you okay?"

"Yeah. I'm fine. I can't say that I'll be fine once I get up, though." She giggled.

Oh God, that sound. The rage in his chest calmed, and he instantly felt lighter. Her laugh had superpowers. "Yeah, sorry about that."

"I'm not. I just ... I hadn't had sex in a while. And I haven't done it like that ... ever."

He thought for a moment. "I don't think I ever have, either. I was so—"

"Mad?"

Well, she opened the door. He grabbed the opportunity to get some answers. "Why did you go out with him?"

"I told you ...." She pulled the covers up to her neck.

"I know what you said. But why him?" He raised up on his elbow. "Do you like him? Do you want to date him?"

"No. No offense to your friend, but he's ... Never mind. Just no."

He exhaled and struggled at tamping down a full teeth-baring grin. Something about the date ending in a brawl and knowing it had gone horribly wrong was satisfying. At least he wouldn't have to choose between her and the guys. Except Seth. But he couldn't figure the Seth situation out right now. "Okay, well, what about us?"

"What about us? We had amazing hate sex last night." She smiled. "So much for always being sweet." She nudged him and winked.

The smile was a good sign. If she'd liked the sex, this was still on the road to a relationship. "Aside from last night, I thought we were going somewhere. The awesome convos, the holding hands, the making out." He was having trouble reading her expression. Why did she seem confused? "Do you get what I'm saying?"

"What do you mean? Like a repeat performance? I'm more than a little sore right now."

"No. I mean somewhere long-term."

"Like, an every-Saturday kind of thing? I can do most of them, but—"

The tone of her voice was businesslike and cordial. This was not the Fortune he'd gotten to know. "No, no. A relationship."

"What?" She laughed a little, but it wasn't her real laugh. It was a tinny, girly, fake laugh.

He cringed when he heard it.

She coughed and cleared her throat. "I thought this was just a fun thing for you."

"'A fun thing'?" He scrutinized her for a few minutes, then got up and began to dress. This didn't make sense. Who dated in their thirties for a sex partner? "Why would you think that?"

"I mean, look at you. You're white. You're gorgeous. Usually, the hot white guys are one and done. Unless they want a repeat performance, of course. Isn't that what you're asking for?"

He stared at her, his body rigid from holding himself back from grabbing and shaking her. "What the—are you high?"

She blinked. "No, I'm sober. When you didn't want to go to the gala, I got the hint. You don't want to get too serious. And then last night ..." She sat up, and some of the covers fell away from her body. "You won the dare, and bonus, you got laid. I think that covers it, right?"

His practical, logical side was telling him to get out now, but the view in front of him was making it difficult. Her arms were lazily crossed over that deliciously ample bosom. With her top half uncovered, a dark purple bruise near her collarbone was clearly visible. He wished he were back at that spot, inhaling her scent and tasting her.

Even as she was spouting this ... *weirdness* was the only word that came to mind, Jason felt no hesitation, no apprehension, only heady desire and a need to be with her. He should have been hearing warnings: *Crazy girl! Step away from the crazy girl!* Instead, he felt protective of her. Like he wanted to shield her and tell her that he'd never hurt her.

Still, if she couldn't love him, where would this even go? He looked at her again, the ache to get his hands on her again so real it hurt. In the daylight, with the sun illuminating her velvety brown skin, he mentally erased everything on his to-do list and imagined himself in bed with Fortune all day. Instead, he pulled on his jeans and breathed in deep, unsure of what to say. The only phrase that came to mind was, "I don't know who hurt you, but I am not that guy."

Fortune looked affronted. "I didn't say you hurt me. I just know what to expect from you. From all of you."

"'All of you'? You mean 'hot white guys'?" A sneer crept onto his lips, but deep down something was aching and hollow.

"Well, yeah, but all guys, honestly."

He was staring again, but he couldn't stop looking. It was like a train derailing in slow motion right in front of him. He couldn't put together the view of this gorgeous woman, the memory of last night, and what she was currently saying. He shook his head, but the action emphasized how sore his neck and back were. "This is crazy talk. I gotta go." Jason picked up his keys and stuffed them in his front pocket.

Fortune shrugged and mumbled something.

"What was that?" he asked, wincing a little at how harsh his voice had sounded.

"I said I'll let you out." She got out of bed and grabbed whatever she could find to wear, ending up with last night's T-shirt, some panties, and a robe that she tied so tightly around her waist, Jason wondered if she could breathe.

He watched her, mentally cringing at the fact she was covering up all those luscious curves he had only briefly gotten to explore, and then they walked downstairs.

At the door, he turned back to her. "I'll text you later," he said to the top of her head.

She was avoiding looking at him. "Um hmm," she responded, shifting from one foot to the other.

He tilted her chin up, but she still refused to look him in the eye, peering down, her chestnut brown irises glassy. So, he touched his lips to her cheek and left.

He didn't know where he was going, but he had to get out of Fortune's house and think. When the car stopped, he was in front of Graham's apartment. Graham's car was outside, so Jason got out and went to the door, not sure what to say to him or why anger was building in his chest again.

"What are you doing here?" Graham stepped out of the way to let his friend in.

Jason had to remind himself that he wasn't angry at Graham—if anything, he should have felt guilty for not telling him about Fortune—but his fists kept clenching, and he had to force himself to unclench them. "I couldn't think of anywhere else to go."

Graham poked him in the chest. "Man, about last night, I swear I had no idea. But then again, you could have told me."

"She said she wasn't going to ask you out. I didn't think ..." Jason sighed. "I didn't want to tell you. Your ego is crazy big, and you know it."

"I'm just saying. You could have told me." Graham went to the kitchen. "You want a beer?"

And like that, whatever animosity had existed between the two dissipated. How was friendship so easy, but even attempting to start a relationship with Fortune was so hard?

"A beer at ..." Jason looked at his watch. It was already fifteen after one. He'd thought it was still morning. "Never mind, yeah." Jason plopped down on the sofa and sighed. "What the hell is going on?"

Graham handed Jason a bottle and sat beside him. "Well ... you punched a good friend for some woman you aren't with because she was out on a date with ... me, and from the looks—and smell—of things, you stayed at her house last night. You did her, didn't you?"

Jason dipped his head to his chest, pulled his shirt over his face, and sniffed. He smelled like sex and ... her. Her vanilla body spray, the cocoa buttery smell of whatever she put in her hair, even the flowery smell of fabric softener from her sheets. She was all over him. It was mouthwatering. He wanted to die. "Yeah."

"Dang, man. How was it? No. Don't tell me." Graham took a gulp of his beer. "I'm lying. How was it?"

Jason rumbled low in his throat.

"Whoa. That good, huh? Why are we even talking about this? You like this woman. Duh. A lot, if last night was any clue."

"The woman is messed up. Like, damaged goods."

"Well, cut her off, then," Graham suggested.

"Nah, man. That's cruel." Her words came back to him: *Usually, the hot white guys are one and done.* It was what she was expecting from him. He wasn't one of those guys.

"The damaged part—did you find this out before or after the sex?"

Jason looked at his friend, confused. "After. What does that matter?"

"If you found out before and still hooked up with her, that's cruel. But if you found out after, then it's new information, and you're getting out while you can."

Somehow, that still seemed wrong. One, he wanted to be with her. That one night would not be enough. And two, he couldn't do that to her and leave. But he had.

Had he broken Fortune by leaving? He had already messed up by not telling her the whole story about the dare and turning down her gala invite. Had she already written him off before they even had a chance to fully talk about this? This was hell. He was in hell. "Okay," was all he could say.

"You don't seem like it's okay. In fact, I haven't seen you like this since Lily."

Lily. Even though he'd been thinking about her for weeks, no one had mentioned that name in a while. His almost wife. They had been together for three years, but he' never felt ready to propose. In hindsight, she'd never pressured him, either. They had been fine as boyfriend and girlfriend. It had been their friends—and his mom—who hadn't been fine with that. So, he'd proposed, and she'd accepted. But even afterward, he'd felt ... off. He had been sure Lily was hiding something from him.

His concerns had been realized when he'd caught her with Sheila, his roommate at the time, the week after he and

Lily had ordered engagement announcements. Since then, he'd been serial dating—and complaining—that there were no good women out there.

Finding Lily with Sheila had hurt, but it had been a relief, too. His instincts had been right. Here, his instincts were telling him something entirely different—that Fortune was right for him. But her view of men was weird. It wasn't an "all men are dogs" mantra exactly, but this woman had been hurt before. Could she even be relationship material?

Here he was again, wanting to be certain, not trusting his gut. He hadn't listened to himself with Lily and moved ahead with the engagement because he'd wanted to spare her feelings. In the end, he'd been the only one hurt.

And here he was, questioning himself again, while Fortune had hedged her bets with Graham.

The night of their second date, Jason had thought he was being reasonable when he'd turned down her gala invitation. They had been on only two dates. But looking back, he saw it for what it had been—not listening to himself. Or her.

He liked Fortune and wanted to spend more time with her. What harm was there in going to a formal fundraiser with her? But instead of accepting that, he'd basically screamed, *Don't take me*, which had opened the door for her to ask someone else. Fortune probably meant what she'd said at the time about not dating Graham, but Jason had practically led her to her crush with his hemming and hawing. But then she'd failed to give him the heads-up that she and Graham were going out, and that wasn't cool.

This was hell, and he couldn't do anything but sit in it and stew.

Graham gave Jason another beer and sat in the chair across from him. He had always sensed when Jason needed some time to think. And Graham wouldn't talk about Fortune or last night until Jason brought it up again. Instead, he chose to address the other elephant in the room.

"We have to do something about Seth," Jason mused.

"Who knew he was a misogynist?" Graham asked.

"Well, he's been a jerk for years. Maybe we were blind to who he was being a jerk to."

"Yeah, probably. What do we do about it, though? I think you knocking the crap out of him should be enough for now." Graham looked over at him and grinned.

"I do have this scratch on my face." Jason dramatically pointed to the small red line across his cheek, now barely visible.

The two bowled over in laughter, the serious portion of the visit clearly over.

Graham clicked on the TV and one of his four game consoles. He tossed Jason a controller, and they continued their saved game session of *The Witcher*. "That whole night was crazy. Well, the part at The Graveyard. Before that wasn't," Graham said.

Secretly, Jason had been waiting for this. When Fortune had uttered her displeasure about the date, he'd wondered what had happened to make it go so badly. And he wanted to gloat. "So, you didn't think it was strange when Fortune asked you out?"

"Not really. She's a regular at the store. We have little chats whenever we see each other, but about produce or sale items. Grocery store stuff. We'd never talked about anything personal until she came up to me a couple weeks ago. I thought that was kind of bold. Had to see what she was about. Plus, I mean, she's cute."

She wasn't just cute, she was beautiful, Jason thought. He breathed deeply through his nose to keep from opening his mouth and letting some choice epithets fly. After all, Graham had been an innocent bystander. He wasn't to blame. And now, he was being supportive, helping Jason sort what he felt for Fortune. It was probably easier to do that when your first date ended with her leaving while you kept your friends from pummeling each other.

He turned back to Graham. "How do you think your date went?"

Graham shrugged. "I thought it was going okay until you started beating the hell out of Seth. But I guess not, if you hooked up with her afterward."

Jason grinned. "Dog, she hated your date!"

"What? I didn't think it was going that bad. I mean, we didn't talk much. She's hella competitive." Graham shrugged.

Jason thought back to the arcade and silently agreed. "What did you do?"

"Some miniature golf." Graham reflected a moment. "Although she did roll her eyes at my 'cute' comment."

"What exactly did you say?"

"I said she was cute. And she had amazing legs."

Jason laughed, remembering what Fortune had said about the backhanded cute-for-a-chubby-girl compliments she'd gotten from other guys. His bro was a nice guy, but wow, was he bad with women. Jason tossed his controller on the chair and headed to the kitchen, bent on making himself a sandwich. "Thanks for the laugh, man."

"What did I say?"

Jason laughed harder. Graham's confused expression made Jason more reassured about where he stood with Fortune. Graham had been one clueless dude.

His phone pinged with a text from Fortune.

> **Fortune:** Wow, you got out of here fast. Guess you're in the one-and-done category. Nice knowing you.

Jason raked a hand through his hair and growled at the phone. She'd sent it right after he'd left, but his phone was doing some weird holding-on-to-texts thing lately. This whole day had been weird. He responded.

> **Jason:** I'm not done. Need to think.

> **Fortune:** What's there to think about? You either want it, or you don't.

Jason: Don't you mean want YOU?

The text bubble appeared and disappeared twice before she responded.

Fortune: Either way, you don't leave what you want.
So I guess I have my answer.

Jason: No, this isn't over.

Fortune: Sure, OK.

Was Fortune really dismissing him after having sex with him and going out with his best friend in the same night? What the hell? Two could play this game. Jason planned to take days, possibly even a week or two, to make up his mind about Fortune. That would show her. He locked his phone and went back to video gaming with Graham, trying to will away the annoying frustration churning in his gut.

He was being petty. Ugly-inside-his-soul petty. That's probably why a little voice in the back of his mind kept saying, *This isn't going to end well.*

Eighteen

Fortune

FORTUNE HAD BEEN IN a funk for three days, dragging into work, then dragging back home to an empty house, watching episode after episode of various *Real Housewives* shows while periodically glancing at her phone.

Jason hadn't come by, called, or texted since their night together. And she wasn't going to contact him; he was the one who'd left her. It was fine; this was not new behavior from guys she dated. She had, in fact, predicted this would happen, because the hot white guys had always been one-and-done with her. He had been spouting *relationship* the morning after, but she knew better.

If she thought about it, she'd never been in what she'd call a real relationship—one where they dated for more than a few months, where he treated her like a prize, where he was so happy to be with her. Most of the time, she felt like a buddy, and sometimes—if she was honest with herself—she felt used.

The last time she'd even come close to something real was Thomas, the one who'd called her Luscious Lucky, and that had been more like a serial fling. He'd loved coming by and doing the movies-and-chill routine—which involved more movies than chill because no one messed with Fortune and her weekend binge-watch habit—but the going-out routine, not so much. She'd had to make a deal with him to get him to go out to dinner with her on Saturdays. He would agree only if they got regular *chill time*. Why couldn't he call it what it was? Sex. Fortune had kept telling herself it was fine because he'd obviously wanted to be around her. If he hadn't, he wouldn't have made deals like that, right?

After six months, when things had gone from movies-and-chill to just chilling all the time, she'd made the mistake of asking him the dreaded *where is this going?* question. Soon after, Luscious Lucky had seemed to turn into sour grapes. He'd constantly fought with her over little things, and one day, he'd flat out said he wouldn't go out with her anymore.

"We don't have that kind of thing going on here."

"What do you mean? We used to go out for dinner and a movie every other Saturday."

"We're more of an indoor sport."

"What? Dinner and movies are indoors. What the heck are you saying?"

"You want me to spell it out? Fine. You asked where this was going. It's going to the bedroom. It's only going to the bedroom. Where did you think it was going?"

"Well, you can go out the door, then. Goodbye."

She'd held the door open for him and watched him leave.

Six months wasted on mediocre dates and lackluster sex. On the plus side, she'd made it through all the seasons of *Ozark*. This was how her dating life had been until Jason.

With Jason, all she'd had was a handful of online conversations, three dates, and a night of wild—but great—sex. She shouldn't be this sad. It had been only another failed dating attempt, but great for the eight weeks it had lasted. Why was she as devastated as if she had lost her best friend? She needed to let him go and move on.

But she couldn't. The next day, she was back to dragging and glancing, and watching her life fall away with each *Housewives* episode. So, when Elaheh suggested they go out Friday night because, "You look like you could use some serious alcohol therapy"—Elaheh's words, not Fortune's, even though inside she agreed—Fortune told her work friend, "Yes, I'll go."

And here they were, back at Sly Foxes, and Fortune didn't have a clue why. Alcohol therapy could've been anywhere else, but Elaheh ended up here. The last two times Fortune had been here, she'd had a bad time—the first kneeing Line Stranger (now known as Seth), the second dancing crazily with Jason. At least with Jason, she'd had a great time at the arcade beforehand.

She should have told Elaheh she was uncomfortable here. But it felt like that was something she would divulge to an long-time close friend, not a work BFF, no matter how close they were. Someone who truly understood being the overweight Black girl when everyone wanted a pale, size-zero supermodel.

Elaheh walked up to Darius at the front of the line. "Hey, Darius, got room for us tonight?"

"Sure," Darius replied to Elaheh's comment, but he was glaring at Fortune. "What happened to Jason?"

"Nothing happened." Fortune's tone was high-pitched and wavered a little. She smiled at him, fearing her smile was too bright and looked forced. "Girls' night tonight."

"Not what he said. But I'm not getting into it." He put up a hand and shook his head at Fortune's pleading look.

But what had he said? She didn't know, because he wasn't speaking to her. She imagined Darius sitting in his living room trying to watch TV while his wife half yelled the teachers' lounge gossip about Jason from their kitchen while stirring a pot of some kind of chili. Darius seemed like he would love chili. Guess he didn't like her so much anymore, though. "So, no more Ms. Delicious?"

"Have a good time, ladies." Darius ignored Fortune's question and let her and Elaheh behind the velvet rope.

"What was that about?" Elaheh asked.

Walking into the club, Fortune briefly glanced back at Darius with a frown. "I have no idea." She sighed and turned back to Elaheh. "Actually, I do know why. Darius's wife teaches at the same school where Jason subs."

"Oh." Elaheh's voice was low, but her wide-eyed expression screamed, *Yikes!*

"Yep. Word probably got around. Guess I know now why he hasn't called. He's madder than I thought he was. Or he thinks I'm crazy. Either way, I got the stink eye from Darius, so I guess that means the fun's over."

"Wow, you do need alcohol therapy." They squeezed up to the bar, Elaheh flagging down the bartender. "What exactly happened with Jason?"

When they settled at their usual table, Fortune relayed the events of the failed date with Graham and afterward, minus a lot of the hate-sex details. As usual, the drinks kept coming from the night's crop of Elaheh's admirers. Fortune drank them all.

By the time they went out on the dance floor, Fortune's vision was blurry, and she was so warm, she started to sweat. Tonight, no one came up behind her, not even a jerk like Seth. For the first time in decades, she felt like the four-and-a-half Marshall had said she was.

Then in walked Elaheh's husband, Geronimo, surprising his wife. People clamored to introduce themselves and snap a selfie with the minor-league third baseman fresh from a winning season. Fortune was swiftly jostled to the outskirts of the throng of fans. Among the chaos, Fortune grabbed Elaheh's hand to get her attention, waved goodbye, and slipped out into the night to wait for her Lyft driver. Yep, there were numbers even lower than four-and-a-half.

The next day, she struggled to stay upright. It took her three hours to get over her hangover enough to retrieve her car. When she got back, she stripped to her underwear, threw on a robe, and went downstairs to watch some movies. The movie marathon went from day well into the night, but it didn't cheer her up. It didn't even matter. Nothing mattered.

As the credits to *Silver Linings Playbook* rolled, she wondered what the heck she'd watched. "I spent two hours watching crazy people fall in love, and I can't even find a man to go to a gala with me without causing a fight," she said aloud to the screen. "Where did I go wrong?" She laughed.

At first, the laughter was a light giggle, but then it grew loud and maniacal. And as the credits rolled and a loud rock song became a sweet melody with a bit of country twang, the laughter became sobbing. Then the sobbing became uncontrollable.

She reached for her phone to send a text to Louis. It was simple. "Come over." But her emotions and the situation weren't.

When he responded, "Be right there," the sobbing slowed, and an uneasy calm settled in her chest. Through the tears, she went back to her bedroom to find something to wear and to sort through her once again tattered love life.

Fortune played back in her mind what she'd said before Jason had left her bed. "I don't get it," she said to the air. "What did I say?" She sniffed, the tears threatening again. "I don't know what I said to make him leave!"

The doorbell rang, and she threw on a ratty pair of gray pajama pants and a blue tee and raced to answer it.

"What. In. The. Hell?" Louis looked her up and down, tsking and waving his index finger in the air in figure eights. "Did you get caught in a tornado?" Louis was tailored and sharp as ever, his slim frame decked out in a pair of designer jeans and a fluffy cream-colored sweater.

"Hey." Fortune backed away from the door to let her best friend in, then slumped into a dining room chair. "Rough night."

He breezed by her to the kitchen and rummaged through her pantry until he found a bag of coffee. "You think?" He brewed a pot while he searched her cabinets for some clean mugs. "Tell me what happened."

Fortune got up and followed the smell of brewing coffee, mentally dismissing the fact she would be up all night on a caffeine high if she drank it. A clear head was a must when venting to Louis. She narrated her entire two weeks since she'd told him she was going to ask out Graham, from grocery store encounter to last night at Sly Foxes, skimming over the sex part for Louis's benefit, although he wouldn't have cared. She was the one who was embarrassed talking about sex; he was never ashamed of anything.

Louis poured himself a cup. "So, you basically lied to this guy, went out with his friend, instigated a fight between them, then let him use you and called him a manwhore for doing it."

"Pretty much." She gulped her coffee. The burn on her tongue and throat felt like punishment.

He raised one eyebrow, giving her a motherly admonishing glare. "Did you like Jason?"

"Yes." It was the only truth in Fortune's world right now—she liked Jason.

"Why did you go out with Graham, then?" He set his coffee on the table and tilted his head as if he were peering into her mind to understand her.

They had been friends too long for her not to recognize his face-the-truth look. She shrugged, the guilt already spreading through her. "I needed a date to your ball."

"Uh-uh, no. Don't pin this on me. You could have gone back to SwipeMatch. But no. You went to the one person you shouldn't have. Why, why, why did you do this?" Louis threw up his hands in surrender.

Fortune laid her head on his shoulder. "Grass is greener."

"Grass is ... What the—that's BS. Try again."

"Louis! Why are you kicking me when I'm down?" she whined.

"Because this is all your doing, that's why. You will get no sympathy from me here. At least not until you tell me the truth. You did everything you could to push that man away. I don't get you. You wouldn't mess up something good intentionally."

"I didn't mess it up. He walked out."

"Because you basically called him a player!" Louis was yelling now.

This was not why she'd asked him over. What happened to the comforting words and hugs while she cried? "I did not call him a player. I simply said—"

"Don't mince words! You pushed him away! Why did you push him away?"

"Because I am not going to be made a fool of!" Fortune gasped.

The two were silent for a beat, faces inches away from each other.

He wore a scowl, but his eyes looked more confused than anything. "What?" he whispered.

She breathed deeply. "He has a racist friend that hates big people. Another friend is a self-absorbed social climber. He only went out with me because they dared him to. I was a joke!"

Fortune sniffed and wiped the fresh tears trickling down her cheeks. A sob formed in her throat, making it difficult to talk without her voice sounding wavy and clipped. "He'd already talked his way out of escorting me to the gala. Those two have probably already convinced him that he wouldn't want to be seen with me in public. It's only a matter of time before he's secretly seeing me to avoid having to answer questions about why he's with a four-and-a-half when he could get a ten."

"Oh no. Sweetie." Louis pulled her in for a hug and closed his eyes. "Not this again."

She sobbed in his embrace, her palms covering her face. How had she Marshalled herself before Jason could?

He patted her gently on the back. "Four-and-a-half? Stop the madness. Don't ever think that thought again. Girl, I've schooled you on this. I thought you were over that high school Marshall crap."

When it came to guys and dating, she didn't think she'd ever be over *that Marshall crap*. In the rest of her life, she karate-chopped negativity into submission—Aileen, people at the office, strangers in line at a club. But when it came to dating, her mind always went back to that moment in the back of Marshall's car when he'd compared her to Kylie and rated her a four-and-a-half.

It wasn't like anyone in society felt differently. Ninety percent of magazine covers sported some skinny—most of the time white—woman as the definition of beauty. She'd never be that, and she never wanted to be. But, dang, why couldn't she realize that some guy out there might be okay with her being plus-size? Would even love her for her curves?

"You've got two problems here. One, you can't see what a good thing you've already got. And B, you can't see what a good thing Jason's already got." He released her and poked her in the arm.

Stated proof that Fortune and Louis shared a brain. She half smiled.

"You like this guy, and you need to get over Marshall. Like, permanently over. Whatever your mind is saying you deserve, it's lying to you. You need to go get Jason."

Louis left her with a fresh cup of steaming coffee in hand and her mind whirling with thoughts. She finally understood what Louis had meant by *painfully single*. It was about him looking at her wallowing in this state of singledom and being physically and emotionally hurt by what he saw. She should have someone who loved everything she was as much as

Louis did. She should have a guy who appreciated her and liked who he was when he was with her.

Louis knew her and cared for her. He didn't want to see her settle for the single life, when he knew she wanted to be loved. That much was obvious from the way she'd been fawning over Graham. And it probably hurt Louis to see her settle for less than what she truly deserved, whether it was a self-absorbed guy like Graham or no guy at all.

Because she was worth it. She wasn't a four-and-a-half. She was a *ten*. And Jason thought so, too. At least before she'd called him a player and turned him off.

After another bout of crying, followed by tons of reassurances that she was fine, she nudged Louis out the door.

Fortune realized through her tears that she had to go see Jason. She decided to test the waters with a text.

Fortune: We need to talk.

Five minutes of no response. Pacing. Pulling out her hair. Pouring Moscato.

Jason: Yeah, we do. Saturday. My place.

Louis had insisted, *You pushed that man away!* She could only hope that Jason wouldn't push her away when she tried to make things right.

Nineteen

FORTUNE WALKED UP TO Jason's door and rang the bell, prepared for a fight and an eventual breakup, but she hoped neither would occur. If she were honest with herself, she couldn't let go of Jason as easily as she had other guys. He'd given her a glimpse of what it was like to be adored. He'd made her feel as special as she deserved. Damn him.

The front stoop was bare except for a withered potted plant. The flower's petals were curling under, and even the stem was brown in places. If Jason would deadhead it and take off a few of the withered leaves and give it regular watering, it could come right back.

No. That plant was dead. Irreparable. Pruning it and coaxing it back to life would probably be too much work for something that was not worth saving. Kind of like their ... whatever this was.

"Hey."

His voice shocked her out of her plant diagnosis. His height and body blocked the doorway, and she stepped back instinctively.

"Hey."

They barely met each other's gaze, but the moment they did, anger and worry creased his forehead.

"Come in." He left the door open for her and went to the kitchen, rummaging around for something.

She heard shuffling and the refrigerator opening and closing, but she couldn't move. *Well, guess you couldn't hope for much*, she thought. He seemed to still be mad with her. Fortune put away her hope and focused on preparing for a fight.

He walked into the living room and set a bottle of pink Moscato, two bottles of water, and a glass on the coffee table. "Aren't you going to sit down?"

She closed the door and scurried to the part of the sofa closest to her and farthest from Jason.

They stared at each other.

She poured herself a glass of wine. "How about last time …. Weird, right?" She took a sip. "I would say that I was off my rocker, but I'm not sure if I was off my rocker, but it sounded like I was off my rocker—"

"Would you stop saying 'off my rocker'? You sound like a grandma." Jason sighed. "What was that about?"

"Well, it all started with this gala—"

He shook his head. "No, I mean that morning. You basically told me I was either a jerk or a john."

"That wasn't how I meant it …"

"Then what did you mean?"

"I need to back up." She took another sip. "Our first two dates were good. Awesome, really. So good I thought you'd be okay with being my escort ... But evidently not ..." She paused, laughing nervously.

Jason didn't smile, hard worry still etched on his face.

Looking at him made explaining things ten times worse. His scowl was pained, his mouth set in a straight line. Was he pitying her or, even worse, disgusted by her? Why did talking seem so difficult? She felt like she was hurting him, and that was hurting her. But she had to get through this if she wanted him to see her as anything other than crazy, because Jason wasn't going to be swayed. "And after the gala conversation—"

"Here we go with that again!"

"Wait." She held up her hand. "After that conversation, I thought you didn't want to be a plus-one. You were acting like a guy who wanted to keep his distance, even though it seemed like you liked me. It's happened before. Mostly in my twenties. Once in my teens." She sighed heavily and wiped a hand across her closed eyes.

"But I didn't—don't—want to keep my distance." He reached out for her hand, but she shook her head, peering at him through barely open eyelids, so he fell silent.

"I didn't think you did at first. I thought I was reading too much into this. Maybe you liked me, but you didn't like galas. But when you harped on the fact that you couldn't dance, I thought it was a nice way of saying you didn't want to be with me. And then taking me to Sly Foxes to show me how bad you were? It was overkill. And kind of a lie, because you are a great slow-dancer.

"But I still needed an escort to the ball, so I thought, 'Why not ask Graham?' It was that, or go back to SwipeMatch, and I couldn't go through that again. There wasn't—isn't—enough time." She covered her face with her palms and sighed.

"Do you really not get how I feel about you? How hurt that made me? You said you had a crush on him."

"What does a crush matter? I mean, really? The chances of him returning that are seriously low. Like, almost zero. No one falls for me like that. And I thought you liked me, but even I didn't think you were *falling* for me. Do you even know how hot you are? You could get anyone you want." She laughed wildly, like the thought of him pining over her was the biggest joke in the world.

But Jason stared hard back at her, as if he was putting a puzzle together in his mind. "So, this is a self-esteem issue."

"No. It's an expectations issue."

Jason's brow furrowed in confusion. "Come again?"

"I don't have a self-esteem issue. I love myself. I know I'm wonderful. I just have low expectations for the rest of you. And I'm not getting that out of nowhere. It's based on what I've found out from almost every guy I've ever dated." She dared to look him in the eye.

He stared back, speechless, but the confused look still marred his gorgeous features.

"You've got to understand. Guys like you don't take girls like me to their office parties or home to their parents, unless they're trying to give their parents heart attacks by showcasing their 'bad choices.' You experiment with us while you find other women you can date without ruining your rep in public."

She sat back into the sofa, satisfied that she'd made her point, because this was where they were. On dates, they had been only to crowded places or each other's houses. And of course, there was the gala—an event where Jason would be introduced to people Fortune knew, an event that her best friend hosted. He was very much against attending. He was hiding her because she was the experiment.

And now they'd been found out. His friends hadn't known they were dating until last Saturday night, and when they'd figured it out, they obviously hadn't approved. It was only a matter of time before he'd make up some excuse to stop seeing her—work was more demanding, he didn't think they could work beyond this ... whatever it was. Sex with benefits?

He should own up to it. After all, this was the goodbye conversation. She'd been a dare, and the game was over. She was a grown woman; she could handle it. If he told the truth, it would make the sting of breaking up easier.

Not *breaking up*—they weren't even together. Still, it was going to hurt. She'd really liked this guy.

Instead, he was silent for a few minutes, a scrutinizing look on his face.

Finally, he asked, "Is that what happened to you?"

Fortune lurched forward, jarred by the question. "What do you mean?"

"Something like what you described must have happened for you to act this way. Who hurt you? And are they still around? Because I think I want to hurt them."

She stared at him, wide-eyed. Anxiety churned in her gut, warning her never to tell Jason anything that could lead him to Marshall. Not only because what had happened between them was humiliating, but because Jason looked like he really might hurt him. Not that Marshall didn't deserve it, but that was over twenty years ago.

"You said 'once in your teens.' Was that when you were hurt?" Jason continued.

Oh no, he wanted the whole story, like he was some kind of therapist or something. *Great. He thinks I'm damaged and wants to fix me.* Embarrassment heated her face and throat. *Why can't he leave me alone?*

But while anxiety hovered on the outskirts of her emotions, her heart wouldn't let it in. Warmth spread through her chest from his soft, deep tone. She felt cared for ... loved even. Was he concerned and protective of her? Labeling him as a Marshall might have been a presumptuous judgment. Emotions flooded her thoughts and paralyzed her response.

"Fortune, I'm serious." He nudged her shoulder so she'd look at him.

But she could look only in his direction; she didn't have the courage to meet his stare. And she wouldn't dare touch him, even though she desperately wanted to throw her arms around him and sob into his shoulder. Instead, her heart hammered, and her mind constantly swirled with myriad paranoid questions.

"Um ... yeah. Uh ..." She inhaled and held it, afraid if she exhaled, a tumble of words would come out that would ruin everything she thought this relationship was.

He held her face with both of his hands, forcing her to look him in the eye. Their knees bumped into each other. "We can't move forward if you don't tell me what happened to make you this way. And isn't that the point of us talking? To move forward?"

Was that the point? Fortune shook her head in disbelief, her movement limited by his cradling hands. This couldn't be right. When she'd knocked on his door, she'd known exactly what she was walking into. She'd been preparing for closure. This was supposed to be her drop-the-mic moment—explain what she'd said Saturday morning, say goodbye, and leave. They were at the end, and she wanted to be the first to say goodbye for once.

So why was he talking about moving forward? He seemed like he wanted to work things out. Why did he care so much, anyway?

This therapeutic let's-work-this-out stuff had to be bogus. He couldn't care that much about a woman he barely knew.

As soon as she told him about Marshall, he'd cry out, *I knew it!* Like he'd discovered the key to understanding all women, and he would usher her right out the door. He wanted to make her relive embarrassing high school trauma to humiliate her and prove a point—that she was damaged—before promptly escorting her out of his life.

No, she wouldn't tell him the Marshall story.

He was still cupping the sides of her face, and now he was rubbing a thumb back and forth across her cheek. "Sweetie, are you okay?"

Part of her wished that he would stop rubbing her cheek, because it was going to make her cry. And the way he'd said *sweetie* in that deep, pillow-soft voice melted her resolve.

Fortune sighed heavily, worn down and defeated, but still refusing to hug him, to even hold his hand. She was the ribbon at the end of a balloon that a child had let go of, barely out of reach of the child's parent.

"Sweetie?"

She hated this feeling.

"Yeah, I'm okay." She sighed again. "The guy's name was Marshall. And I had a crush on him junior and senior year of high school. Me and my ridiculous crushes."

She told him the Marshall story, not because she wanted to, but because something in the way he sat beside her, his arm now around her shoulders, buoyed her spirit. He was literally holding her together, because she was crumbling apart.

"And he said, 'Have you seen Kylie? She's a ten! You're like a four-and-a-half.'" Tears fell from her eyes like water from a dripping faucet, but she swiped them away and shook her head angrily, mad that she was letting this get to her again. "And ever since, I've been trying to prove to every man I've ever dated that I'm better than a four-and-a-half.

"But guys see what they want to see. So, for the past I don't know, five? Ten years? Instead of expecting the moon and the stars from men, I've just taken whatever scraps I can get from a guy without expecting it to go anywhere. You want a few dates and some sex? Don't want to meet my friends or vice versa? Cool. That's all I'm going to give you. No emotional entanglements, no falling in love. I can handle that. It's really your loss, though. I'm a great girlfriend."

"Come on, Fortune." He squeezed her shoulder. "Give us—give *me* more credit than that. I'm not this jerk, or any other jerk, from your past. I see you." He leaned in at the same time she reared back.

"You're best friends with a narcissistic sycophant and an idiot who hates fat chicks. Everyone in your social circle is a Marshall jerk! How long will it be before you're one, too?"

Jason released her from his grip and gaped at her. "Is that what you think?"

"It's not a stretch, believe me."

His stare was hard and lasted for a full minute. Then he raked a hand through his hair and closed his eyes so tightly, the skin crinkled at the corners. "If you can't see and trust how I feel about you right now, I don't know how we can move past this."

Yep. Just what she'd thought. This was the familiar brush-off she understood. Even with the dates, the sex, the revelations, it all came back to guys needing distance from her. Jason didn't seem any different. "I don't, either."

"I ... I need some time to figure this out." He got up. "Maybe you do, too?"

She echoed his movements, then headed to the door. "Maybe." *Or maybe you need to figure out how to tell me goodbye. Glad I don't have that problem.* "Goodbye, Jason."

When she got to her car, she quickly left his house so he wouldn't come outside and try to continue the discussion. Not that he would have anyway. Defeat and loss rounded her shoulders, and she frowned, blinking back tears. Instead of heading home, Fortune pulled into a dark, empty parking lot of an abandoned building down the street from his subdivision.

She didn't want to run away from Jason. She wanted to run away from this whole Jason *thing*. A guy caring for her? Wanting to find out who had hurt her? Guys didn't do that, except gay ones who were also your best friends. She couldn't fathom a guy having a sexual attraction to her, caring about her as a person, and on top of that, looking like Mr. June in a Lumberjack pin-up calendar. This did not happen.

They'd had only three dates and some great hate sex. That didn't amount to a relationship. It sure didn't amount to love. This was getting out before it got too hard. She could say goodbye. She could go it alone.

But why did it hurt so much?

"What am I supposed to feel?" she yelled to no one, slamming her fists on the steering wheel. And then the tears came. Rivulets sliding down her cheeks. She mentally held back sobs and guttural cries until she couldn't anymore.

This was worse than the ODating4U.com summer fiasco. At least then, she'd recognized exactly what she was getting—an endless line of Marshall jerks. Asking to go dutch until they slept together, looking like bums for first dates because she was "just a big Black chick," assuming she had low self-esteem and was easy because of her weight, and getting pissed when they found out neither was true. All jerk actions.

For so long, this had been her dating life. She had taken pieces of men—experiences with them, a few dates here and there, an occasional fling—and used those pieces to make a love life. She was so used to men not taking her seriously that she didn't take them seriously.

And now, she was afraid she had turned a serious one away. She was—for the first time in weeks—lonely.

Twenty

W HEN FORTUNE LEFT HIS house after unloading all her relationship baggage on him, she was sure he'd end things the next day. She'd come off as a big bowl of damaged crazy, and who wanted to deal with that? But he hadn't ended things.

Instead, he'd left their relationship—if she could call it that—in limbo. Despite Fortune texting him a few times, Jason hadn't acknowledged or texted back. He hadn't called or stopped by her house, either.

That had been almost a week ago.

He'd ghosted her instead.

And here she was, alone. Again. She had poured her heart out to this guy, and even though she'd known better, some part of her had wanted his eyes to go soft and his arms to stretch out to her. Instead, she'd somehow moved him from being stern and protective to offended and guarded. Fortune had become too good at this—pushing men away. She thought she was revealing them for the condescending jerks they were for judging her. But this time, she thought, I pushed him away.

Thursdays at the office were usually a flurry of activity with people wrapping up projects and tittering about week-end plans. She'd been one of those excited titterers for a few weeks, gushing to Elaheh about how wonderful Jason was. Now, Fortune was a sad sack in her cubicle, whining to her work BFF before they went into their last department meeting for the week. Fortune cringed about how lovesick she'd been only two months ago, getting caught chatting with Jason on SwipeMatch. Now, she was just sick.

"I came in ready to break up, then he made me spill my guts and gave me hope, only so he can shut the door in my face and ghost me? Why do that?"

"I think you're looking at it the wrong way," Elaheh ventured. "You went in thinking one thing, but he could have thought something different. Maybe he needed your explanation to decide. Making a decision with emotions and hormones mixed up in it—those take a while to figure out."

"Meanwhile, I'm going to Louis's ball solo again." Fortune toed the carpet under her desk and sighed. There was a small spot that was frayed, and she ran her boot over it, thinking it would free that strand of carpet. But perhaps she had caused the carpet to fray in the first place by nervously rubbing her foot across it in the same spot. Bringing her own problems to a situation to cause another problem—sounded like her forte.

"See, you're on a deadline. He's not."

Fortune thought about what Elaheh had said. She didn't want to admit that Elaheh was right, but dang it, she was. Jason and Fortune were working toward two different things. She remembered what her goal was when they'd first talked on SwipeMatch: She'd been working to get a date to a ball and hadn't even thought that she would feel something for a guy. His goal had been more long-term. Even though he had lied about the real reason he was on SwipeMatch, he could have told the truth about the relationship part. Her goal had a timeline. His goal didn't.

So, while Fortune's emotions had already been on a roller coaster after the second date, maybe Jason's hadn't been. He'd already opted out of the gala, so that had had no bearing on his decision whether to date her. To him, it had probably been a nonissue. He probably wouldn't have thought that anything was wrong until the morning after they'd had sex. When she'd opened her big mouth and said that hot white guys were one and done. Ugh. She had probably sounded deranged and messed over.

Then, when he'd responded to her text to come over, she'd assumed it would be goodbye. That's what she'd thought he was doing. But what if it hadn't been goodbye? What if he'd only wanted to understand her? To understand what he would be in for if they started a long-term relationship?

Panic set in that what she'd feared that night might have been true. She had pushed him away. Or maybe, it was like Elaheh had said, he needed time to sort out his thoughts.

Had Fortune sorted out hers?

She looked at her phone for the millionth time that week, hoping for a text from Jason. What she saw instead was the last text she'd sent:

> **Fortune:** It's okay if you don't want to talk again. It was fun knowing you! :)

She'd sent it late the night before, frustrated and halfway into a bottle of Moscato. But Fortune had been so hung up on Jason's disinvite to the gala and being the chosen one in his Truth or Dare game that she hadn't even let her heart imagine what being Jason's girlfriend could be.

They'd had only three dates and some great hate sex. That didn't amount to love. Did it?

It amounted to something, or she wouldn't be like this—wrung out and torn up like her emotions had pushed her out into a tornado funnel.

Did she even want to be his girlfriend? Fortune looked at her phone again, and a hollow ache formed in her chest as her thoughts came together like pieces of a puzzle. Her mind flooded with memories of those three dates. She tingled with the memory of his hot skin pressed against hers as he'd pushed her to multiple orgasms. She wanted him, missed him, maybe even loved him.

Yikes. She loved Jason.

The admission scared her. Whenever she'd even attempted to put her heart out there with other guys, they'd thrown it away, neglected it, or they'd run from it. And that had hurt worse than a guy turning down one formal invite. Yet, she couldn't ignore the warmth and happiness in her chest at the declaration. Fortune loved Jason.

That doggone Elaheh, making Fortune think.

As if she'd heard her thinking, Elaheh peeked around Fortune's cubicle. "Are you coming to the department meeting? I need you to back me up on this crazy campaign idea."

Fortune grabbed her phone and her laptop, shaking her head and pasting on a smile. "Of course. Anything to stop thinking about this love stuff. You know I've got your back."

"Did you say 'love'?"

Fortune sighed heavily and sucked in her lips to keep her expression blank.

Elaheh's face scrunched into a cute grin. She looked like she'd discovered a basket of puppies at Fortune's desk. "Tell me everything."

Twenty-One

Jason

AFTER FORTUNE HAD LEFT his house, Jason had sat for hours in stunned silence, his mind racing, his soul full of jumbled emotions. For days, he'd racked his brain, wondering how he could have been so wrong about her, wondering if what she'd said justified going out with Graham and the mayhem that had ensued.

Every day at work, he broke down their conversation while he and his team built the concrete walls on his latest construction project. And every evening, he pieced the conversation back together to make some kind of sense of it. But nothing ever resolved, and he spent the nights dreaming of sex with Fortune and waking up with longing and confusion all over again.

The stuff she'd said, the accusations she'd made, none of them had been pleasant, and yet he missed this woman. More than missed her, he needed her. His body shivered with the memory of being inside her. His mind wondered how he would do without that fun, witty woman who made getting through every afternoon easier. Nothing inside him said, *Stay away from the crazy girl.* No, that was his friends talking.

What she'd said about his friends—that had hurt. And she thought so little of him, too, as if nothing he'd done while they were together could erase the potential jerk she saw in every heterosexual man. This was why she had distanced herself the morning after. It was her defense mechanism—take what she could get, but don't get too close. Relationships will only get your heart broken.

No, this wasn't self-hatred, like he'd thought then. This was self-preservation. She had basically been screaming that to him—from her stiffness and refusing to touch him while she'd explained what she'd meant by *low expectations*, to her tear-filled voice when she'd talked about Marshall.

But Fortune was wrong about Jason. From what she'd told him about her crush-turned-jerk from her past, Jason was nothing like him. Not even in his heart of hearts. And Jason didn't want to be done with her. In his living room, she'd argued and ended things before he'd even absorbed what she'd said. Apparently, she'd already declared them over. They weren't. He'd just needed quiet and time to think.

Everything she'd said that night had shocked him. This must be what it was like to be marginalized. Having to adjust who you were to be seen, to be ... included. Surely, this wasn't how all plus-size women felt. This had to have been because this Marshall guy had hurt her.

And then Jason was back to thinking about this Marshall douche and what he'd done to Fortune. What should have been a happy memory for her—winning the powder-puff game—he'd tainted. Not to mention scarring her so much he'd messed things up for guys like Jason decades later. If he could have taken the DeLorean back twenty-two years, he would have smashed this guy's face in.

DeLorean. Now, he was thinking in '80s terms like she did. Man, did he like this woman! Damn. He more than liked her, and he'd felt that way since he'd walked into Diamond Steak Co. and seen her. But, like Fortune had been waiting for him to be a Marshall, Jason had been waiting for her to be a Lily.

Jason had been guarding his heart, exactly like Fortune had.

In trying to prevent another failed relationship, he'd been overly cautious, making sure not to rush. But that wasn't the lesson Jason should have learned with Lily. He should have learned to listen to his instincts. To trust them. *I have to talk to Fortune.*

With that revelation, he grabbed his phone to text her. Oh no. It was Tuesday. It had been a full nine days since they'd spoken. She probably thought he'd ghosted her. He scrolled through their muted conversation, reading all the unread texts. Her last one confirmed it. She'd added the winking emoji to make him feel guilty. Fortune wasn't happy. She was probably angry, or hurt, or both. She'd probably written him off as a douchebag days ago, the same as she'd done to other guys before him.

But he was not those guys. He wanted to be her plus-one. He had to work things out because he wanted her back. Because he loved her.

He *loved* her. Whoa.

They'd had only three dates and some great hate sex. That didn't amount to love. He paced the length of his living room, tossing his phone from hand to hand, shaking his head. Nah, this couldn't be *love*. He needed to talk to her, though. To be sure.

He tested the waters, responding to her texts, phone calls, and DMs—everywhere she'd tried to contact him. He waited a day, then tried to make contact again. Nothing.

There was only one way he'd be able to talk to her. The gala.

He looked up the number for UICC and called, hoping his call would go through.

"This is Louis Grainger. How may I help you?"

The nonprofit's receptionist had said she'd connect him with Louis's assistant. Instead, Jason had gotten Louis himself. "I was expecting your assistant."

"Restroom again. Pregnant women. Who's this? I can tell her you called."

"Uh, no. I wanted to speak to you. I just—um." Jason cleared his throat. "Let me start over. I'm Jason Reed. Fortune's friend?"

An uncomfortable silence hung in the air for a couple of beats. Then Louis huffed. "Why are you calling me? If she's not talking to you, I'm certainly not going to send her a message—"

"No! I understand. That's not why I'm calling. I want to buy a ticket to your fundraiser."

"The gala has been sold out for weeks. Javier Firestone's a draw. Sold us out way ahead of schedule."

"Surely, you could add one seat to a table? It doesn't have to be a table near hers. I just need to be in the room."

"Do you know how many people want me to 'add one seat'? I can't do it for you and not for everyone else."

A twinge of panic burst in Jason's chest. He had to get into this ball. This same freaking gala that he had previously been invited to and had been dead set against going. The irony hit him like a cheap shot to the jaw. "This is the only place I can talk to Fortune. I have to talk to her."

The seconds of silence on the other end were maddening. "I don't know—"

"Louis, please." He held his breath for a moment before saying more. This would be the first time Jason had said it out loud. "Louis, I love her. I've got to tell her. I can't let her be at this ball alone."

After a long pause, Louis responded with a heavy sigh that ratcheted Jason's urgency down a few notches. "Meet me at Free Range for lunch. And bring your checkbook."

Jason entered Free Range and stood near the case for the sugared treats, away from the lunch line, but in plain view of the door and the other diners. The little bistro was crowded with mostly office people in suits and business-casual out-fits, standing stoically in line, tapping away on their phones, or huddled around tables with their colleagues or friends. Standing there, he ran a hand through his wild hair, feeling out of place with his scruffy face, jeans, and work boots.

Everyone was looking at him. Their stares were prickling his skin. Seth was right, he was a big emo, but that was for another time. He rethought logistics and got in line, wishing he was sitting in a dark corner of the dining area. From some of the stories Fortune told him, Louis had probably picked this place on purpose to make Jason feel ill at ease.

"There you are, sweetie," Louis called from across the bistro, waving his hand toward Jason. A few heads turned to Louis, then to Jason.

Jason's neck and cheeks burned with embarrassment. He wasn't usually this vulnerable or discomfited, even with a gay man calling him *sweetie* across a crowded room. But Louis was throwing him off his game. Maybe because Jason's future with Fortune lay in Louis's hands.

"So, coming in from the job site, I see?" Louis met Jason at the line, looking him up and down.

Jason turned and met Louis's gaze. Louis didn't look anything like Jason had expected. Despite what Fortune had told him about Louis on their first date, Jason had still pictured Louis coming in wearing a shawl and full makeup. Perhaps a crown of some sort. Instead, Louis was dressed in a tailored navy suit, white shirt, and pink-yel-low-and-white-striped tie. That and his comment made Jason feel even more out of place, and a tad disgusted with himself for stereotyping.

"I'm actually substitute teaching a shop class in a couple of hours," Jason responded.

"Oh." Louis looked Jason over again with an inscrutable expression. "All righty, then." He cleared his throat. "First off, let me say, I spoke up for you, even though you got yours and left. And I wouldn't have even entertained this last-minute notion if I didn't think that you belong with her. And secondly, don't ask me how she is, because I'm not going to tell you."

Jason nodded. "Fair enough."

The cashier took their orders and gave them each a number. Louis led Jason to a table in the middle of the bistro, and they sat. They stared at each other for several seconds before Jason got the hint that Louis wanted to get down to business. He pulled his checkbook from his inside coat pocket.

"How much?"

"First, let me ask you, what are you going to say when you see her?" Louis asked.

At least this he was prepared for. Jason had known Louis would never just hand over the ticket. He would want to keep Jason from hurting his best friend more. "I'm going to tell her I love her, and I'll be different next time if she would—"

"No, you aren't," Louis interrupted.

"What?" He was taken aback. Was Louis attempting sabotage? Maybe he thought Jason needed to be taught a lesson.

Don't mess with my bestie like this ever again, and thanks for your generous donation to the gala you will never attend. A pang of anxiety throbbed in his chest. "But I want her to know I love her."

"She's not going to hear that." Louis shifted in his seat, leaning in closer. "You say, 'I love you,' and she's going to hear, 'I pity you, and I'm sad about it.' Then she's going to grab a steak knife from the nearest table and murder you."

Jason inhaled sharply. He looked away from Louis, unable to find words to respond.

"How else do you think she'd stop all that white male privilege coming out of your mouth right now?"

"I don't understand." Jason reared back and crossed his arms, instantly on guard at the term. "What about that was privilege?"

"You don't think some ... dude has played the 'I love you, and I'll do better' card to get back in her pants? Like, just because they deigned to love her despite her ... size"—he rolled his eyes—"that she's supposed to forgive them, accept their mistakes, and take them back? That's privilege."

Louis's tone was packed with condescension and disdain. "She doesn't need to accept you and all your flaws. You need to accept her in all of her glory." He closed his eyes for a moment and leaned back, as if forcing himself to calm down. "You need to be the guy that's different, the one who acknowledges she's hurting because, in fact, she is a ten and always will be, and you'll spend every day showing her if you have to."

If he got the chance, Jason planned to do just that. Perhaps he should tell her that.

"It's not about your feelings. It's about understanding her and supporting her. When she asked you to my gala, she was already into you. Probably even falling for your ass. You were getting the best parts of her before you even earned the right to them."

Jason's mind went back to after their second date, and he flinched. While Fortune had been falling in love, all he had been thinking about was her on top and how she made a bowl of ramen sexy.

"Now, you've got to work to get her back. But first …" Louis took out a ticket to the gala and slid it halfway across the table. The price stamped on the top left was $250. "The UICC thanks you for your generous donation of five hundred dollars."

Jason hastily wrote the check, afraid Louis would tack on another $500 before Jason finished, just for spite.

Louis took the check and tucked it into his jacket pocket. "Pleasure doing business with you. Don't mess it up." He gathered the remains of his lunch and headed toward the door, but then turned back. "Fortune was right. You really do look like a lumberjack." He winked and threw Jason a wicked grin before he left.

Now that Jason had at least gotten on the best friend's side, what was he going to say to Fortune?

Twenty-Two

Fortune

THE WEEK BEFORE THE ball was an emotional upheaval for Fortune. She'd thought that admitting to herself that she was in love with Jason would bring some measure of peace, but it made her feel worse when she didn't hear from him.

After she'd had the revelation, Fortune had waited for a day to hear from Jason. It had been two full days since her fun-knowing-you text, and he hadn't responded. Racked with sobs and sadness so sharp it had felt like hot pokers in her chest, Fortune had blocked his number, deleted her SwipeMatch profile, and blocked him on all social media.

His silence the week before had told her that she'd lost something more real, more fulfilling than she'd ever had. After meeting a guy who finally understood what she was worth, he was gone. And that hurt felt like nothing she'd ever felt for any other guy she'd dated.

But Fortune couldn't dwell on him or the love she might have lost. She had to move forward. No more tears. She had a gala to attend.

When Louis picked her up, Fortune slunk out her front door, a silvery, glittery purse standing out against her blood-red dress. The dress was high-necked and sleeveless with a V neck front and a fluted A-line skirt that hit her right above the knee. Her sandals were strappy with a chunky heel and as glittery as her purse. The only thing out of place was her neon purple manicure and pedicure.

Louis yelled, "Sweetie, pick up your bottom lip off the ground. You look gorgeous!"

"Thanks, bestie. I thought this year would be different than last year."

"Oh, it will be. Wait until you see where I've seated you." He rubbed his hands together craftily, then they took off for the ball.

Arm in arm, Fortune and Louis walked into The Providence ballroom of the Zed hotel. The room was filled with dozens of tables, all covered in gleaming white tablecloths and decorated in shiny metallic and floral centerpieces. Places were already set for dinner, and numbered metallic cards stood out to help patrons get to their tables.

The ballroom had three front doors and two doors on either side for entry. Bars in each corner of the expansive room were already busy fulfilling donors' orders. A rectangular row of tables at the front of the room spanned the entire wall, and in the middle of the row stood a podium with the hotel's name on the front, just in case the media filmed any of the speakers. It had been a while since she'd been to a wedding, but she'd recognize Zed's wedding setup any day. The only things different were the podium front and center and, behind it, a huge banner with the gala's theme: "Have fun giving today to remember tomorrow."

Well, it would probably be another long while before she attended another wedding. Most of her friends were married, and Louis was against traditional wedding ceremonies, so she wouldn't be a maid of honor again anytime soon.

Louis's assistant was already there, barking orders at a group of volunteers.

"Got to love having an assistant for these nights. Finally, I can enjoy myself during cocktail hour." Surveying the room of donors, Louis sighed contentedly.

"Don't enjoy yourself too much. I need an anchor for cocktail hour." Feeling skittish as she walked beside Louis, Fortune peeked at other guests and hoped that the impossible would happen—that Jason would appear and sweep her away. She shook the thought out of her mind. *Stop hoping for a pipe dream. He's done with you.* "Might be some sharks in these philanthropic waters."

No sooner than she'd gotten out the words, she spotted Aileen Davenport across the dance floor at the other bar. She shifted, turning her back to Aileen, but it was too late. She'd been spotted. "Fortune? Is that you?"

Fortune turned to face Aileen and the man on her arm. "Ah! Mrs. Davenport. How nice to see you."

"Likewise!" She gestured to the man beside her. "This is my husband, Chip. Chip, this is my miracle worker at Davies Marketing, Fortune Edwards."

Miracle worker? Yes, Fortune thought. She'd own it. The glow of respect and recognition from Aileen Davenport felt great and well-deserved.

Chip was only a few inches taller than his wife, which made him about five six or five seven at most. He had a head full of white hair and eyes deep set in a wrinkled but masculine, angular face. He resembled a short Karl Lagerfeld. "Nice to meet you, Fortune."

As they shook hands, Chip stared at her with a blank expression.

Fortune plastered on a smile and forced herself not to snatch her hand out of his grasp. One probably had to be a little creepy to put up with Aileen Davenport.

"I'm surprised to see you here," Mrs. Davenport remarked.

"Yes, I'm here every year. Louis is my best friend." She smiled up at him, but he was half turned away and talking with someone else. Fortune tugged on the hem of his suit jacket.

"I'm surprised I haven't seen you at one of these before. UICC is our sister organization." Davenport scrunched her face into an unflattering, confused look.

"I'm usually volunteering."

Louis turned back to their group, interrupting before Fortune could elaborate. "Mrs. Aileen! Lovely to see you, darling!" He pulled her into a European-style air kiss. "How are Bitsy and Mitzie?"

"Oh, they're wonderful, Louis! How are the totals looking tonight?"

Louis plastered on a fake frown. "Not as good as they could be. I'm hoping the auction will make up some of the difference."

Mrs. Davenport leaned in. "What are we auctioning off this year?"

"Oh, darling, you know it's a surprise! And you can't get it out of me, not yet. I've got my eye on you! If you'll excuse us, I've got to handle some event business." He whipped around with a flourish, almost throwing Fortune off balance as he towed her along.

After they left the Davenports, Fortune whispered, "I thought you said your totals had already surpassed last year this time?"

"Of course they have!" He grinned. "But I'm not going to tell her that! That midget on her arm and his friends are loaded."

Then, with a caring frown around his eyes and a serious horizontal line of a mouth, he led her to her seat. "Fortune. Sweetie. You've got this. I swear your table is going to be the table where everyone wishes they were tonight. Trust me on this."

"I swear, if you are lying about this, I'm gonna—"

"Here's your table."

When she cast her gaze over the table, seven pairs of eyes belonging to seven gorgeous hunks of masculinity in identical black tuxes and bow ties gazed back at her. They smiled, some with mischievous eyebrow raises. Well, at least they wouldn't ignore her when she asked for the bread. Everyone at this table looked like they understood the value a good warm dinner roll.

This was the table of her dreams—if she'd looked like a runway model. A pang of insecurity hit her and wouldn't let her go. In some ways, this could be worse than last year. How could she hold these guys' attention? In her mind, she was cursing Louis from here to Sunday. *Thanks a lot, BFF,* she thought in the most sarcastic tone she could muster and mentally kicked him in the shin, imagining he felt the sting of insecurity coursing through her nervous system right now.

"Guys, this is my best friend, Fortune. Fortune, this is Jeffrey, Tony, Mark, Chase, Paul, Michael, and Big Shawn. Guys, be nice to my BFF."

As if on command, the guys stood and greeted her. Big Shawn pulled out the empty chair beside him for her to sit. The insecurity dissolved in her veins, replaced by a warm comfort and acceptance. *Okay, BFF. I take it back. Thanks a lot.*

The corners of her mouth upturned slightly, she glanced at Louis and nodded.

"Have fun," Louis whispered and disappeared into the crowd of people getting to their seats.

Fortune sat and smiled nervously at the expectant stares coming at her from around the table. Dinner was being served, and she watched for a moment while the guys devoured steak, chicken, vegetables. As she'd predicted, no one touched the bread baskets, but no one cared that she did. "So how did you guys get stuck at the singles' table?" She laughed.

"Singles' table?" Jeffrey was on her immediate left. "Is that what this is?"

"Only if most of us are gay," Michael quipped.

"Hey, nothing wrong with being gay," Tony said. "I'm not, but there's nothing wrong with it."

The group laughed.

"No need for a disclaimer, bro," Mark said.

Dessert came around, but only Big Shawn and Fortune took one. The rest asked for more water or a glass of wine.

Jeffrey turned to her. "We're here for the auction."

Fortune nodded. "You're the presenters."

Big Shawn leaned over and whispered loudly, "No, we're the merch."

Another bout of group laughter.

"What?" Fortune struggled to keep a straight face, but broke into hearty laughter.

"You have a great laugh," Chase said. "Like Julia Roberts."

"Yes, she does," a voice behind her remarked.

Fortune turned to face a wall of tuxedoed torso. When she looked up, she met Jason's gaze.

The corners of his mouth lifted in a half smile that caused her stomach to flip. "This looks like the fun table."

"You're here." She couldn't stop staring at him. What was he doing here? Her heart was beating so fast, she hoped she wouldn't pass out. *He's here for you, silly girl.* She wanted desperately to touch him, to hug him, but her body wouldn't move. "You're really here."

"Yeah. Well, sort of. I'm at table twenty-six. It's practically outside the door." He chortled. "Eh, what can you do when you bought the last ticket?"

Had Jason figured out what he felt for her? Was he as in love as she was? She wanted to jump into his arms and kiss him until her lips were puffy. But he hadn't given any indication that he felt the same as he conversed with the group of guys.

"Are you part of the auction?" Paul asked Jason. He eyed Jason with an envious glare, his forehead furrowed with worry.

"No. I'm just here to support the charity. My grandmother had Alzheimer's. This is a different take on supporting those with the disease. If I could see her laugh one more time as she told us stories about my dad as a teenager. Those were her favorites. She kept those memories the longest." He sighed. "But she would have loved this. This would have made her laugh whether she remembered or not."

Fortune hadn't known that one of Jason's grandmothers had had Alzheimer's. She didn't know a lot about Jason, but she wanted to know more. A whole lot more.

The lights in the ballroom lowered noticeably, and like clockwork, waitstaff cleared plates and topped off drinks, and hotel staff brought out mic stands and other props.

Louis was nowhere to be seen, but Louis's assistant was headed toward their table. She leaned in as far as her pregnant belly would allow. "Guys, I need you to follow me." She made a gesture to a set of double doors across the room and walked in that direction, not looking back to confirm the well-dressed guys were following.

Fortune was alone at the table, Jason behind her seat. She refused to look at him, afraid that the man behind her was about to formally end things.

Jason leaned in and caressed her shoulder. "Can we talk outside? For one minute?" He gestured toward the nearest door. Everything was so inviting about him, from his stance to his open jacket and buttoned vest to his half-amused smile. It made her want to follow him anywhere he was going.

She took his hand. "One minute. I'm sure Louis will miss me if I'm gone too long."

He led her to the lobby entrance, which was dark now that the sun had set and the recessed lobby lights had been turned down.

Mark and Chase from her table were at the far end of the entrance, nervously pacing and giving each other pep talks before going back into the ballroom to be auctioned.

Their exchange struck her as comical, but she barely cracked a smile, sensing that Jason wanted her undivided attention.

Jason started, "I wanted to explain the last couple of weeks. I couldn't go without—"

Someone burst through one of the hall doors right as Louis was shouting in a high-pitched voice, "Everyone, get ready for our secret auction in ten minutes! This year's merchandise is sure to wow you—" And then the door closed.

"Wow, is he loud," Fortune mumbled.

"That's your friend," Jason retorted.

She rolled her eyes, but grinned. "You were saying?" She looked at him, and for the first time that night, she really saw him.

Even though he'd cleaned up, signs of fatigue were obvious. Jason shook his head as if he were shaking himself awake. He'd let his hair grow, and it flopped into his eyes, emphasizing the faint shadows under them. His stubble was growing into a beard, and it was uneven. Had he been as harrowed about their whatever-it-was as she had been?

"Anyway," he began again. "Our last conversation was ... It was a lot to process. I needed some time—"

"You could've told me that before now," she interrupted.

"I wanted to be sure of—"

Fortune continued as if she hadn't heard him. "I mean, a little text—"

"I didn't know what to feel!" Jason yelled.

She fell silent, hearing the words she'd yelled into the ether two weeks ago echoing back to her off the lobby's cavernous walls.

He looked around the lobby, but no one was there. "I was angry at so many things," he said in a loud whisper. "And I was hurt that we hadn't connected like I thought we had. After you told me about Marshall, I got it—sort of—but mostly I was still confused." He paused.

"Confused?" She tried to keep the pain out of her voice. "About what?" Hadn't revealing her past hurt cleared everything up? The story was simple enough. Girl has crush on guy, guy breaks girl's heart by trying to have sex with her behind his girlfriend's back, then guy denigrates her when girl says no, and every guy who likes girl after that gets the side-eye. What's confusing about that?

"I couldn't understand why you didn't realize that I'm not Marshall or any of those other douchebags in your past. I see you. All of you. Your kindness, your beauty, your awesome personality. You're right. You would make a great girlfriend. But you aren't the only one that knows it. I do, too."

She was stunned. She'd never been so wrong about a guy since Marshall. At least this was wrong in a good way. What had she done to deserve this man? Oh yeah, she had been her true self, and he'd seen it. He knew what a prize he was getting. She was the one who needed to be convinced. Jason must have seen what the other guys hadn't. He saw her as a potential girlfriend, someone he could take home to his mother, possibly even ... love ... one day. The thought warmed her inside, and a small smile formed on her lips.

"I figured out what I needed to do now." He leaned down and pressed his lips gently to hers, his growing beard tickling her skin.

"What's that?" she asked, lost in a fog of longing from his kiss.

"I needed to come here. The one thing you asked me to do, I had to do it. Not only because I wanted to see you again, but because you asked. You deserve to have someone be there for only you like you're there for probably everyone you know, if Louis is any indication."

She gasped. "Jason." No other words were coming.

He pressed his cheek to hers. "You know what else?"

"What?" The friction of his scruff against her cheek sent a shiver through her.

"I want to see you naked again," he whispered, his breath tickling her ear, heating her and making her shiver at the same time. "This time in my bed."

Goosebumps raced down her arms, and her nipples beaded into throbbing points. For a second, the Zed lobby vanished, and the only things that existed were her and this tall, sexy man. She closed her eyes and inhaled his scent of aftershave and ... chocolate? Oh right. Dessert from the gala. Her mind came back to the present. "I need to—"

"No, you don't. Louis gets it. Let's go." He released her from his embrace and tugged her hand in his.

She glanced up at him, grinning. "This is so *Pretty in Pink.*"

His gaze raked over her, stopping somewhere near her cleavage and then going back to her face. "But you're wearing red," he said, a look of slight amusement on his face.

"We can't do this if you're not going to get my '80s references." She raised a skeptical eyebrow.

He laughed and leaned in close, their foreheads touching. "I got it. Only this time, Duckie's gay and Blane's not a jerk, so there's no ambiguous ending. You're supposed to be with me. Now, do you want to go?"

"Yes. Let's go. Now."

He met her lips in a slow, lingering kiss.

She wasn't sure if the excited jitter coursing through her body was because of his '80s movie analysis or his kiss. It was probably both.

They made their way to the valet booth, exchanging kisses and pinches and caresses. She couldn't stop touching him, and he was glued to her side, curling his arm around her protectively every time they met someone in the corridor to the garage. When they got to the parking garage, they parted long enough for Jason to give the valet his ticket. As soon as the valet turned to his coworker, Jason was back by Fortune's side, dipping his head to whisper what he wanted to do to her later. She pursed her lips and crossed one leg in front of the other, attempting to look unaffected, but the quickened rise and fall of her chest gave her away.

They got in the car, exchanging quick kisses until the valet interrupted them. "Sir, we need to pull another car around."

"Sorry." Fortune turned to see if there was really a car and spotted a plush corgi dressed as an astronaut in Jason's back seat. "Uh ... what's that?"

"That's Sporgi, my niece's toy. She left it in the car the other day."

"Your niece? Yeah, right. You've got it belted in!" She giggled.

"*She* did it!" he huffed, overly dramatic and self-righteous.

"This is hilarious!" she said through laughter. Tears gathered in the corners of her eyes. "OMG, I love you so much right now ..."

She stopped and stared at him, her eyes wide with panic. What had she just said? Realization spread through her, and her stomach clenched in a cringe. Why did she always mess up a good thing?

He stared back at her, the corners of his mouth slowly lifting.

She stammered, unsure of what to say to fix it. "I didn't—I—mean—"

He interrupted, "I love you, too." He stopped at the garage exit, framed her face with his hands, and closed his mouth over hers.

A horn honked behind them, and they jumped apart.

"Now, let's go find out what's under that little red dress of yours."

Twenty-Three

J ASON LOVED HER. FORTUNE silently turned the phrase over in her mind as he maneuvered his way through traffic out of Uptown. With a few turns, the city skyline became a blurred, dark canopy of centuries-old trees as they wound through the Dilworth neighborhood. It felt like they were protected, cocooned in a world of love that held only the two of them. A world where he kept saying those three words to her over and over.

Well, that and *under that little red dress*. She stole a glance at him and imagined peeling off layers of tuxedo and running her hands all over his smooth chest and tasting his skin along his collarbone. Her breath caught as she thought about his teeth grazing her neck and his fingers sliding in and out of her. She clasped her hands on her lap to keep from grabbing his.

"You're deep in thought." He wedged his hand in between hers, breaking the clasp to hold her hand. "What about?"

"Your hand between my legs." The words would have sounded bold without that hitch in her voice.

"Like this?" He let go of her hand and grasped her knee instead, then made his way under her dress and up her thigh. "Is this what you were thinking about?" His voice was deep, rumbling through her like a freight train, speeding away with her inhibitions.

"Yes." She breathed in small pants.

He pushed in higher, closer to her center. She let out a small moan when he rubbed a knuckle against her underwear, the lace deliciously scratchy on her sensitive skin.

"Fortune, you're so hot here," he said in a low murmur.

She leaned her head against the back of the seat and closed her eyes. "I'm hot everywhere."

He chuckled softly. "Yes, you are." He pulled her thigh to his side of the car, spreading her legs, and ran his hand up and down her panty-covered seam. "I love touching you here."

"I love you touching me there." She swallowed against another moan rising in her throat. "But don't you think you need to slow down a little?"

The car decelerated, and Jason hooked a finger around her panties. She panted at the warm press of his skin against her sex.

"I meant your hand!" She made a sound that was somewhere between laughter and whimpering. She grabbed his hand with both of hers and tugged it away from her, enfolding it in a clasp. "Please don't slow the car. We can't get to your house fast enough."

"That was the sexiest thing I've ever heard you say. I think I love you even more right now."

She laughed softly.

He seemed reluctant as he slid his hand from her grasp, and as soon as he let go, she craved his touch again. He was like water, and she had been parched for years. If they didn't get to their destination soon, she would crumble into dust and blow away.

Finally, they stopped in front of his house, and she was out of the car and on the porch before the engine had shut off. A mum with bright orange blooms had replaced the dying plant that had been there.

"You got a new flower?" she asked as he unlocked the door.

"The last time you were here, I saw you staring at it when you came in. I guess I had forgotten all about it. I'm surprised Mrs. Kosinski didn't say anything. That nosy old lady is always nagging me about something."

"Kosinski. Your neighbor." Something snapped into place in her mind, and she faced him. "Wait. You saw me?"

"I told you, I see you. Your awesome personality, your kindness, your judgmental glare." He stepped toward her, a half grin turning up the corners of his mouth.

"I wasn't judging—"

"Your gorgeous full lips, your tits in that dress, your purple fingernails that I want digging into my back ..." He wound his arms around her, taking her parted lips in a rough kiss.

She moaned into his mouth, a beg for more.

He obliged, twirling his tongue around hers.

She reached for the lapels of his tuxedo jacket and freed him of it.

He lifted her, backing her against the door and leaning in to kiss her deeper. He kissed like he had been parched, too, like he had craved her as much as she craved him. He could do this all night, and she would—

A loud, incessant, yapping bark startled them, and they broke apart, panting to get air.

"Must be Mrs. Kosinski about to take Babsie for a walk. Her and that miniature noisemaker." Jason pressed a quick kiss to her cheek, then opened the door. He led her to the kitchen and rummaged in a cabinet for a moment before extricating a wineglass. "I just realized you never had the tour. Do you want it?"

Fortune leaned on the island and thought back to the first time he'd asked. That night had gone from awesome, fun date to disastrous nonsex. Her body had not been responding to him at all then, as cool and dry as the concrete countertop under her forearms. Not the case now, she thought, pressing her thighs together to keep the damp heat between them.

"Sure," she said slowly, wondering how long it would take to get to the bedroom.

Jason pursed his lips, then bit the bottom one, failing at holding back a smile. "The abbreviated tour, right?"

She breathed and laughed. "Um, yeah. Is it that obvious?"

"Is what obvious?" He broke out into a full-on grin and handed her a glass of sparkling pink wine. "So, bathroom and master bedroom it is." He motioned to the kitchen behind him. "This is some room with food and Moscato." He paused. "And one day, one of Fortune's homemade cheese-cakes."

She stared at him, her breath caught in her throat.

Jason winked, grabbed her empty hand, and led her up the stairs. As enthralled as if he were a riveting TV show, she watched his back as he ascended. She could see his muscles move even under his jacket, and that butt ... Jiminy Christmas. If she hadn't been holding a glass, she would have reached out and pinched it.

When they got to the second floor, he opened a door on their right. "Guest bathroom. You seem like a woman who needs her own bathroom space." He pointed to the small stack of linens on the vanity. "Those are yours. And they're clean."

He assumed correctly; her own bathroom space was a must. And he had *prepared* for her. Who was this guy? And why hadn't she met him sooner? She stared at him in disbelief.

He shrugged. "What? My mother taught me well. Plus, I'm a grown person."

She laughed. "That second one's debatable."

He raised his eyebrows and shook his head. "Anyway, I'll wait for you down there." He pointed to an open door at the end of a short, shotgun hallway, then took her glass and walked toward his bedroom.

Fortune hurriedly used the facilities—taking a little time to snoop in drawers and behind the shower curtain, all immaculate—and followed Jason's directions. A bluish-orange glow that hadn't been there before spilled through the doorway. She gently pushed open the door.

Entering Jason's bedroom was like walking into a piece of art. Bathed in candlelight from dozens of tealights around the room, he stood at the foot of his bed, still wearing his tuxedo pants and unbuttoning his shirt. The king-size bed was turned down with military precision, the comforter dyed with various swirls of blue, from Carolina sky to navy. His sheets were steel gray, as was the wall behind the bed. The rest of the room was painted a bluish white. The colors made Fortune feel like she was floating in the sky, about to hop on a cloud. And with candles lit, it looked like a sky at sunset.

"Wow. This is … wow." Her gaze traveled around the room, then landed on him. "Well, now we figured out which Golden Girl *you* are. Sweet, naïve Rose," she said, the awe taking away the bite in the joke.

He responded with a squinty smile as he shrugged off his shirt and tossed it across the room near a chair where a towel and other pieces of clothing were draped across the seat. In one motion, he cradled her face and slanted his mouth over hers.

Kissing him in his candlelit bedroom was like being in the middle of a movie. The oddball, lovesick girl in her was twirling on the side of a mountain, singing about hills being alive with music. Jason wanted her—not for one night, or a few nights, but he wanted all of her all the time. It was so different from the rest of her love life that it seemed like fiction. But his mouth, now trailing hungrily down her throat, was very real.

The heady giddiness flowed through her, emboldening her. She reached for his pants and undid them, pushing them to the floor, then ran her palms around his waist and to his perfectly round backside.

He leaned back to look in her eyes. "Guess the abbreviated tour was the right choice." He chuckled as he carefully stepped out of his pants and toed them to the side so she wouldn't have to let go of him.

She realized, as bold as she was, this was not going to be like before, with him running the show and her snapping back at him. This was not hot hate sex. This was ... She couldn't even say it. Because, dang it, she'd never done this. She'd never made love before. How could she have gone her whole existence without ever making love to someone?

Until now, Fortune had never thought about the negative side effects of a half-lived love life. Pleasing a guy who wasn't planning on sticking around was different than making love with him. Now that she'd found a guy she loved who loved her, she didn't know how to show him that love. Fortune bit her bottom lip, unsure what to do next.

"What's going on in that gorgeous brain of yours?" Jason tilted her chin up. With his thumb, he worked her bottom lip free of her teeth.

"I ...." She sighed. "I don't know how to do this."

He raised an eyebrow. "Once upon a time, we already did this."

"No. We did something like this. But not this. This is … different."

He cradled the back of her head and touched his lips to her cheek. "Why are you worried?"

She hesitated. The paralyzed knot in her stomach wasn't worry, exactly. It was more like a ball of lust encased in anxiety. What if she messed this up, and he fell out of love with her?

"You can't mess this up. I'm already in love with you. You get that, right?" he asked, voicing her thoughts.

Oh, he was good. "It's … I can't believe this is really happening." The paralyzed anxiety eased, giving way to pure excitement.

"It's happening," he said in a low voice. His hand moved from her neck over her collarbone to her breast, stopping to stroke her through layers of fabric. "All you have to do is let it."

He took her mouth in a slow kiss while he reached behind her and unzipped her dress. She was putty in his embrace, loose and malleable, as he peeled off the dress with painfully slow, methodical movements. The now-familiar rainfall scent mixed with his own and the gentle scratch of his scruff made her dizzy with need. His hands caressed her, and everywhere they touched, her skin ignited until her whole body was one big conflagration of lust.

The dress fell to the floor in a red shiny pile, and she stepped out of it.

He trained his gaze on her every move.

Under Jason's stare, Fortune felt need and vulnerability bubble inside her even though she was bound tighter than a sausage in black corset-style shapewear, a black strapless bra, and lacy cheeky panties.

He stepped back, appraised her, then ran his fingers up and down her corseted midriff, throwing the butterflies in her stomach into excited chaos. "Am I going to be able to get this off you?"

"Doubtful." She grinned.

Jason answered with a nod and walked around behind her. His breath was warm on her neck and smelled like cinnamon. His body heat radiated against the back of her from her ankles to the top of her head. His callused fingers went up the backs of her thighs, over her butt, and up and down her back. She shivered under the rough caress.

"No laces," he commented idly, then his touch and heat were gone.

Fabric rustled, and the bed creaked.

"No laces," she repeated. Fortune grasped each thin strap and pulled her arms out of them, then pushed the top of the corset down.

"Turn around," he ordered, maneuvering her with a grip on her thigh.

She eagerly obeyed, facing him. Jeez Louise, this man was gorgeous, Fortune thought as she took in the scene—over six feet of chiseled naked masculinity sitting at the foot of the bed. Well, almost naked. He still wore charcoal-gray boxer briefs that bulged, straining to hold him inside.

"I want to see all of you." The gravelly tone that tinged his voice reminded her of Hot Hate-Sex Jason.

She bit back a whimper, her hands itching to touch him instead of wrestling with tight lingerie.

He took his hand off her thigh and leaned back, staring at her, his eyes intent as if he were committing to memory every inch of her.

Fortune continued peeling the top of the corset down. She wiggled the shapewear down her body and stepped out of it.

Her heart thudded so hard she felt like one big heartbeat. She reached behind her and unhooked her bra with unsteady hands. Fortune had never stripped while a lover watched. Taking off clothes was a feat of engineering most of the time, with the guy fumbling and Fortune trying to keep his hands away from the wobbliest parts of her body. And then, when she was finally naked, there was the awkward avoidance—looking away from her jiggly thighs or avoiding touching her belly. There was nothing more humiliating than a guy being turned off when he saw her stomach or her arm flab.

But Jason was different. He loved her. He wanted to touch her and demanded to see her. And if she hid from him, he'd call her out on it, she thought, remembering how affronted he'd acted when she'd moved his hand away from her waist. She stopped thinking of past lovers and her own insecurities and focused on Jason's eyes, those dark blue pools of desire fixed on her, craving to see even the parts she wanted to hide.

"You're holding back." He sat up and grabbed her at the waist, his thumb settling into that notch at her side above her pelvis, and tugged her to him. "You've got to let it happen."

The move jerked her out of her insecure thoughts, and she gasped as a bolt of lust-fueled heat pulsed up her spine from deep in her core. She threw her head back briefly, her chest heaving.

In one swift motion, Jason moved from her waist to her neck, pulling her mouth down to meet his. His other hand yanked her bra off from the front, then grabbed the back of her underwear, stripping them to her feet. When she sidestepped out of them, his fingers pushed into the soaking heat between her legs while his tongue pressed into her mouth.

She held on to his shoulders to steady herself, his tongue and his touch blasting away every emotion except need. No more concerns about stretch marks or love handles, whether he was turned off by the fleshy parts of her, or whether her underwear had highlighted instead of down-played the cellulite on the backs of her legs.

There was tasting and relishing. And then it was just relishing as he kissed his way down her throat to her breast—the stinging pleasure as he gently pulled her nipple between his teeth, the rough friction as he circled her sensitive bud with his thumb, the firm ripple of his muscles as she gripped his shoulders. The sensations were coalescing, building, reducing her to a whimpering ball of need.

"I'm close," she panted as her knees weakened. She leaned into him, half draping herself over his shoulder and hugging him around the neck.

"Let it happen, baby." He lifted her left leg, bending it so her shin rested on his thigh, opening her up to him.

She pushed back, a second of panic shooting through her at the fear that he would lift her other leg, and all her weight would be on him. Her own words echoed in her head. *I'm too heavy*.

As soon as she shifted, he threw his arm around her waist, holding her close. "It's okay, baby," he soothed. "I've got you. Sweetie, I promise. I've got you."

He repeated it over and over until she felt the building inside her again, and then he was calling her beautiful and coaxing her to come. Then a dam burst inside her, and she went from one sure foot on the floor to shaking in his lap.

Twenty-Four

Jason

JASON ROSE WITH A still-trembling Fortune in his arms. He laid her on the bed, planting kisses on her neck and chest while her panting slowed to normal breathing again. Then he ditched his boxer briefs and reached in his nightstand for a condom.

As much as he'd love to have her straddling him, she was obviously still too self-conscious for that. But he had time. He'd show her how much he loved her, how he couldn't get enough of her body, and then one day she'd be confident enough to be on top.

Of course, the only reason he was rationalizing this now was to give him enough time to roll on the condom before he freaking burst. When she'd been in his lap, he'd felt her—all her soft, wet heat on him—and it had taken everything in him not to free his erection and plunge into her. He was having a first, too—he'd never felt this ... urgency, his body demanding he throw caution to the wind so he could be surrounded by her. It was like wrestling a hungry bear, only the bear was inside him.

In front of him was pure beauty. Her skin glistened with a faint red undertone from exertion. Those roller-coaster curves of hers made him ache to touch her again. Her forever buttery, musky, vanilla scent made his mouth water. Man, he was in love with Fortune. He was taken with her. His friends would laugh if they knew how soft he'd gotten over this woman. But screw them. They didn't know what he had. She had her hand between her legs—not touching herself, more like shielding herself—blocking his view of that magnificent entrance that he never wanted to exit. He smiled slightly.

"What are you doing?" Fortune asked.

"Appreciating the view. Almost ..." He sauntered over and moved her hand to the side. "Perfect." God, she was beautiful everywhere. Rich brown gave way to shimmering pink. It made him think again of cherrywood, specifically cherry trees in full bloom in spring—an explosion of various shades of pink that mesmerized him.

"Can you look later? Kind of in the middle of something here." Her lips turned up in an arrogant smile.

Now, this was the Fortune he loved—witty and a little brassy. Confident. Jason stared into her eyes and matched her smile. "Now you want to get cocky? Give her an orgasm, and she bosses you around."

"I believe you're the one that's cocky right now." Her gaze seared him as it traveled down his body.

"So, you've got jokes, huh?" He climbed over her and positioned himself at her entrance, nudging her open.

She whimpered.

Warmth radiated from inside her, and it took every bit of restraint he had not to bury himself right then. "Still got jokes?" He slid in a little farther and waited.

She answered with a low moan and a shake of her head.

"Thought not." He leaned in close, pressing his cheek to hers. "I can't not stare at you. You're too damn sexy," he whispered, then sank in her to the hilt.

Her breath caught for a moment. But then she whispered back, "You're not so bad yourself," and laughed, throaty and soft.

Her laugh dissolved his crumbling restraint, and he thrust in and out of her, groaning in delight. She was so smooth and tight around him. "You feel so good," he growled. What surprised him was that for the first time with anyone he felt like he fit. Like this was where he was supposed to be.

She answered in a keening groan.

He kissed her lips, her throat, and licked his way down to her breast. Beans & Bread's best cinnamon roll couldn't compete with Fortune's skin. He wanted to slow down to savor every moment, but her moans, her shivers, and her neon purple nails raking up and down his back edged him on like a spur to a horse's flank.

"Jason! Harder," she begged, wrapping her legs around him.

He would do whatever she asked to hear those small moans grow into high-pitched cries. And she didn't disappoint him. She didn't talk dirty, but when she called out his name with that sultry, breathy alto, it was like she was caressing the base of his spine.

"Oh! Jason, I'm—" The orgasm took the rest of her words as it slammed through her.

He'd never get tired of seeing her like this—head thrown back, plump full lips parted, body arched up to him in a sensuous curve that showed off tantalizing breasts that were more than a handful. In that moment, it was as if she'd forgotten all her hang-ups and insecurities and succumbed to passion. And she was sexy as hell.

Her walls clenched tight around him, and he felt it, too. The uninhibited freedom, the overwhelming pleasure, and the pressure to let go. So, he did. His own orgasm shuddered through him so hard, for the first time ever he saw stars. Bright, shimmering pink stars.

Fortune

Fortune woke to the weird sense she was flying. She looked around the room as memories of the night before came back to her. How could sex be so scorching hot and so syrupy sweet at the same time? If this was what making love was like, she would never get enough. Her back was to him, and his arm was across her, strong and protective even while limp with sleep. In his arms, she was small enough to be the little spoon. Cuddling was not normally her thing, but this was ... nice. She belonged in his arms.

Jason stirred. "Morning," he said into her hair, his voice deep with sleep.

"Morning." She turned her head toward him. "So, last night was nice."

"Nice? Really? That was some of my best stuff!" Jason attempted a flabbergasted tone and failed.

She giggled and shifted under his arm to lie on her back, turning her head to face him.

He smiled. "Yeah, it was."

He rolled onto his stomach and slid to what was becoming her favorite spot—his head on her shoulder. His weight on her side comforted her. The light came in through the blinds and shone on his back, lighting the hammer and anvil on his left shoulder. She ran her fingers across the tattoo and wondered why she hadn't asked him about it. Probably because she'd been too caught up in how he made her feel. "So, what's with the tattoo? You're not really a blacksmith."

"No, I'm not a blacksmith," he began, "but my great-grand-dad and his dad were. It was the profession in my family for generations until Grandpa James went into construction. I'd like to think the reason I love the trades is because of them."

He paused, briefly looking into space. "But when I got it, I was trying to prove something to the guys. I was complaining about something—I can't remember what—and they nick-named me Emo." He let out a snort of laughter. "I wanted to do the one macho thing none of them had done at the time—get a tattoo. And this was the most macho tattoo I could think of that, if my parents saw it, they'd be okay with it." He rolled his eyes and shook his head. "Didn't work. They still call me Emo sometimes."

"Well, you rant about bad dates, probably while your 'bros' are trying to play *Fortnite* or beer pong. I'd call you Emo, too." Imagining his friends walking behind him taunting him in song all the way to the tattoo parlor door like they were in a Broadway musical, she doubled over in giggles.

"I'm going to ignore that because I love hearing you laugh."

They lay quiet for a moment, listening to the birds outside chirping like mad, the faucet in the bathroom dripping, and each other's hearts beating.

Fortune couldn't tell what Jason was thinking, but she was brimming with questions.

"When did you fall in love with me?"

"When I saw inside your refrigerator." Jason grinned.

Fortune remembered the cheesecake and laughed.

"This is going to sound tired, but ..." he started.

"What? Just say it." Fortune stretched out lazily beside him.

"I think I fell in love with you when I first saw you. Remember when you were standing at the hostess stand? I called you, and you turned around?"

"Yeah?"

"I swear at that moment when I saw you, I heard 'Locked Out of Heaven' by Bruno Mars, and I knew I couldn't let you go. I had to get another date with you." He flashed a sheepish grin.

"Ew, mushy much? Did you see me with a glitter filter, or was I in plain HD? And you put a soundtrack to it, too!" She pretended to gag.

"Cut it with the filter madness." He reared up on his elbow, peering up at her. "And what do you mean 'soundtrack'? The song was playing while we were waiting for our table."

His hair was a tousled mess, and his almost-beard had a week's worth of growth, ratcheting up his sexy factor by ten. As if it could go any higher.

"Really? I didn't notice." She remembered thinking his marriage hint on their first date had been a little—no, a lot—weird. Now it made sense; if he fell in love before dinner, surely envisioning a wedding by dessert was logical. Thanks, Bruno Mars.

She raised an eyebrow. "You know that song is about wanting to get laid, right? You're coming off like every guy I've ever talked to online."

"Well, I think I've more than proven I'm not like every guy you've ever talked to online."

No, he wasn't. And this hadn't been like any online fling she'd ever had because ... Well, there was romance. More romance than disappointment, that was certain.

But there was still the question of the dare. Exactly how much had his friends been involved? She didn't want to come out of this cocoon of happiness, but she had to know. "Um ... about SwipeMatch." Fortune tamped down the worry to keep it from showing on her face, but her mind was racing. "Did Seth ...?" She sat up, pulling the covers up with her. "Um, did he ... pick me?" Had Seth picked her, thinking she was the worst Jason could do? Had he recognized her from the club? Insecurity prickled under her skin.

Jason's eyes went wide. "No! He dared me to find someone. I found you. I talked to you. I asked you out. That was all me. Seth sucks at making dares, but I totally won at this one." He leaned over and touched his lips to hers, instantly calming her.

Warmth flowed through her, and she felt wanted. Desired. Loved.

If she were honest with herself, SwipeMatch hadn't been her first choice, either. Louis had almost forced it on her. And she was glad he had. He'd seen how much damage Marshall had done, even when she hadn't.

Being *painfully single* wasn't about being perpetually alone, it was about using her experience with Marshall to sabotage herself into loneliness. She constantly made choices that kept her single and believing the plus-size, odd chick could never find true happiness. But here was happiness, staring at her, waiting for her to acknowledge it.

"Wow, you're like twenty questions today." Jason chuckled.

"What can I say? Orgasms make me inquisitive!" She smiled and snuggled closer to him. "I want to know everything about you. I love everything I know so far."

He stared at her for a full minute, his eyes full of adoration.

It felt strange but right having a guy look at her that way.

He pulled her into his arms. "How about a proposition to break up this little Q and A?"

"Okay." She shifted back to face him.

"You said you're a great girlfriend."

"I am."

"I'd like to find out for myself."

A thrill zipped through Fortune's chest. Be Jason Reed's girlfriend? She could do that. "Only if you'll be my boyfriend."

"That's the only way it works for me." He pressed his lips to her temple. "I love you, Fortune."

She snuggled into him, ducking her head to his chest, and smiled in contentment. This had to be the best place she'd ever been and the happiest she'd ever felt. "I love you, too, Jason."

Did you want more of Jason and Fortune's love story? Or maybe you identified with Jason and Graham's gaming or Fortune's geekiness about '80s TV and movies? Be a Nerdy Romantics newsletter subscriber and get your nerdy and romance urges fulfilled.

The Nerdy Romantics newsletter is a monthly newsletter packed with book recs, first looks, a little about me, and behind-the-scenes podcast episode info with links to show notes. Sign up here and get a copy of "Star Date" a steamy romance about two Trekkies who meet at a *Star Trek* convention.

http://ymnelson.com/subscribe

Sneak Peek

While this book is totally fiction, it was inspired by my real-life experimental dating on Tinder, which I documented on my blog. (If you missed it, check out #MyTinderSeries https://ymnelson.com/category/mytinder-series/)

Because readers really responded to the series, it inspired me to write a fictional what-if story that ended in an HEA. And *The Accidental Swipe* was born.

This is why reviews are so important. They tell other readers about great books, and they tell us authors what you really liked (which can inspire more books you want).

So, please review *The Accidental Swipe* on Amazon or wherever you bought your copy, GoodReads, and BookBub. Read on for a sneak peek of the next book in the Accidental Lovers series, *The Accidental Proposal!*

The Accidental Proposal
Chapter One

Jason

Buzzz, buzz, buzz. Jason's phone buzzed so much it threatened to fall off the nightstand.

"Would you get that already?" Fortune demanded, eyes closed, lying on her back.

Jason forced himself to turn away from her and grabbed his phone as it bounced off the nightstand's edge. He wanted to silence it and put it back, but the long line of text messages from Graham made him pause.

> *8:03 PM, yesterday*
> Waiting on you again

> *9:54 PM, yesterday*
> Where are you, you didn't say you weren't coming

> *7:49 AM*
> I'm headed to your house with a couple of cops.

When had Graham become such a nag?

"Who was it?" Fortune asked.

"Just Graham."

"Well, answer him."

"It's already over. Not important."

"He's your best friend. Whatever it is, it's important enough for him to text at the crack of dawn on a Saturday. Answer it. Trust that I'm never ignoring Louis or Celeste for you."

So, everyone was chiming in on his life. "Okay. Fine. I'll text him."

"Thank you," Fortune sighed, sounding exasperated, though she didn't move. She was in that half-spent, half-zen place she usually got to after they made love. It was the moment he could talk her into going again.

And Graham was spoiling that moment.

Jason sent a quick text to Graham, calling off the cavalry, but he knew that wouldn't be the end of it. Jason had done the unthinkable—he'd ghosted the guys for a girl. At some point today, he'd have to answer for his crime and see his best friend in person.

He'd been putting off seeing any of the guys since getting together with Fortune. What had it been? Three months? The longest they'd gone without hanging out. But who wanted to hang out with a buddy when sexy Fortune was around?

With a simple text, he possibly could've avoided them for another three months. But last night, he'd ghosted instead of just flaking, and they were going to want to know the cause.

Which meant everyone would have to meet. For real this time. Time to get back to reality.

In a few minutes.

He twirled one of her short auburn curls around his pinky. The curl slid across his skin like silk. At the root, it was a rich sienna brown, which he was a little excited about. He wished she'd let it grow, so he'd have more of the luscious curls to run his fingers through. But she liked it short. He was simply happy she let him play in it because, evidently, not all Black women wanted you to touch their hair. It was so soft like everything else in Fortune's bed—her sheets, her mattress, her.

Usually, she kept curls wrapped up in some kind of head-scarf at night, but right now in a post-coital haze, her top half was completely uncovered, and only the bed sheet they were both under draped over her hips. He loved seeing her like this—naked, her medium brown skin like a piece of finished cherry, with swirls of darker brown in places. The sight of it awakened the creative spirit in him—the need to get his hands on something to hone it and bring out its beauty. Her skin begged to be touched, and he did. He couldn't stop when she was like this.

Come to think of it, where *was* her scarf thing? He searched among the sheets and found the scrap of satin fabric underneath her shoulder, near where he'd pushed it off so he could get his fingers in her hair while they made love.

He slid the head covering under his pillow. He wasn't hiding it; he just wanted to get it out of the way. If she never found it again that might be okay with him. "Speaking of friends, you know you need to meet mine."

"I've already met your friends. It didn't go well, remember?"

"Yes, of course, I remember." Who could forget the night he'd spotted Fortune on a date with his best bud, Graham, and Jason had punched his other friend, Seth? When they all met for the first time, a disastrous accident ensued, ending with Graham breaking Jason and Seth apart during an all-out brawl in the Graveyard's parking lot, and Jason and Fortune almost didn't get together.

After a hot night with her and a couple of emotional conversations afterwards, he'd had to make a decision: leave Fortune, or get to know her and take some time away from the gang to do so. So, he chose Fortune. He could use a break from the gang. They'd understand. After all, they'd been back and forth with each other for over twenty years.

His pursuit of Fortune was his way of rationalizing avoiding them. But he couldn't anymore. "That's why you need to meet them again. Erase the bad first impressions and all. They're better guys than that, I promise."

He leaned against her—his front against her side with one of his legs draped over hers—and breathed her intoxicating vanilla scent. Her eyes were still closed, so he took the moment to get his visual fill of her. His gaze lingered, taking in the fullness of her lips, the curve of her throat, the ampleness of her breasts.

"Why are you harshing my buzz?" She folded her arms over her chest. "And stop staring at my boobs."

"I wasn't staring!" He laughed. He'd definitely been staring. Who could blame him? They were perfect.

"Yes, you were. I could feel it."

"So, what if I was?" He reached his hand under her folded arms and nudged them loose. "And you haven't felt anything yet." He cupped a breast while he licked and kissed her neck.

She playfully pushed him away but quickly succumbed to his seduction and arched to him, pushing more of her breast in his hand.

As he kissed his way down her body, her hums and moans were a drug he couldn't live without. He fondled her nipple until it became a hard bud, then he moved to the other to hear more of that sensual melody. He drank in her rich vanilla buttery scent, nuzzling deeper and drowning in Fortune. Thank goodness he didn't have anywhere to be today.

Then he remembered Graham's frantic texts, and his own hastily-typed response: Forgot to tell you I got held up and couldn't come. Come by the house later. I'll text you.

He had to pull himself away from Fortune and get back to his life. She was so damned sexy when she was being no-nonsense.

Get a hold of yourself, Reed. He leaned away from her and took a few gulps of air, clearing the heady fog of laziness and lust. Slowly, his memory returned. He was asking her something, and ... He looked at her, and this time their gaze connected.

An innocent expression lit her face. A fake innocent expression.

His brows furrowed.

"What?" she asked.

He countered with a classic detective stare. "You lured me right in and made me forget what I was asking."

"I did no such thing."

Sugar almost dripped from her lips when she smiled.

"You're like a pot of honey. But you're still avoiding the issue. Sweetie, these are my friends. You've got to meet them. Properly this time. I don't want them to think you're my secret." He moved his hands from her breasts and circled her waist protectively, hoping she recognized he wanted her in his life, not only in her bed. "And I don't want you to think that either, especially after that Mike guy."

"His name was Marshall, and ... yuck. I don't think that." Her tone was light, but her smile disappeared. She grew rigid under him, the soft compliance of her body gone in an instant.

He shouldn't have mentioned Marshall.

"Why?" she continued. "They already hate me. No need to remind them."

"They do not hate you!" He gave her a brief squeeze. "They just need to get to know you. And you haven't even met all of them. Ranjan wasn't at The Graveyard that night. I think you'd like him." He remembered his and Fortune's first conversation on-line when she mentioned accents. "He's the one with the British accent."

"So, *he's* the one I should have fallen in love with." Her lips parted in a wide grin.

"No. That would have been doomed from the start. He's not into girls."

"Hmm, okay. Seems I'll have to settle for you, then."

"Guess so," He trailed his index finger along the bridge of her nose. "Oh yeah, and 'harshing your buzz'?" He raised one eyebrow. "Reclaim that from the nineties, did you?"

She shrugged. "Whatevs, man. I say what I want."

"Hmm. Does that mean I get to do what I want?" He kissed her behind her ear and licked a path along her jaw to her chin.

Her sigh came out like a moan, and she shifted away. "As fun as that would be, I need to meet Louis for some errands this morning."

"Tell me you'll meet my friends, or I'm not letting you leave." He continued his pleasure journey, kissing his way from the tip of her chin to the hollow of her throat.

She laughed and squirmed and wriggled until he was forced to stop kissing, lest he get an accidental elbow to the stomach. "Fine."

She pushed her lips into a sexy pout that made him want to kiss them, but he waited for her response.

"You know that could've backfired on you." She grabbed an empty box from the nightstand and tossed it his way.

He released her to avoid getting hit with it.

"We're out of condoms, so you get your wish. I'll meet your friends." She slid from under him and made her way to the shower.

Clutching the empty prophylactics box, he felt cold without her heat, but the view as she walked to the bathroom was heavenly. He would settle for that view every morning.

"And stop staring at my ass!" she yelled before she closed the door.

Playlist

1. "Crush" by Gavin DeGraw

2. "I'm So Tired..." by Lauv & Troye Sivan

3. "Getting Started" (Hobbs & Shaw) [feat. JID] by Aloe Blacc

4. "I Don't Care" by Ed Sheeran

5. "Nothing Even Matters" by Lauryn Hill Feat. D'Angelo

6. "Locked Out of Heaven" by Bruno Mars

7. "I Will Follow You" by Rivvrs

8. "Sucker" by Jonas Brothers

9. "Out Loud" by HRVY

10. "Natural" by Imagine Dragons

11. "Where Your Heart Goes" (feat. SYML) by Uppermost

12. "Drew Barrymore" by Bryce Vine

13. "Fallingwater" by Maggie Rogers

14. "Dancing With A Stranger" by Sam Smith & Normani

15. "boyfriend" by Ariana Grande & Social House

16. " PILLOWTALK" by ZAYN

17. "Better" by Khalid

18. "In My Blood" by Shawn Mendes

19. "Someone You Loved" by Lewis Capaldi

20. "Too Good at Goodbyes" by Sam Smith

21. "Right Now" by Nick Jonas & Robin Schulz

22. "If You Leave" (From "Pretty In Pink") by OMD

23. "So Beautiful" by Musiq Soulchild

24. "Best Part" by H.E.R. feat. Daniel Caesar

25. "Pretty Mess" by Erika Jayne

Listen to *The Accidental Swipe* playlist on Spotify

Acknowledgments

I've been writing for fun since middle school when I wrote a two-stanza, emotional and reflective poem. In high school, I handwrote a novel between junior and senior year. The feeling was glorious, and I've been chasing that feeling ever since.

Thank you to my very first beta readers (and longtime friends): Peggy, Laura, author Bethanie F. DeVors, and John; and to my current beta readers of this book: Sara L., Gracey, Marcie, and Staci. Most of this was written in a branch of the Charlotte-Mecklenburg public library with author buddies Gracey Evans and G. S. Carr, and I can't be more grateful for the support of writing buddies and a library that encourages indie authors.

My editor and proofreader Suanne Schafer and Joyce Lamb are awesome helpful women. My cover designer Amber Daulton is accommodating and patient, especially after I basically took one model photo and ran amuck (ha-ha). Thanks Jen Graybeal for being an unofficial—for now—book coach and the most enthusiastic nerdy romantic. Thanks also to Womens Fiction Writers Association (WFWA) and Contemporary Romance Writers (CRW) for your support, advice, awesome craft and marketing courses, and feedback during workshops and contests. The WFWA WritingDate attendees are amazing virtual writing partners and a wealth of information. Thanks to NaNoWrMo virtual writing sessions (especially NaNo Writers of Color). Without them, the Sporgi scene would not have been a thing. I've learned so much from Clubhouse's Romance Author Community (led by Jen Graybeal), Writers in the Storm, and Authors Clubhouse, to name a few.

Most of my co-hosts on Nerdy Romantics Podcast are longtime real-life friends. Without them, I wouldn't have that daily boost of support that you don't realize you need until it's not there. Dana, Marcie, Staci, and Pam thank you for putting up with all my cover iterations, my testing on my websites, retail sites and other places, and my wild podcast conversations that go on long after we've heard "the recording has stopped." To the rest of the 8-Ball crew, I feel your support in spirit (and on social media❤❤).

Thank you to my family, who have always encouraged me by reminding me not to waste the gifts God's given me. Mom, Dad (RIP), Stacey, and all my extended family that's supported me before that two-stanza poem and since — thank you.

And of course, thank you, Readers. This book wouldn't have happened without the readership of my blog where this idea was born. I hope to continue to entertain you, make you laugh, and most importantly, show you that you are loved.

Also By Y. M. Nelson

The Owen & Makayla Trilogy
"The Owen & Makayla Trilogy, Vols 1-3"
Secret Second Chances, a novella (coming soon)

Accidental Lovers Series
The Accidental Swipe
The Accidental Proposal (coming soon)
The On Purpose Wedding (coming soon)

Standalone Novels
The One You Slept On (coming soon)

Short Stories
"Introverted"
(featured in *North Carolina's Emerging Writers: An Anthology of Fiction*)

About the Author

Y.M. Nelson is based in Charlotte, NC and writes about love, women's journeys, and amateur DIY. After she spent most of her writing "career" ghostwriting for companies, Y. M. decided to produce and share her own work with the public. Her debut romantic comedy *The Accidental Swipe* is based on her #MyTinderSeries blog serial. When she's not writing, Y. M. hosts the Nerdy Romantics Podcast which she created. She can also be found teaching college English, baking something sweet, upcycling random pieces of furniture, or watching reruns from one of the *Star Trek* franchises.

Follow her at https://ymnelson.com for the latest news and links to her social media.

amazon.com/stores/Y.-M.-Nelson/author/B01MUAO9A5

bookbub.com/authors/y-m-nelson

g
goodreads.com/ymnelson

f
facebook.com/authorymnelson

p
pinterest.com/authorymnelson

instagram.com/authorymnelson